THE PHOENIX KEEPER AND THE FIERY WATERS

MARGARITA ARTISTA

For Nicole,
Thank you for your
Support! Hope you enjoy!!

MARGARITA ARTISTĂ

PUBLISHED BY AZALA PRESS
COVER DESIGN BY RACHEL MCEWAN DESIGNS
EDITED BY IOANA CHELDIU

© *MARGARITA ARTISTA*

THE
PHOENIX KEEPER
—AND THE—
FIERY WATERS

A Note From The Author:

This novel and its affiliates are a work of fiction. The ideas, discourse, and actions presented throughout the development of this story are not meant to be taken as historically accurate. The manner in which people, places, and institutions are named and described throughout this story are not intended to be whole representations.

This work is not intended to encourage, discourage, idealize, or romanticize any thoughts or actions. This work is intended to make you think.

A conscious effort to maintain equal representation of different genders, sexualities, ethnicities, religions, lifestyles, and other significant markers of individuality has been made in the creation of these books. No representation throughout this story is meant to be taken as a whole representation of the entire group to which that person belongs.

This work is intended to act as an acknowledgement that we all have differences and similarities, endure hardships and celebrate accomplishments, and can be good or bad, no matter our walks of life. We are not defined by our skin tone, who we choose to love, the religion that we follow, or any singular detail in itself. Rather, these things become small ingredients that are mixed into the recipe of who we are. They are not us; they are parts of us.

- Safe in Our World provides links to global resources for mental health and substance use. Visit www.safeinourworld.org/find-help/ for more information.

"All that is solid melts into air, all that is holy is profaned, and man is at last compelled to face with sober senses his real conditions of life and his relations with his kind."
Karl Marx

"When man discovered the mirror, he began to lose his soul."
Émile Durkheim

"A man is but a product of his thoughts. What he thinks, he becomes."
Mahatma Gandhi

For anyone who is struggling and who needs to feel seen and heard - know that you are valid and worthy of living a life free from your personal difficulties, whatever they may be.

.

PART ONE
THE DALLIANCE

CHAPTER 1

"You know you're supposed to catch the frisbee, right, Keiffer?"

"Can it, Roscoe! We can't all be star athletes!"

"This isn't about athleticism, dude! It's about incompetence!"

"Nobody asked for your opinion, Sajan!"

I threw a glance over my shoulder at the boys as I flipped the burgers on the grill in front of me. "Would you guys chill out? It's a game of beach frisbee, not an Olympic championship."

"Yeah, get a grip," Emmanuella chimed from the picnic bench where she was preparing a salad. Chenoa and Everly were setting out bowls of chips and other munchies beside her.

"Hey, you don't know what's at stake here," Hakeem replied.

"Losing team has to clean out the lounge fridge this week," Elijah added. "And Keiffer's forgotten cheese is growing whole new ecosystems in there."

"It wasn't forgotten," Keiffer argued, his blonde hair blustering in the ocean breeze as he faced us intently. "It just got wedged in between some things at the back and I didn't find it for a while." The frisbee flew straight into his head not even a second later, prompting a yelp from him and roaring laughter from the other boys.

Myra brought the burger buns over to me. "That cheese sounds forgotten to me," she murmured quietly.

"Keiffer will realize that soon enough," I whispered back as I began plopping the burgers on the buns. "Remember, his brain hasn't been oiled in a while." I nodded towards him. "And if he keeps taking impacts like that, it'll be a fruitless effort to keep it lubricated anyways."

"It may be pointless already," Chenoa added from behind me as she hauled over some cheese slices. The traditional Cherokee tattoo of a feathered dreamcatcher on her arm seemed mightier under the afternoon sun, as if it had somehow absorbed its energy and manifested it into a pronounced, proud splendour.

"It's a good thing he's pretty," Everly noted, shaking up the lemonade she'd mixed.

Chenoa frowned at her. "You still think he's pretty, huh? I thought you and Hakeem kind of had a thing going."

Everly sighed. "Hakeem is sweet, all right. But I'm just not sure he's my type," she mused. I noticed Myra perked up a bit at this, her dark eyes twinkling in the sunlight, but she didn't add anything to the conversation.

"And Keiffer is?" Emmanuella snorted as she began setting the picnic table.

Everly smiled shyly. "He's just got this…goofy charm about him, you know?"

Emmanuella rolled her eyes. "More like all goof, no charm."

Everly huffed as she crossed her arms. Her deep, rich skin glimmered with the remnants of her sunblock. "Not all men can be as smooth as Elijah, okay?"

I felt my cheeks flush a bit.

"How's he liking the new car, Seraphine?" Chenoa asked me. "Has he taken you for a ride in it yet?"

Elijah had just bought a Honda Civic a few days prior – it was old and a little worn, but it got the job done. "He loves it. We drove here in it, but I guess the first real ride will be tonight when we go to the drive-in."

Everly squealed. "So cute!"

I smiled, more to myself than anything, as I finished preparing the burgers and turned once again to address the boys. "Lunch is ready!"

Immediately, the game of frisbee became an afterthought as they all scrambled up from the sand and on to the grassy area, where our picnic bench was. Everyone grabbed a plate, and we all sat down to eat together. The fact that we were at the beach in early October had still not quite registered with my Canadian mind, but I certainly had no complaints about spending my Saturday that way.

"Hey, Seraphine, isn't that your lab partner over there?" Chenoa asked, nodding her head behind me.

I turned and indeed saw Felix running on the path towards us. With the time difference, we'd ended up returning from Heliopolis last Monday morning. Assignments and quizzes had swamped us, so we'd agreed we'd wait until after we were all caught up before we got back to our Phoenix adventures. I hadn't seen him since our last lab on Wednesday, which admittedly had felt a little odd, what with all the time we'd been spending together as of late.

"Yeah, that's him," I answered Chenoa as I waved at Felix. He noticed my movement and waved back, reaching to remove the headphones from his ears as he slowed to a walk and headed over. The last time everyone had seen each other was when he'd given me my dress back. I hadn't received any further questions about that incident, though I'm sure that didn't necessarily negate their existence.

"Hello, everyone," Felix said to us, smiling at me as he

wiped the sweat off his face with his tank – combined with the black athletic shorts, it was perhaps the most casual outfit I'd ever seen him in. "Lovely day for a picnic."

"Sure is," I patted the spot beside me. "Care to join? I think there's a few extra burgers."

"Oh, I wouldn't want to intrude," Felix replied.

Keiffer waved him off. "Nah, it's all good man. You deserve some power food after a run, anyways." He smirked at me. "We promise she's not drunk, so she shouldn't puke and need any dry-cleaning, either."

I rolled my eyes. "I made apple crumble for dessert, too," I added.

"She makes the best desserts," Hakeem exclaimed.

"Oh, yes, I'm quite aware," Felix said with a chuckle. "Well, if you all insist."

He sat down beside me as Everly poured him a glass of lemonade. "Here – you're probably thirsty," she said.

"Indeed. Thank you."

"This is a good running spot, hey?" Sajan asked him.

Felix nodded as he took several gulps of the sugary drink. "I run here often," he responded, nodding towards the ocean. "It's worth the drive for the view."

I'd seen the view from his place, which wasn't too shabby, either. But I suppose no matter how beautiful the view from home was, a change in scenery was always appreciated.

We continued eating, my friends and Felix engaged in conversation that I admittedly found heartening. Despite her initial suspicious reaction to him, even Emmanuella seemed to ease up on the sarcastic remarks as the two conversed. Considering both Felix and my friends were relatively significant presences in my life, it was helpful if they all got along.

There was, however, one person who did not seem as enthusiastic as the others about Felix's company. It was impossible to miss the expression on his face, the one that had noticeably hardened since Felix sat down.

"So, Felix," Elijah started at the next break in conversation. "You've been lucky enough to try Seraphine's desserts, too?"

Immediately, everyone's eyes landed on either Felix or Elijah. I suppose not everyone in the group had made the connection earlier by the lights that went off in some of their gazes.

Felix, though, only returned a small smile. "She brought some over once when we had to work on our lab report," he lied smoothly.

Elijah tried – and failed – to soften his expression. "Oh, I see," he said, his gaze flickering over to me as he attempted to smile. "That's kind of you."

I shrugged. "It's my way of thanking him for putting up with me as a lab partner." I snorted. "You know, with my limited brilliance on the subject."

I could see Felix's lips twitch a bit with amusement.

Elijah simply shook his head. "I'd love it if you were my lab partner."

I smiled. "You say that without any experience," I reminded him.

"But I have experienced your desserts," he countered.

To this, Felix gave him a single, nonchalant nod. "They are pretty convincing," he agreed. The smile on his face was still there – unbothered, unthreatened, almost light-hearted. He sat straight, but not tense, with a natural calmness to his energy. Nothing Elijah could say would crack the even river stone I saw in him.

Elijah, on the other hand, was still presenting a feeble pleasantry that was only working because nobody had called it into question. "You wouldn't happen to have some extra goodies we can take with us on our date tonight?" he asked hopefully.

I could hear Emmanuella let out an amused breath. She knew what he was doing, too. Anyone with half a mind could see it from a mile away.

I let him see my smile thin. "I'll see what I can do," I said quietly. The look in his eyes bore that insecurity he was desperately trying to bury by engaging with me in front of Felix. It was as if he were a dog claiming his bone. I found it pitiful and...degrading.

It was then that Felix stood. "Well, thank you all for letting me grab a delicious lunch," he said, patting me on the shoulder. "I've got to head home now."

"Good to see you," I said to him. "Drive safe."

"Hey, man, we should run together sometime," Roscoe suggested, motioning to himself, Keiffer, and Sajan. "We do a lot of it for basketball."

"Would be a pleasure," Felix replied, waving at everyone else. "Take care, everyone."

He had just turned on his heel when Elijah suddenly stood himself. "Actually, I need to grab something from my car, so I'll walk with you," he said quickly.

Felix just gave him a brief nod. "Sure," he said, motioning for him to follow.

Elijah smiled briskly at him as he walked over, and together in stride, the two began walking towards the parking lot. We all watched them with bated breath, as if that would somehow prevent catastrophe from striking.

As soon as they were out of earshot, Roscoe whipped a concerned look across the entire group. "Anyone else getting bad vibes there?"

"I don't think they'll be best friends anytime soon," Chenoa remarked, looking at me. "Elijah probably thinks you and Felix have something going on."

I shrugged. "We don't." A small, nagging voice in the back of my mind brought the memory of the Autumn Ball and his drunken advances, but I shoved it away before it could get any louder.

"Yeah, but he doesn't know that," Everly chimed in.

"And how is that my issue?" I remarked.

Sajan frowned. "You seem upset, Seraphine."

I waved my hand in annoyance. "I can clear any confusion up with a simple conversation. The fact that he'd rather do – " I gestured towards where Elijah had been sitting " – *that* instead of talking to me privately is not my fault, nor my problem."

The group exchanged glances. "She has a point," Myra admitted.

Emmanuella sighed as she took another bite of her apple crumble. "Well, hopefully it's not a gun he's grabbing," she told me.

I only let out a humoured breath, mostly to myself. I knew a gun would be no match for Felix.

- F -

I hadn't the slightest clue what she saw in him. He was hardly anything special – almost painfully plain, if honesty is the language I must speak. Frankly, I couldn't picture anyone being a perfect match for her, regardless of their qualities. She was in a league of her own, so much so that even a man made of gold would not live up to the expectation. But despite that, I would hope that her pick would be better suited for her; seeing them together was like watching a turkey romance a swan.

"So, you said you drive out to run here?" Elijah asked as we walked, his pace quickening to match mine. "Do you live far?"

"Just around La Jolla," I answered him swiftly.

"Ah," he said, clearing his throat. "That's a nice area."

I gave him my most convincing smile. "It has its ups and downs."

"I guess that's everywhere, huh?"

I shrugged. "Suppose so."

He nodded in front of us. "This is me."

I turned to look at the car we'd walked towards – a weathered, gray Honda. "Reliable cars," I noted, tapping its hood – just to give him something to feel good about.

He stretched a bit. "Oh, yeah. Just got 'er a few days ago. Glad to finally have a whip." He chuckled. "Everything's just easier with a car, you know?"

"Sure, sure. Well, I best be going."

"Right. Hey, listen man – "

Elijah leaned against his car. "Look, I don't know if Seraphine told you about us or anything, but I just wanted to chat with you, man to man. She and I have a thing going, and it's a little weird to me that you keep coming on to her."

It was a struggle to hide my humour and feign that I was at all interested in his stupidity. "Coming on to her?"

He motioned to where we'd all been sitting. "You know, the whole dessert thing, and then you getting her dress cleaned a few weeks back."

My forehead creased. "So, let me just confirm I have this correct – because you two are a...*thing*, as you say, I'm not permitted to enjoy her baking or assist her when she's soaked in her own vomit?"

He gave off a nervous laugh; perhaps he'd realized the foolishness of his statement, too. "I just get the sense that you're into her and kind of...stepping in my place, is all."

I stared at him. "And what, exactly, is that place?"

He shifted his eyes. "I just told you. We've got a thing going."

"Are you married?"

He looked at me with befuddlement. "What? No."

"Are you in a relationship?"

He seemed taken aback. "Well, we aren't official yet, but – "

"It sounds to me like you're trying to create a place where none exists," I interrupted, raising an eyebrow. "If you're so intent on ensuring her commitment to you, then perhaps you should start with committing yourself to her, hm?"

Elijah didn't seem too thrilled with my logic. "Do you even know how dating works, dude? It's only been about a month."

"And yet, you like her enough to try and keep other men away from her," I replied, cocking my head to the side. "Either that, or you enjoy the gratification of keeping your options open without interference from others...a bit of hypocrisy, if you ask me."

He immediately grew offended. "What the hell is your problem, man?"

I shook my head. "I have no issue. You're the one who created a mountain out of a molehill." I lifted my chin. "Seraphine is my lab partner. We work together on our labs, and then we part ways. I can't change how you read that."

He scoffed and turned towards the car. "Whatever, dude," he muttered as he unlocked the vehicle and began rummaging inside it. I eagerly took the opportunity to leave, promptly heading for my own car.

It was only when I had locked the door to my Aston Martin, parked far away from the moron and his idiocy, that I let my façade crack. Flames danced at my fingertips as I grumbled furiously under my breath, an angry fever crawling its way through my bones.

How dare he act as if he *owned* her.

If laws and morals didn't exist, I would have burned his fingers off one by one so that he could never touch her again. Perhaps I would have burned something else off, too. But that was a scene I could only enjoy in my own mind as I gripped my steering wheel with rage, gritting my teeth to keep from setting my own car on fire.

The thought made me pause.

Slowly, I loosened my grip on the wheel and laid back in my chair. I swirled my tongue around my cheeks, my lips eventually lifting involuntarily. As sinister as it was, I could admit that I was no stranger to a little…meddling. And given he'd shamelessly tried to do a little of his own – pitiable as it was – I didn't feel too remorseful about my ideas.

I glanced out the front windshield. In the distance, I could still see where his car was parked.

My smirk widened – this scene would play well.

- S -

We didn't stay too much longer at the beach after Elijah returned to the picnic. Thankfully, we had some leftovers to last us through the weekend, and we packed them up before heading out.

"You want to go straight to the drive-in?" Elijah asked me as we all headed towards the parking lot.

"Sure," I replied. I was still a little miffed about his actions with Felix, but I'd decided I'd talk to him about it later.

As we rounded the corner up the lot, several firetrucks, as well as a crowd of people, came barreling into view. The flashing lights were muffled by the wafting of a thick plume of smoke.

"What the hell is that all about?" Sajan noted.

"Looks like something must have caught fire," Myra offered.

"That's where my car's parked," Elijah noted. I threw him a quick glance at the hint of concern in his voice.

We approached the commotion, Elijah's footsteps growing noticeably apprehensive as more details came into view. As we found a gap in the crowd, I was able to finally catch a glimpse of the full scene. A fire had wreaked havoc on a vehicle, which was already put out by the firefighters, leaving a burnt carcass in its wake.

Though it was charred and blackened with soot, I could still make out the familiarity of the Honda Civic – or whatever remained of it.

Elijah's hands were on his head in dismay as soon as he realized. "That's my car!" he exclaimed.

"More like it *was* your car," Roscoe muttered. "That thing is a bit overcooked at this point."

"Holy guacamole," Emmanuella said with a shake of the head. "How does that even happen?"

A tall, stocky firefighter made his way over to us. "Are you the owner of this vehicle?" he asked Elijah.

Elijah nodded, his eyes scrambling to take it all in. "Uh, yeah, unfortunately."

The firefighter's hardened features grew sympathetic. "I'm sorry about all this. As you've probably guessed, your vehicle is totaled."

"Yeah, I gathered that." Elijah sighed, shaking his head. "I just got the damn thing…"

"Do you know what happened?" I inquired.

The firefighter shrugged. "Seems to me like either a fuel leak or an electrical short. Happens in older cars sometimes." He grasped Elijah on the shoulder. "You'll likely need some documentation for your insurance claim. Come with me and we'll get you sorted."

Elijah nodded, glancing at me. "Sorry, Seraphine. I guess we'll have to postpone the drive-in."

I gave him a trying smile. "That's all right. It's not your fault." I placed my hand softly on his arm. "Want me to wait with you?"

He shook his head. "There's no point, really. Just head back with everyone else. I'll catch up with you guys later."

"All right. Let me know if you need anything." I turned to my other friends. "Let's go."

Everyone took turns wishing Elijah good luck before we all made our way to the bus stop.

CHAPTER 2

"THAT'S RISKY, SERAPHINE."

I pursed my lips, narrowing my eyes a bit as I wiggled the wooden Jenga block on the side of an already precarious tower. "Risky is my middle name," I murmured back to Roscoe, my concentration fixed on the piece I was trying to remove.

"No kidding," Keiffer noted, watching me with wide, terror-stricken eyes. "That piece has risky written all over it."

I tuned the boys out, focusing entirely on the block. I felt it loosen enough that I could swipe it out, and in one fell swoop, I cleared it from the tower, which barely moved in response.

Roscoe let out a low whistle. "That was a work of art. Truly."

I made a bowing motion with my hand. "*Merci, merci.*"

"Great. Now I'm more screwed than a nail," Keiffer muttered, scanning the tower for a potential block to remove.

I didn't have enough time to argue that nails got hammered, not screwed, before Emmanuella, Everly, and Chenoa all burst through the door to the lounge, decked out in various shimmering crop tops and black jeans. "Who's ready for one hell of a concert?" Emmanuella cheered.

Sajan stood up from the couch and stretched. "It's about damn time. We've been ready for ages."

Myra and Hakeem, who were sitting across from him, both looked up from their phones. "We should get going. We're cutting it close if we want to grab dinner," Hakeem noted.

"Nothing a McDonald's drive-thru can't solve," Everly said vivaciously.

Roscoe nodded towards me. "You sure you don't want to come? There might be tickets at the door."

They'd bought the tickets for the show weeks ago off some resale site, and since Elijah and I had originally planned to go to the drive-in, I hadn't given it too much thought. I had serious doubts I'd find tickets that weren't a complete scam on the night of the show – especially for a concert so popular.

"It's all good," I replied, smiling at Roscoe. "I'll have a nice night in – maybe get some homework done or something. You guys go have fun."

He gave me a few pats on the shoulder as he stood. The room was alive with chatter as everyone bustled around, and as they made their way out the door, the lounge slowly fell silent.

I started putting the Jenga blocks back in the box, pausing once only to check my phone. I'd texted Elijah asking if everything was okay several hours ago. He still hadn't responded.

I tried not to think too much of it and instead focused on getting the game cleaned up. When it was packed, I replaced it on one of the coffee tables and headed back to my dorm. I half-heartedly reached for one of my textbooks, but I wasn't even a full page into reading when I realized work was certainly not what I wanted to do with my Saturday night.

I contemplated my options on the edge of my bed for a moment; then, I reached once more for my phone.

- F -

"You are absolutely diabolical."

I drummed my fingers on my legs, my chemistry textbook propped in my other hand. *"What a lacklustre description for such fine handiwork,"* I replied nonchalantly to Fuego in my mind. My free fingers found my pencil with ease, and I began writing out the next chemical equation I needed to balance on the lined paper beside me.

"Do you not feel even a hint of remorse?" Fuego interrogated.

"No." I looked up from my textbook. *"Oh – hang on."* I paused for dramatic effect, then proceeded to look back down at my chemistry. *"Nope. Nothing."*

My Phoenix let out a frustrated huff in my mind. *"I give up."*

"Thank you. The chastising was becoming a bit tiresome."

"That poor kid probably saved up for a long time to get that car, you know," Fuego lectured.

"Well, perhaps he shouldn't have been an absolute wanker," I countered. *"Besides, I thought you were giving up?"*

I could see Fuego ruffle his feathers in my peripheral, but he said nothing more. I was left in peace with my chemistry – that is, until my phone rang.

I glanced at it on the coffee table, my lips twitching upwards when I learned who it was.

"Hello?" I asked when I picked it up.

"Hey. You doing anything tonight?" Seraphine inquired, her usually lilted voice a bit monotonous.

"Just some chemistry. Why?"

"My evening's cleared up. Elijah's car is…not very usable, to put it nicely, so we couldn't go to the drive-in."

I smirked to myself. "Not very usable?" I questioned with as much surprise as I could muster. "What do you mean?"

"I guess it had some kind of mechanical issue and sort of… uh…caught fire. That's what the firefighters said, anyways."

"What? How awful! I'm terribly sorry to hear that," I replied innocently.

"Meh, it's no big deal. I was wondering if you wanted to ditch the chemistry for a mysterious riddle about a blending temple?"

I chuckled. "Well, how could I ever say no to Little Miss Adventure?" I could hear her let out an amused breath. "I'll pick you up in half an hour."

"Thanks. I'll see you soon."

She hung up the phone, and I couldn't help but grin to myself.

One point for Team Diabolical, zero for Team Wanker.

- S -

I stepped into the familiar, modern foyer of Felix's villa with a glow to my heart. I never thought the space would feel comforting to me – Felix's interior design, though spotless and uncluttered, had always felt a little empty and cold to me. Nevertheless, I found myself grateful to be back on his property, so close to the creatures who'd changed my life.

"You know, I've always found it strange that you have so little furniture," I noted as we walked through the home.

"Oh? And why is that?"

"I guess I just thought rich people always had lots of stuff."

Felix shrugged. "I prefer quality over quantity."

I thought for a minute. "But you have five cars."

His response was delayed. "I suppose quality is sometimes quantifiable."

I huffed with amusement.

He looked at me. "How would you fill the space?" he questioned.

"I don't necessarily think it needs filling."

"Sure. But I'm curious. Theoretically speaking – " he

motioned all around us " – how would you have furnished this place?"

I stopped where we stood, looking over the monotone palette, the sleek lines, the lack of curves. "I would have used more colours," I started as my eyes drifted to one of the recliners in the space. "And less leather."

"What would be used instead of leather?"

"Soft fabric." I tried to reimagine the space in my brain. "Maybe a light grey sofa, and the same colour on the walls. Then pops of reds and golds, and a touch of teal blue. The pillows, the art, the frames. And an ornate rug." A corner of the room in particular spoke to me. "In the winter, the Christmas tree could go there. Where the sun from the window gives it a little spotlight. The ornaments would sparkle in that."

Felix studied me, a softness encasing those lavender eyes. "That sounds…homey."

I gave him a small smile. "But this is your home. And the nice thing about your home is that it's entirely yours," I added, nodding towards the current furnishings. "I think this décor suits you."

He glanced around, the softness becoming troubled. "Perhaps," he eventually conceded before turning back to me. "Are you hungry?"

"A little."

"Good." We walked into the kitchen, where he poured himself a glass of whiskey and threw in some ice cubes. "I'll have the chef start on supper. My father said he wanted to join me. I'm sure he'll be happy to see you as well."

"Cool," I said, eyeing his whiskey on ice. "Got any alcohol that isn't gross?"

He scoffed. "This is a Macallan double cask that was matured for thirty years," he replied. "Goes for about four thousand dollars a bottle."

"Okay. So it's a really expensive and really old yucky juice," I said bluntly. "Do you have…maybe…a Strongbow?"

He blinked at me. "You mean the cider?"

I gave him a look. "No, I meant an archery bow. Preferably strong enough to go through your head."

He rolled his eyes. "No. I have no ciders. I have wine, though."

I sighed. "Wine will do."

He motioned for me to follow him. He led me to a doorway around the corner, and opening it revealed a spiral stairway. I followed him down into the largest wine cellar I'd ever seen – besides the one that had been converted into the Phoenixes' home, of course. Glistening marble covered the walls and floors, and head-to-toe wine racks lined the perimeter of the room. There were several oak barrels in the center that I could only assume contained ageing wine, too.

"Shit," I mumbled. "That's a fuck-ton of wine."

He shrugged. "Pick one."

"Can you point me to one that doesn't cost four thousand dollars?"

"Certainly. White or red?"

"White, please."

He reached to his left, pulled out a bottle, and handed it to me. The label read *Joh. Jos. Prum Wehlener Sonnenuhr Trockenbeere-nauslese.*

"What kind is this?"

"A Riesling. From Germany."

"Okay, I like Rieslings. And it's not four thousand dollars?"

"No, that one goes for about five and a half thousand."

I threw my free hand up and huffed. "Oh, for fuck's sake."

"What? You said, 'not four thousand dollars.' You didn't specify if it had to be more or less."

I shook my head and sighed. "Lesson noted. Got anything cheaper?"

"I don't really know. I'm more drawn to expensive taste, I'll admit."

"Yeah, I gathered that. All right, this German one will do if you have no reservations wasting it on me."

He shook his head. "It's no waste at all. I hope you enjoy it."

I gave him a small smile. "Thanks."

We made our way back up the spiral staircase and into Felix's dining room. It was smaller than Luther's and less busy. No china hutch, no extravagant décor. Just the black table, the twelve black chairs, and a small, marble fireplace, above which hung a marble-framed mirror. The large windows provided a spectacular view of the gardens.

Just as we entered from one doorway, Luther arrived through the one opposite us. "Seraphine, Felix! So good to see you!"

I gave him a big hug. "It feels like it's been forever, what with Egypt, and Italy before that."

"Why, it certainly – " he stopped midsentence as he pulled away, his eyes darting from Felix to me and back again. "Wait – I beg your pardon?"

"It's a long story," Felix said. "We can discuss it over dinner."

———

"So it's all true!"

Luther's incredulous statement was the loudest thing said since we'd sat down for supper. We had told him the entire story, from the fire and fight with Alchnost to our trips to Italy and Egypt. Felix brought the Legend of Sedaurea to show him, and he'd studied it with wonder amid our conversation, the same way I imagine an archaeologist lingers amongst the artifacts he's been searching for his entire life.

"Incredibly, yes," Felix replied. He sat with his back pressed against his chair, swirling a third – or maybe it was his fourth – glass of whiskey. His gaze was distant, and it seemed to fall not on the Legend of Seadaurea, but rather through it, beneath the table, and past the floor below.

Luther shook his head slowly as he chuckled, looking at me. "You must be really glad you didn't listen to me, young lady," he exclaimed.

I gave him a soft smile and shrugged. "My parents will tell you that I've never really been a good listener," I replied. "Maybe, just this once, it's paid off."

"Well, I'll say," Luther said. "This is quite the discovery! Have you any idea what happens next?"

Felix cleared his throat and reached into his pocket, pulling out his phone. "There was another riddle on the pedestal in Heliopolis," he explained, scrolling through his photos. "We've got to decode it."

"What does it say?"

"Here." He enlarged the photo he'd taken and handed it to Luther, who read it aloud.

"My light has hatched and shall brighten the way
On your journey to the land where a temple lays
In the vastest region of its kind
The temple hides away from the blind
Nestled in fauna with which it blends
Where the trees dance around the river bend
The temple sleeps through sweltering heat
And the cries of the clouds who often weep
Like to each other, this temple will draw
My brothers and sisters in feather and caw
And within it slumbers my wings of Earth
Who awaits your hands to awaken its birth."

"A temple!" Luther exclaimed. "My word, this is turning into quite the quest!"

He turned to me. "Your intuition was really on to something here, my dear. I mean, this adventure was practically sitting here and waiting for you to happen upon it!" He shook his head, tutting. "I can't believe I nearly talked you out of this. You two will certainly have to keep me updated on your findings."

Felix nodded, taking the phone, and looked over at me. "We will."

"Good, good. I'd best be going, now. I'm in the middle of a quarterly report that won't finish itself, you know." Luther stood and smiled at me. "Always good to see you, dear. Stay safe, you two."

"Chat soon," I told him, and I watched as he left the room.

The echoes of Luther's footsteps disappeared shortly after he did, and a peaceful quiet enveloped the room. I finished my glass of wine and turned to Felix, only to find he hadn't stopped looking at me. His eyes seemed intent, as if he were looking at something within me, something of great interest.

I formed a crease in my brow. "What?"

He blinked, but he didn't tear his eyes from mine as a little smile flitted at the corners of his lips. "Nothing. It's just – nothing."

I eyed him. "Is something funny?"

"No. Well…"

He cleared his throat, his smile widening a bit. "I've noticed your cheeks get a bit rosy when you drink." His eyes travelled across my features. "It makes you look like you're blushing."

"Huh," I considered, tapping my cheeks softly with my fingers. The warmth I felt on the inside had certainly transpired atop my skin. "Interesting. I've never been told."

Without warning, his fingers were suddenly on my skin, just where mine had been. He brought his thumb across my cheek with a touch softer than cashmere, his smile softening as he did so.

"It's like the wine has tickled you pink," he noted, slowly bringing his fingers down.

I nodded, my eyes shifting a bit timidly as I instinctively tucked a strand of my curls behind my ear.

The moment had been…unexpected.

It appeared he realized this, too, for he then abruptly shook his head before throwing back the rest of his third – no, wait, fourth – glass of whiskey. "Anyways," he began, motioning to my empty dinner plate. "Are you full?"

"*Oui*, thank you. It was delicious."

"Good. Are you too full for dessert?"

I eyed him. "Well…what's dessert?"

He gave me a humoured look. "Not sure. But the chef rarely disappoints with desserts."

I thought for a moment. "I could go for dessert."

Felix chuckled and reached behind him, towards the mantle of the fireplace, where a small bell was placed. He rang it, and immediately, two maids bustled in to clear our plates.

"Tell the chef we're ready for dessert," Felix said to one. She nodded and scurried off with the other. Shortly after, Francis the butler appeared in the doorway with the chef. Each carried a plate of what looked like decadent sticky toffee pudding and a scoop of creamy butter pecan ice cream.

My eyes widened a bit, and I glanced at Felix. He grew amused at my excitement. The dishes did not disappoint, and minutes later, I'd finished devouring mine.

"Wow," Felix noted as I swallowed my last bite. "I think that was record time."

I let out a sigh of satisfaction as I slumped back in my chair. "That was so good," I muttered, scanning my plate to see if there was another crumb I could gobble up. I'd cleaned it pretty well.

Felix stood and tapped me on the shoulder. "Don't get too comfortable. We have work to do."

———

When we'd reached the Phoenixes' home, I immediately recoiled at Lumina's size. The last I'd seen her, she was a newly hatched chick. Now, she was fully grown, standing with graceful white plumage that glowed like the halo of an angel in the light.

"That's right," Felix chimed at my gawking. "You're not the only Light Keeper in the house now."

I turned to him. "Can you access the magic?"

He outstretched his palm towards me with a grin, and in the center of his hand, a ball of light bloomed seconds later.

"Wow," I said, looking over at Fuego. "So, can you use both fire and light magic at the same time?"

Felix considered this. "I haven't tried yet."

I motioned to his other hand. "Well, now seems like a swell enough time."

He chuckled and outstretched his other hand. As a ball of flames burst from the other palm, the light flickered in the other. I saw a bit of struggle in his face as he attempted to brighten the light again, only for the flames to shrink in the other hand.

"It's a bit…difficult," he said with a strain in his voice, as if he'd lifted something heavy.

"Maybe it takes some practice," I suggested. He nodded as he ceased both sets of magic, letting out a huff of relief.

I walked over to the bookshelf, scanning the spines of the old literature. "Got any particular preference on where to start?"

"Just pick some at random," Felix replied. "Anything that looks promising."

None of them were titled "A Convenient List of Temples in

the World," but nevertheless, I grabbed a bunch of books and brought them over to the sitting area, where Felix and I made ourselves comfortable. "Good luck," I told him as I propped open my first choice.

———

After several hours and twice as many books later, it felt like it was going to take an act of God rather than luck for us to find any relevant information.

"I can't read another word," Felix groaned as he slammed his current book shut. He had taken it upon himself to sprawl across the floor in a dishevelled heap of frustration.

I huffed, blinking up at the skylight – admittedly, I had blanked out several moments prior and had been staring up at the ceiling. "My head hurts."

"Maybe because you haven't blinked for three minutes. Are you struck by my dashing reflection in the skylight, kindling?" I heard Felix tease.

I grabbed one of the couch pillows and threw it at him. "I was thinking."

"About me, right?"

I threw another pillow. "You're so full of it."

I heard him snicker. "Someone's grumpy."

"I told you my head hurts."

"Aww…want me to kiss it better?"

I made a gagging sound. "I'd rather stick a cactus up my own ass," I muttered as I stood.

Felix blinked at me. "…That's concerning."

"Can you take me home, please? I'm tired. We can pick this up another day."

He got himself up from the ground. "By all means – especially if it'll prevent any cactus-induced injuries," he replied. I rolled my eyes, but said nothing more as I followed him out of the cellar.

CHAPTER 3

THE NEXT MORNING, I still hadn't heard back from Elijah. The strangeness of his radio silence was hard to ignore.

Sajan was the only one in the lounge when I entered. I assumed everyone else was taking advantage of the Sunday morning to sleep in after the concert.

"How's it going?" he asked me as I waddled over to the fridge, rubbing my eyes.

"Living the dream," I grumbled in return, grabbing some bread and butter. "How was the concert?"

"Super good. Sad you couldn't be there, though." He eyed me. "Everything okay?"

I sighed as I plopped the bread in the toaster. "I texted Elijah yesterday to check in on him, but I still haven't heard back."

"Really? That's weird." He shrugged. "Maybe he's caught up in all the insurance stuff or something."

"Maybe. I don't know." I looked towards him. "Where's your other half?"

"He's at the gym."

I pretended to gasp in surprise. "Without you?"

He chuckled. "It's my rest day."

"Fair enough." My smile thinned a bit as I poured some coffee. "Can I ask you something?"

"Yeah, shoot."

"Is it hard to hide your relationship in front of everyone else?"

I heard him loose a breath. "You sort of get used to it."

"Do you think you'll ever tell the others?"

Sajan didn't reply right away. "I don't know. It depends." He sighed again. "I'm worried about my family finding out. That's the only reason I keep it a secret."

I turned to face him, studying his expression. "Is it worth them not finding out – living in all this guilt?"

His eyes traversed my features. "They won't accept me. They'll disown me – I'm sure of it."

"But Roscoe loves you," I countered. "And your friends will support you. You know they will. As will many, many others. You deserve to be able to share your love with the world – there's nothing wrong with it." I shrugged. "If they think disowning you for loving freely is justified, then maybe losing them isn't so much of a loss."

His gaze wandered as my words carried their weight to his shoulders. "It's…hard," he eventually replied.

I nodded. "I know." I gave him a trying smile. "Just think about it, all right? I don't think it's right for you to live in so much fear, is all."

Sajan returned a single nod. "Thank you, Seraphine."

The doorknob turned then, and Chenoa burst into the room looking unusually perturbed. "Ugh," she groaned as she stomped over to the kitchen.

I raised my brows at her. "You good?"

"Everly had some guy over last night and they didn't stop banging until, like, three in the morning."

Sajan made a face. "Yikes."

"Was it Hakeem?" I questioned.

Chenoa shrugged. "Don't know. Don't care. Just need coffee," she muttered as she made a beeline for the fresh brew.

Sajan and I only exchanged titillated glances in response.

———

Later that afternoon, after still not hearing from Elijah, I decided to walk over to his dorm and check on him. Something about his lack of a response was bugging me, and I thought it would be better to simply talk to him instead of bombarding him with text messages.

Elijah and Hakeem shared a dorm in a building about a ten-minute walk from mine. It was a bit older, but still quite livable. Their rooms were the last ones on the first floor.

I knocked on Elijah's door and waited a few seconds. To my absolute shock, a red-headed girl opened the door.

She blinked at me, her hair dishevelled, and the shirt draping her small frame clearly one of Elijah's. "Oh. Hello. Can I help you?"

My mouth opened, but all I could do for a long while was stare back at her. My mind whirled with thoughts and feelings, the most prominent of all being a sense of indignation at the hypocritical pretense. There was no mistaking the look of a girl who'd spent the night in a boy's dorm – and given the disastrous mess I saw behind her, I had no doubts Elijah was so comfortable with her that he didn't feel the need to clean up. Perhaps it had not been her first sleepover.

And to think he was jealous of my friendship with Felix…

I eventually managed to clear my throat and smile at her. "Sorry. I was just seeing if Elijah was around," I said as innocently as I could muster, so she wouldn't know how instantly irate I was.

"He just went to grab us some coffee," she replied, studying me a little curiously. "Who are you, if you don't mind me asking?"

"He tutors me in physics," I lied quickly – well, he had once, so it wasn't completely a lie. "I was just checking to see if he was available, but I guess not."

She relaxed a bit. "Oh – well, do you want me to let him know you stopped by?"

I shook my head as I stepped away from the door. "No, no – that's okay. I'll just text him later." I nodded once at her. "Thanks, though."

"No problem. Have a nice day," she said as she shut it. I flipped on my heel and hurried out of the building, my breathing quickening as my anger bubbled over.

Phony, two-timing son of a bitch.

I gritted my teeth as I walked, crossing my arms and gripping my torso tightly. I tried my best not to let any of it get to my head, to remind myself that this boy fumbling me was no indication of my worth. It was the mantra I'd repeated so many times. So many damn times.

It would be a lie to say it didn't sting. But I wasn't sad about losing him. I couldn't care less if I never saw his face again.

In a way, the worst part of it all was the same feeling you got when someone broke a cherished keepsake, like a family heirloom. It wasn't just that the item was destroyed; it was the value behind it, the sentimentality attached to it, how it had travelled through time and space, maybe through generations, to end up in your hands. And then, you trusted it with someone, only to see it fall to its demise. A reminder, once again, that some things are better kept with you. That, sometimes, the safest place for you and your things was with yourself.

I could feel the barbed wire squeeze my heart like a boa constrictor as I stomped up my dorm building steps. I huffed as I threw open my door and fell onto the bed, rubbing my temples as my frustration fizzed out of my mouth in sighs.

"Seraphine?" I heard Emmanuella ask.

"It's me," I called back.

There was some rustling before she appeared in the doorway. It looked as though she'd just woken up, with her hair unkempt and her sleep shirt hanging off one shoulder. "What you up to?" she asked with a yawn.

I glanced out the window. "Just got back from Elijah's dorm."

"Oh?" she asked as she perked up. "And?"

"Well, a pretty redhead answered the door."

Her eyes widened. "What? Who?"

"Don't know. But it was clear they'd had a little sleepover." I rubbed my eyes. "I'm just over it all at this point."

"Fuck, dude. I'm sorry." She frowned. "Was he there?"

"No. He was out getting them coffee."

"Are you going to confront him?"

I sighed. "I don't know. Seems pointless."

She shrugged. "You could give him an ultimatum. Her or you."

I snorted. "I have no interest in salvaging anything with him. I'm sure I could very easily find another guy who cums too fast if I wanted it."

She cackled.

I nodded towards her. "Slept in?"

"Oh, yeah. Definitely needed it," she replied as she stretched.

"That's what Sundays are for."

She nodded in agreement, and then there was a knock on my door. "It's open!" I called.

It was Keiffer who strode in. He also looked like he'd slept in – majorly. "What's crackalackin', ladies?"

"Not much," I replied. "Just chatting."

"Cool, cool. Anyone up for a smoke?" he produced a joint of marijuana from his pocket.

"I'm good, thanks," I replied, while Emmanuella considered, then shrugged. "Sure, why not?" she responded as she made her way over to him.

"Dope," he said, fumbling around in his other pocket. Then he frowned. "Shoot. My lighter's gone."

"Gone or lost?" I teased.

"…Misplaced," he eventually replied, sighing. "Do you have one?" he asked Emmanuella.

Em snorted, but went into her room. She came back seconds later with a lighter.

"Sweet. Hey, keep an eye out for mine, will you?" Keiffer asked of me. "It's light blue with cartoon cheese on it."

"Why am I not surprised?" I retorted. He rolled his eyes before he and Emmanuella left the room.

I sat on my bed for a moment, pondering what to do with myself. I decided catching up on homework wouldn't hurt. I set myself up at my desk and pried open my chemistry textbook.

Just as I did, my phone buzzed.

Felix Clarkson
Hey. Are you free?

My stomach rumbled a bit as I reached for my phone.

Me
Depends. Is food involved?

Felix Clarkson
You only hang out with me because I feed you well, is that right?

My lips twitched.

Me

I can't confirm nor deny that.

Felix Clarkson

I'll make my own determination, then. Food can be involved. There's also a surprise.

Me

A surprise? What's the surprise?

Felix Clarkson

Well, it wouldn't be a surprise if I told you, now would it?

I huffed.

Me

Smartass.

Felix Clarkson

I'll pick you up in half an hour. Lose the sass by then, kindling.

Me

Nah, I'm good.

Felix Clarkson

When they diagnose me with high blood pressure in my fifties, I'm blaming it on you. See you soon.

My amusement was impossible to hide on my face as I shoved the homework aside and went to get my things.

CHAPTER 4

THE LATE AFTERNOON light was warm. It was a comforting feeling against the skin.

As we entered Felix's gardens, I saw what seemed like exercise equipment set up in a sort of circle on the grass. More specifically, they were boxing equipment – some punching bags, speed bags, and a dummy who'd seen better days. A fit, stout woman with short, spiky black hair stood by the equipment with a clipboard in her hands.

I slowed and frowned at Felix. "What is all that?"

He cleared his throat. "Seraphine, it has occurred to me that although you can be quite reactive – " he gingerly touched his stomach " – you seem to lack some…coordination and skill when it comes to fighting."

I stopped and stared at him. "You want me to learn how to fight?"

He nodded. "I think it would be a good idea."

I snorted. "Why? So the next time I elbow you, I actually break your ribs?"

"I'm hoping your days of elbowing me are over," he retorted, lowering his voice a little. "Rather, I'm drawing on our recent experience with Alchnost. He may not be something we have to deal with anymore, but we don't know what else lies ahead. I think it's best to be prepared with some self-defence."

He lowered his gaze. "I agreed to be a part of this little adventure. Think of this as a…condition, shall we say, to my acceptance of the invitation."

I guffawed again. "That implies that having you along for the adventure is something worth compromising for."

He cocked his head to the side. "Wasn't it you who wanted me to be a part of this, anyways?"

I sighed and looked over at the equipment. It wasn't the worst idea in the world to be prepared for a fight. He was right. We didn't know what else we might face in our quest for the Phoenixes.

I turned back to him. "Fine," I said, and we both continued on to the equipment.

The woman approached us as we came closer. "Hey, there," she said, extending her hand. "The name's Uma. Felix asked me to get you fighting."

"So I hear," I replied, shaking her hand. "I'm Seraphine. Nice to meet you."

"You're in good hands," Felix noted, nodding at Uma. "She taught everyone in my family to fight, too. We try to stay out of trouble, but money sometimes brings it to you." He looked at her. "I can't exactly kick her ass without there being dire social consequences, so do it for me, will you?"

"Consider it done," Uma said with a small smile.

Felix gave me a pat on the back. "I'll be inside. Catch up with you when you're done."

He disappeared inside the house, and Uma motioned for me to follow her over to a punching bag. "We're going to do some offense and some self-defence," she told me. "The moves draw on a few things – boxing, kickboxing, martial arts. Ever taken a class along those lines before?"

"*Oui*, when I was younger," I said.

"Nice. All right, let's start with some punches. Show me what you got."

I punched the punching bag.

She nodded once. "Okay, we've got some power in there. Just needs some finesse. Let's work on that form first."

I did not realize how technical punching was, but apparently, a correct punch relied on more than just pure anger alone. We spent what felt like a while working on my punches to get them right.

"Cool. Let's put a pin in that for now. On to kicks." She motioned to the dummy. "Give ol' Daryl Dummy a kick or two for me."

I kicked Daryl Dummy.

"Good. Kicking is your best bet – we ladies carry most of our muscle in our legs. If you're ever in trouble, try and get yourself kicking at the sweet spot. It's the same for both men and women, you know."

I nodded. We spent a little while working on kicking techniques, too. Then we moved on to what I called 'Ifs' – if I found myself pinned to the ground, do this. If I found myself pressed up against a wall, do that.

The sun was beginning to set when Uma gave me a high-five. "Nice work, chicka," she said. "Good first session. Couple more and you'll be a pro."

"Sounds good," I said, wiping away the sweat from my brows. It had been a good workout.

She began packing up her equipment, and I turned to head for the villa. As I neared, I saw Felix through a window, leaning against a wall in the kitchen with a glass of whiskey in hand. He waved for me to join him.

I made my way inside and met him in the kitchen, where scents of delicious cooking wafted through the air. "How do you feel?" he asked.

"Like I could properly break your ribs next time," I answered.

He sighed. "I like the energy, but stay away from my ribs, please."

I huffed at the ceiling. "Killjoy."

He rolled his eyes, but nodded towards the dining room. "Dinner's on the table. After, let's head to the cellar."

I was more than happy to comply.

———

"Look what I've set up," Felix said proudly as we entered the cellar, directing my attention to him. He stood before an easel, on which was a large whiteboard complete with markers, magnets, and an eraser. On the coffee table by the sofa and chairs, he had also placed a globe alongside some of the books we'd left out from the last research session.

I grinned. "Someone's an eager beaver."

He picked up a black marker. "It's like solving a puzzle."

"It is," I said, spinning the globe. "Hopefully, these things help us organize our thoughts a bit more."

"Agreed," he said. He then turned and began writing the riddle we were trying to solve on the whiteboard:

> "My light has hatched and shall brighten the way
> On your journey to the land where a temple lays
> In the vastest region of its kind
> The temple hides away from the blind
> Nestled in fauna with which it blends
> Where the trees dance around the river bend
> The temple sleeps through sweltering heat
> And the cries of the clouds who often weep
> Like to each other, this temple will draw
> My brothers and sisters in feather and caw
> And within it slumbers my wings of Earth
> Who awaits your hands to awaken its birth."

"There we are," he said before walking over to the bookshelf. "Shall I just pick some books at random to start sifting through?"

I didn't respond right away. "Hold on a second."

He turned back to look at me as I brought myself directly in front of the whiteboard, studying the riddle. "I think we're looking at this the wrong way," I continued.

Felix frowned. "How so?"

I looked at him. "The first riddle was four lines, and it told me where the sanctuary was quite directly. That meant all I had to do was decipher what the City of the Sun represented, which called for further research in books or atlases as a starting point. But I don't think it's the starting point here."

His gaze flitted to the riddle. "You don't think a hidden temple is mentioned in any of these books?"

"That's not what I'm saying," I replied. "It could be written somewhere, which we can come back to later if this thought process doesn't work. But look at what we've already got – " I motioned to the board – "this is a description, and a very detailed one at that. Maybe instead of searching for what books may say about this riddle, we should first see what the riddle has to say about itself."

"It's highly elegiac, though," Felix countered. "Doesn't that leave a little too much room for interpretation? What if we end up in a completely different direction?"

"Well, let's look at it piece by piece, and then put the pieces together and see if it makes sense," I said.

He considered this for a moment, then shrugged. "All right."

I grabbed a red marker as he sat down on the sofa beside the whiteboard. "Okay," I said. "*My light has hatched and shall brighten the way; on your journey to the land where a temple lays.* I see that as stating that this riddle's presentation is contingent on the fact that we hatched the Light Phoenix, and now we are looking for a temple. Agree?"

"Agree," Felix said.

"The next two lines. *In the vastest region of its kind; The temple hides away from the blind.*"

"From the legitimately blind, does it mean?" Felix asked with a frown. "That seems like an unrelated clarification."

"No, I would say that's too literal an approach, given the context of the riddle. To me, that just says that wherever this temple is located is in the largest area of that particular environment, and that it hides away from those who don't know anything about it very well."

"Oh. That makes more sense," Felix remarked with a nod. "Carry on."

"All right, and the next two. *Nestled in fauna with which it blends; Where the trees dance around the river bend.*"

"Okay, see, here's what I was talking about," Felix said, standing up and outstretched his hand. "Pass me the marker for a second."

I did, and he circled the words '*blends*' and '*dance.*' "The words are poetic, so what constitutes the meaning here?" he asked. "Something that blends could just be situated in the right place at the right time, or it can actually change appearance, like a chameleon. And how do trees dance? Does it mean wherever this is, it endures a lot of wind?"

"I think you're approaching it too narrowly," I answered. "Look at the bigger picture. *Nestled in fauna with which it blends.* I don't think she's trying to say the temple actually physically changes in any way. All she's saying is that the surroundings of the temple and the temple itself are so similar that it acts as a sort of camouflage. *Where the trees dance around the river bend* – to me, that just says the river is not straight, and there are a lot of trees. I'm focusing more on the fact that there is a river at all in this place. That in itself is a clue."

Felix considered this. "All right. *The temple sleeps through sweltering heat; And the cries of the clouds who often weep.* So, utilizing your methodology, that says this place is hot and rainy?"

"Exactly – now you're getting it."

"Okay," Felix said. "So we've got a large, hot, place with a lot of trees, a lot of rain, and a river."

I paused and then shook my head. "No. We've got the *largest*, hot place with a lot of trees, a lot of rain, and a river."

His brows shook. "Hm?"

"Could I borrow the marker?" I asked, and he promptly handed it to me. I underlined the *'est'* in *'vastest.'* "Remember this part? She could've just said 'vast,' but she didn't. She said 'vast*est*.' I think that's worth noting."

Felix stepped away from the board, cocking his head as he looked it over. "A lot of trees imply a forest of some kind."

I nodded slowly, my eyes darting over the words we were dissecting. "And a forest with a lot of rain is a rainforest. Given that it's hot too, it's probably tropical."

"Hm…the largest tropical rainforest…"

There was a pause as his eyes widened a bit, and he straightened his head atop his neck. "We're talking about the Amazon Rainforest, are we not?"

"I think we are."

"Interesting," Felix said, running a hand over his jaw. "But the Amazon is huge. How are we supposed to find the temple in such an expanse?"

"I think she answers that question in the next two lines. *Like to each other, this temple will draw; My brothers and sisters in feather and caw.*"

Felix hummed. "That says that the Phoenixes will sense it, doesn't it?"

My heart began thumping with excitement in my chest as I nodded enthusiastically. "And the final two lines are just our indication that this is the Earth Phoenix we're after, as we've previously discussed."

He turned to me, his violet irises luminous. "Well, look at that. Learned to fight and solved a puzzle."

I smiled. "It's been a productive afternoon. So when do we leave?"

He glanced at his Rolex and then back up at me. "It's almost seven. We probably won't have time to make it to the Amazon and back before classes tomorrow. Maybe we should wait until Friday afternoon?"

I groaned, giving him a look of bewildered exasperation. "*Friday?* Are you serious?"

"Seraphine, we really shouldn't be skipping classes for random excursions."

"They're not random," I replied, crossing my arms. "We conducted a thorough analysis to come to a likely conclusion. That's not random."

He sighed, rubbing his eyes with his fingers. "Don't try to manipulate the argument with a logical fallacy."

I squinted. "I haven't the slightest clue what you're talking about."

"It's called a red herring," he explained. "When you distract from the original argument at hand with different information of lesser relevance. People use it to redirect conversations in their favor."

"Well, sure, except the information *is* relevant," I retorted. "You're suggesting we shouldn't skip classes for random excursions, but I'm saying the excursions aren't random – they're well thought out, and have proven to be lucrative in the past. And that means they're more meaningful, which therefore makes it easier to justify skipping classes for them."

He blinked at me. "Things would be a lot easier for me if you weren't so mouthy," he finally replied with a bit of disgruntled defeat.

I raised my eyebrows. "Now *that's* a red herring."

He thought for a moment, then let out a sad breath. "I'll go get a bag," he muttered.

————

The flight to the Amazon was supposed to be a little shorter than the flight to Heliopolis. By the time Aurora and Fuego were soaring Felix and I high above the rainforest's trees, it was late evening. The moon shone in the clear evening sky, giving off a mystifying illumination of the greenery below. The atmosphere we flew through had gotten more humid, too, and it was obvious it had rained over the forest not too long ago. We had left Lumina behind – it would have been more cumbersome to take her along.

Felix and I flew side by side, and as we found ourselves over the bulk of the forest, we both simultaneously let our Phoenixes take control of their flight pattern in the hopes that they would lead us to the blending temple. All we had to do was wait for them to find it.

As we continued to fly over the vast expanse of rainforest, I became enthralled with watching the stars above me whizz by. I had stared at the night sky before, but there was something more captivating about it now that I was much closer to it. Without really thinking, I reached out my arm and attempted to entrap the stars in my grasp. I knew there was no chance of that ever happening, but it was the childish joy the action brought to me that made me repeat it over and over, putting a smile on my face.

"I used to do that when I was young, too."

I turned to look at Felix, who was watching me with a nostalgic smile.

"When I still lived in my father's mansion, I would sneak out of the house in the middle of the night and go for flights with Fuego, always trying to get closer and closer to the stars. And then I would reach for them," he continued.

I cocked my head to the side, intrigued.

Felix turned his gaze to the stars, his eyes becoming somewhat misty. "The stars...they're all so far away and so far apart from each other, and each of them burns differently from the next. I couldn't help but think that even though we all appreciate the beauty and the shine they give off in the night, it doesn't make up for how lonely they are."

He reached up and tried to grab a star, like I had done just moments before. "I thought that if I grabbed all of the stars in the night sky, I could bring them together. I could make them see that even if they were hundreds of thousands of miles apart, and even if they felt like they were the only ones out there, that they were not alone. They would understand that there were many others just like them, all burning faintly miles and miles away from each other. And they would see that, although they were just specks of light when they were separated, together, they displayed a beautiful painting on the canvas of the night sky."

He brought his arm down and looked at the back of Fuego's neck; I could feel the sadness enveloping him. "But I guess it's a bit juvenile to assume the stars even have feelings. Or that, if they did, they wouldn't prefer the loneliness they're used to. We tend to get used to being alone, so why wouldn't they?"

There was a long pause after this as I processed the gloom of what he had just said, looking back up at the stars with a newfound sympathy for the things in life that found themselves in solitude, and could not fathom another way of being. Then I glanced briefly at the star tattoo on his hand, pondering it, remembering how he'd been an advocate for reading the stars. Was that the meaning behind it?

Moments later, Aurora and Fuego burst into a frenzy of activity. Loudly squawking and feverishly flapping their wings, they rapidly began descending, and like two shooting stars, we found ourselves plunging down beneath the trees.

"They must have found it!" Felix yelled as we dashed towards the ground.

The Phoenixes both coasted abruptly to the forest floor, and the blur of motion came to a sudden stop as they landed shakily and came to a halt. Felix and I both hopped off our

Phoenixes' backs onto the moist dirt and took in our surroundings.

The forest was damp and reeked of humidity and moisture. Every which way I looked, the dense jungle greeted my eyes in the shadows of the night. Various greenery in the form of trees, mosses, vines, and ferns lined every nook and cranny, and an ominous hum caused by the sounds of forest bugs zipping to and from in the air buzzed around us. Fireflies danced between the vines that hung from the branches of the trees, and I could tell just by the sight of movement that numerous creepy crawlies were spread about the vegetated forest floor. It was hard to tell exactly what life was present in the near vicinity due to the low light, and frankly, I didn't really want to take a closer look, especially because I had a pretty good idea of what lived in the Amazon Rainforest.

I could hear running water coming from somewhere nearby, which indicated to me that there may have been a stream or possibly a section of the Amazon River flowing not too far from where we were. And in the near distance, I could also hear a stifled orchestra of songs and chirping from what sounded like many different species of birds. I found this odd; from what I understood, most birds slept as soon as night fell.

Aurora and Fuego, who seemed a bit restless and disturbed, extended their necks towards a section of dense vines that hung from a rather large tree. Flapping their wings in an impatient way, they seemed to convey the message that something of importance was in the direction they were motioning towards.

"What's the matter, girl?" I asked Aurora, soothingly rubbing her neck. She cooed back towards me with strain.

"I think the temple's this way," Felix said, walking towards the vines. "They're very distracted and drawn towards whatever it is."

"Well, go on – do the honours," I said, motioning to the vines expectantly.

Felix nodded quickly at me, his lavender eyes possibly the brightest things around us, and then reached for the long, twisted greenery. Slowly, he pulled them to the side.

An unusually large expanse was revealed to be hiding behind the vines. Huge trees surrounded what seemed like a purposefully cleared dirt floor and provided a covering of large leaves up above, making it impossible to see from the sky. It was dimly illuminated by the multiple fireflies that hovered lazily in the air. There was a stone pedestal placed in the center of the space, and in front of it were flat rocks that formed an unconnected path leading to a relatively big structure. It was made of the same stone as the pedestal and was covered from top to bottom in vines, mosses, and other plants, so much so that if you blinked and looked away, you had to struggle to make out the outline of the building beneath the greenery. Large steps led to a huge, ancient-looking slab of rock – what could be the entrance, I assumed. At the top of the structure, and the only part partially uncovered by vegetation, were three statues of identical Phoenixes, lined in a horizontal row across the width of the building.

All around the temple, be it on the branches of the trees, perched on the ground around it, or flying overhead, were birds of nearly every size, shape, and colour. The songs that had been muffled were now very clear, as all the birds chimed in with their unique and individual sounds. I concluded that perhaps the temple drew more than just Phoenixes to its locale. Personally, I was fascinated by the possibility of the phenomena.

"I don't know about you, but that looks like a temple that blends in with its surroundings to me," I said quietly.

"I would have to agree with you there," Felix responded. "Come on."

We brushed past the vines and slowly made our way into the temple's courtyard, our Phoenixes following closely behind us. I stopped in the middle, standing by the pedestal, and became consumed with the detail I could make out beneath the plants covering the temple. It seemed intricate Greek designs had been meshed with traditional Amazonian art on its walls, making it unique to any kind of ancient architecture I had ever seen before. Walking past the pedestal, Felix approached the temple's entrance, and Aurora and Fuego trailed in his footsteps eagerly in their little mesmerized trance.

The dark was a bit of a hindrance, so I reached deep down to grab hold of the magic. I found it, grasped it, and then shut my eyes as I expressed the light as hard as I could. Upon reopening my eyes, I saw I had now brightened the previously dark area we were in, and I could see details much better in the yellowish light.

"Good thinking!" Felix yelled out to me. He had stopped in front of the building and was now studying it closely.

I took the opportunity to glance around once more at the surroundings, now that I could see more clearly. The most striking thing I noticed around where I stood were footprints, the depressions of which I hadn't picked up on in the dark. I approached one set of them closely, frowning – they seemed relatively fresh, and it looked like there were several different sets with several different types of markings. Different shoes – that likely meant more than one person.

"Someone's been here," I noted. "Recently."

Felix turned to me, his eyebrows raised. "What?"

I nodded at the footprints. He came over and inspected them. "Hmph," he said decisively. "You're right."

I pondered the thought of who it could be. Were there other Phoenix Keepers who somehow knew of the same legend? We may have had the book, but maybe through hearsay? It wasn't impossible. And I knew there were lots of indigenous tribes who still lived within the Amazon. Maybe they'd stumbled this way on a hunt? Maybe they knew about the legend, too? Maybe *they* were the Phoenix Keepers?

Felix considered the footprints for a moment before he

made his way back up to the presumed entrance of the temple. "There's no handle," he said, motioning to it.

"There isn't?"

Felix shook his head, placing his hands on either side of the large rock slab and pushing forcefully to the right, left, and then up and down, which yielded no result. "Nope. And it won't budge, either."

I bit my lip. *Excellent.* Now how the hell were we supposed to get in?

Clearly as confused as I was, Felix looked around the front of the temple, and then turned his attention back to where I was standing. "What's that?" he asked, nodding towards the pedestal.

I glanced at it. Upon closer inspection, I realized there were two parts to it. The top part had a similar structure to the temple that lay before it – in fact, I soon realized it was a miniature model of the temple. The top of the model contained three separate but similar indents, all in a horizontal row. The lower part had a large, stone wheel, made ancient by what looked like years of wear and overgrowth of moss.

"It seems to be some kind of mechanism," I answered him. "Maybe it opens the door."

"Well, then, open it!" Felix exclaimed.

Not really thinking about it, I stood over the pedestal and tried to spin the wheel. It didn't move. A second and third try proved futile.

"Huh," I muttered, taking a step back and studying the pedestal again with perplexity. I had been almost certain that it was the solution.

"What? Is it not working?" Felix asked, and his tone implied he was a little frustrated.

"No," I answered him.

He sighed and rubbed his face with his palm. "Well, this is just swell."

Ignoring his whining, my attention was drawn back to the

top part of the pedestal. As I studied the indentations, I slowly began to recognize that it was intended for something to be placed in them. The depth and shape of the gaps indicated moving parts, like some kind of ancient machinery.

"Something's not right," I said, mainly thinking aloud to myself.

"Yes, and that something is *you*," Felix stated, looking at the door. "That thing must just be for decoration. There's got to be a different way to open it."

"No, no, that's not what I meant," I retorted. "Something's not right with the pedestal."

Glancing upwards, I got another look at the three Phoenix statues atop the temple, and it hit me.

"Felix, the statues are missing!" I blurted.

He gave me a squinty gaze. "The statues?"

"*Oui*," I said, pointing to the indentations in front of me. "It's a replica of the temple. There are three Phoenix statues on top of the temple, and none here, even though there are places for them. I think we need to find them and put them in their spots so the pedestal matches the top of the temple, and *then* spin the wheel!"

Felix's eyes returned to normal size, and he pursed his lips together. "Well, I guess that makes sense. But where are they?"

I glanced around the temple's courtyard. "They're probably around here somewhere! Look around!"

We began scurrying around the surrounding area, searching every possible location for the Phoenix statues – in the holes of logs, underneath rocks, hidden behind vines and plants. It took about fifteen minutes of feverish searching before we both reconvened, yielding empty hands.

"They're not here," Felix breathed, leaning against the pedestal.

I rubbed my forehead with my hand, my eyes falling back to the footsteps. I considered them again. Then I lifted my gaze back up to Felix, who had also been looking at the footsteps.

We made eye contact, and I knew we were both thinking the same thing.

"Maybe whoever was here took them," I suggested for both of us.

He let out a long breath. "Well, that doesn't make our lives any more difficult at all," he said sarcastically.

I felt a flood of discouragement wash over me. Who could have taken the miniature statues? Why would they have taken them? And, most importantly, how were we supposed to find them and get them back?

A bug landed on me, and I swatted at it in annoyance. "Yeah, I'm getting eaten alive here, too," Felix mentioned at my movement. "Maybe we should get out of here and think of a plan."

I didn't respond right away. "You mean go home?"

I saw him shake his head. "No – just out of the forest." He looked up at the canopy of trees. "I think we're close to the border of Colombia. We could fly to Barranquilla."

I frowned, looking at him. "Why Barranquilla?"

"My father's got a hotel there."

My brows relaxed. I should have seen that one coming.

I turned to the Phoenixes, who were standing at the edge of the clearing, watching us. I didn't really have an alternative solution.

"To Colombia it is, I guess."

CHAPTER 5

As soon as we had made our way out of the trees, we flew north, towards the northern coast of South America. Once we could make out the coastline and the hints of city light down below, we followed it west until Felix announced he could see Barranquilla.

It was still night, and so landing in some brush at the edge of the city was stealthy enough to keep us secretive. We sent Aurora and Fuego off into hiding before making our way into civilization.

The city was quite alight for a very early Monday morning. Different coloured lights twinkled from the buildings, most of which were vibrantly painted. The night sky seemed to dance with colour, as if a million neon lights were flashing within it. There were a few cars and people out and about, and music seemed to evaporate from some of the clubs and bars on the street corners. While not as muggy as the rainforest, it certainly was still humid and warm. In the distance, I could see towering high-rises glistening in the illuminations of the night around them, the glass a sort of reflective mirror, bouncing the colours off in prismatic rays and blending into the darkness.

Felix nodded at the high-rises. "That's where we need to

go. The hotel's in the Vizcaya area." He glanced around at the roads, spotting a taxi at a red light. He whistled and hailed it, and the taxi pulled up promptly beside us. We shuffled in, and Felix told the driver the name of the hotel. The driver nodded, and we were off.

I watched the lights and colours whir past us as we drove by. It was an enchanting city – in the day, it must have been full of life, just like its people. I thought about Julius and his Colombian side; the Colombian architecture and atmosphere perfectly embodied him and his essence.

"Did your father meet Marlli in Baranquilla?" I asked Felix out of curiosity, turning to look at him.

He was on his phone, and he shook his head. "She was from Medellín – that's where they met," he replied. "Only major city in Colombia where we don't have any businesses." He glanced up at me. "Not anymore."

I raised my eyebrows. "Not even a hotel?"

"Certainly not a hotel," he remarked, looking back down at his phone. "I don't think my father could build a place to rest there in good faith." He was quiet for a moment. "He spent a lot of time there, back and forth from San Diego, doting on a woman who ultimately did him wrong. I'm sure the city has drained him as much as she did."

I turned to watch outside the window again, considering the world and what it meant to us. The places we loved, the places we didn't – where we went and where we came from. How the places we lived in made us feel, and how the places we travelled to made us long for home, whether that be where we'd arrived or where we intended to return. It was amazing how the world shaped us, made us experience things, summoned us, or sent us away. I thought about Montreal and San Diego, how they both meant something entirely different to me, but how they also were both so important to me; there was the place I was molded, and then the place that would paint me. I thought about Heliopolis, and Stignano, and the

Amazon, and now Baranquilla. I wondered how long the list would grow, and wondered what would eventually come of it – what I would learn, what I would leave with. Where I would settle down, marry, and raise a family.

And ultimately, where I would…

I swallowed as I shook my head a bit.

The thought of death was frightening to me, a harsh reality I hadn't quite come to terms with. The intrusive, nagging truth sometimes meandered into my head when I least wanted to remember it all might – *would* – end someday. I'd heard people describe mortality as a blessing; after a certain point, living became bothersome, or painful, or tiring, and all you longed for was eternal sleep. I couldn't fathom it. My life was my most beloved possession. I never wanted it to end – besides, what came next? *Was* there anything that came next?

I shivered, letting the thoughts wriggle out of my head.

"What's the matter?"

I turned to Felix. I hadn't realized he'd been watching me, but the look on his face carried concern.

I grew a bit flustered – I didn't want to dwell on the topic. "Nothing. I'm fine."

I knew by the way his finger tensely traced the length of his jaw, as if writing further worry in his features, that he didn't believe me. "Are you sure?" he persisted, his eyes intent.

I sighed a bit. "I don't know. I was just thinking about dying." I bit my lip. "It scares me."

He didn't respond right away. "A natural fear. Though I'm surprised to hear it from you, given how gung-ho you seem about – " he glanced at the taxi driver – "…well, you know."

I found myself a bit tickled at the irony. "I tend to forget as much about death as I possibly can," I explained. "I try to live as if I'll never die. It keeps me…less anxious. But occasionally, I remember I'm not immortal. And I'm forced to face the feelings that come with it."

He considered this with a slow nod of the head, his eyes

flitting over my face like moths over a dwindling light. "Well, if it's any consolation, you'll likely live long after me," he then offered.

I frowned deeply. "Why do you say that?"

He grew amused. "Well, for starters, I'm the only smoker between the two of us," he ruminated. "And I'm a man. Statistically speaking, that gives you an advantage."

His amusement was not contagious. In fact, if anything, the thought was a bit distressing. "That doesn't really console me."

He chuckled. "Don't worry, kindling. When I'm dead, I promise to haunt you regularly."

The nonchalance of his delivery on such a morbid matter seemed odd to me, but before I could comment further, the taxi came to a stop in front of a tall, shimmering high rise. My attention was drawn to the grand fountains lining the incline leading to the large, glass doors of the hotel.

"*Gracias*," I told the driver as we exited, and Felix paid him with a considerable tip. We made our way up the incline, through the glass doors, and into the ostentatious lobby of the Clarkson Hotel. A young man with cinnamon skin and dark hair stood behind the check-in counter, and he smiled at us while we entered.

"*Buenas noches,*" he said with a nod, and then he seemed to recognize Felix. "*Señor* Clarkson, it is a pleasure to have you here. What may I do for you?"

"Is the penthouse available?" Felix asked.

The man made an open gesture with his hands. "For you, *señor*, it is always made available," he replied, bustling around under the desk for a room key and handing it to Felix. "Any bags we can take care of for you? Anything we can have brought to the room?"

"No bags," Felix said, taking the key. He seemed to pause. "But whiskey and cigars would be good," he then added. He glanced at me. "And cider. A Strongbow, if you have one."

"*Por supuesto.* We will have that up to your room as soon as possible," the man said, grinning at us both. I returned the smile and thanked him before we made for the elevators.

The penthouse was on the thirty-sixth floor of the building, and it was absolutely ridiculous. It had two levels, the first of which contained a sitting area, a private pool table, a mini bar, and a huge terrace with an infinity pool. On the second level were two bedrooms, which you reached by ascending a gorgeous, glass spiral staircase and passing a red velvet chaise lounge. Each had a gorgeous adjacent bathroom, complete with a large Jacuzzi tub. There was gold and silver detailing all around – on the walls, on the decorative pillars, and on the fixtures. Outside the massive glass windows, I could see an incredible view of the cityscape, illuminated by warm lights in the dark of the early morning.

I threw my stuff down on one of the armchairs and plopped onto the black leather sofa, staring out at the view. "Wow," I murmured in disbelief.

Felix shuffled over to the window, leaning against the wall. "It's a beautiful country," he said in agreement. "It's unfortunate it has to be so tainted by its past."

I considered this. "You could make that argument about a lot of places, though," I remarked. "Even the United States."

He nodded slowly. "But some places in the world get more forgiveness than others," he added. "Whether deserved or not. Especially the United States."

I couldn't really disagree with him. We were quiet for a moment, until there was a knock on the door and Felix went to answer it. A hotel employee handed him a box of cigars and a silver ice bucket containing his whiskey and my cider – they had managed to find me a Strongbow. Felix took it and tipped him before sending him on his way and shutting the door.

"Here," he said, handing me a glass and the can of Strongbow.

"Thanks," I said, pouring the cider into the glass and sipping on it. Light, fizzy, sweet, fruity – just what I needed. It refreshed my insides in a much-needed way, the same way I desperately needed my outsides refreshed. Even in the short time I'd spent in the humidity of the rainforest, I had perspired and dirtied in a way that made me feel disgusted with myself.

"I'm going to go shower," I told Felix.

He shrugged. "All right."

I went upstairs to one of the bathrooms and gratefully stepped into the rainfall shower. I ran it as hot as possible, sipping my cider whenever I wasn't directly under the torrent of steamy water.

When I emerged back downstairs in a fresh pair of shorts and a cropped tee, I was surprised to see Felix putting on his shoes. He glanced up at me as I entered.

"I'm heading out for a bit," he murmured quickly, as if he wanted to start and end the conversation in a hurry.

I frowned. "Out where?"

He motioned to the window. "Just out on the town. For a walk."

I studied him. "That's unlike you. Aren't you a bit of a homebody?"

He sighed. Perhaps he'd come to accept the inevitability that I would pick up on any behaviour that didn't remotely resemble the norm. "I need a few things."

"What things?" I asked, crossing my arms.

"Just…things. Some snacks I like."

"I have snacks."

"I said snacks I *like*, Seraphine."

I made a face. "What's wrong with my granola bars?"

"Nothing's wrong – " he huffed, making for the door. "I'll see you later."

He opened it, but before he could leave, I started for my own shoes. "I want to come, too."

Felix whirled around to face me in shock, as if the idea was unheard of. "What? Why?"

I shifted my eyes. "It's a city I've never been to. It'd be nice to see what it's like."

He scanned my face. At first, it seemed like he was going to object, which made me even more suspicious. But then, he eventually relaxed his startled gaze into a more defeated one.

"Well, all right, then. Let's go," he mumbled.

We were quiet as we made our way down to the lobby and stepped out onto the streets. The night air and soft breeze felt refreshing on my now clean skin. Felix began walking, clearly with a direction in mind, and I simply followed.

We turned down several main streets, drawing closer and closer to the sounds of liveliness and nightlife. I was surprised Felix would be going towards the sounds of social butterflies and parties. People were out and about, laughing and chatting and singing and even dancing where there was music, without a care in the world. It was as if they hadn't realized night had fallen and it was time to rest.

Eventually, Felix rounded a corner where the stone streets could only carry pedestrians. There were some small businesses – clubs or bars, it seemed – that had certainly seen some wear and tear, but it didn't seem to hinder their teeming clientele, who lined up patiently for entry. I studied our surroundings, the people gathered who were drinking together and having a good time. Everyone seemed in good spirits – very good spirits, considering it was the early hours of a Monday morning.

I was so distracted by the sights around me that I almost didn't notice Felix had made his way over to a man outside one of the bars. I watched as the man leaned forward to say something in Felix's ear. He simply nodded and handed the man some cash – a lot of cash, it seemed, for the small box of cigars that was returned to him.

Cigars – didn't he already get cigars from the hotel?

"*Hola, bonita.*"

I whipped around to find a tall, handsome man beaming down at me, his pearly white teeth a bright flash against his tanned and heavily tattooed skin. He looked to be about my age, perhaps a little older, with luscious, dark brown hair that fell past his shoulders and warm, brown eyes that clung to mine.

I was taken aback, more by his attractiveness than anything else, but managed to smile in return. "Oh. *Hola.*"

"*Por qué no estás bailando?*" he asked me, tilting his head as if to pronounce his strong jaw even further.

The Spanish language was somewhat similar to French, so I could gather he was asking me something about dancing. Nevertheless, I just laughed a little awkwardly and clarified, "Uh, no Spanish. Sorry."

His grin somehow grew bigger and brighter. "*No hay problema, chickita,*" he assured, taking my hand and pulling me towards him. "*No necesitas hablar español para bailar.*"

Though I was a bit wary of a stranger in an unfamiliar place, I was also a little too enthralled with his prettiness to resist. I let him take my other hand and bring me closer, his body leading mine in beat with the music that blared in the background.

But before I could fall into rhythm with him, a firm hand on my shoulder yanked me away.

"She's with me." Felix's stern words came from behind me, drawing the attention of the man who I'd suddenly been parted from. I peered up at Felix; his lavender eyersbore a piercing scowl, his lips pressed with displeasure.

The man threw his hands up defensively as he backed away – Felix was only a few inches taller than him, but the man suddenly seemed comparably small. "*Lo siento, señor,*" was all he said before he turned and disappeared into the crowd.

I turned to frown at Felix just as he made to glare at me. "I leave you alone for five minutes and you start frolicking about with random men?" he asked, unimpressed.

"I didn't have much of a chance to frolic before I was so

rudely interrupted," I grumbled back, trying to catch a glimpse of where the pretty man had gone.

His hand shot down from my shoulder to grip me by my forearm. "I thought we agreed that I was your dance partner."

I surveyed him, my eyes narrowing. His features were laden with a begrudged indignation, his jaw strained, his brows furrowed low above his eyes. There was no humour to be found within him – only ice, save for the ember of aggravation that flickered in his stark lavender irises.

"This isn't one of your father's events," I replied bluntly, pulling my hand away from him so I could cross my arms against my chest.

"If it will keep you away from strange men in foreign countries, then it applies everywhere," he countered.

I lowered my gaze, the corner of my mouth twisting. "Why does it matter?" I pounced. "Are you jealous?"

He scoffed immediately, his nose crinkling. "Perish the thought," he sniped.

"Good. In that case, please excuse me."

I tried to turn, but he grabbed me again. "Where the hell are you going?"

I gave him an innocent expression. "To find my little friend and finish our dance, of course." I raised my brows. "You know, since it won't bother you."

He gritted his teeth, releasing his grip on me a bit dramatically. I could see his hands flex at his sides as he clenched and unclenched them, but whatever words were trying desperately to escape the barricade of his lips never came.

"You could always find a pretty girl to dance with," I suggested with a smirk.

He scoffed. "Of course I can. Not that I need your permission."

Something roiled deep within me, a little fiery, and at the same time, a little chilled. "Good. Glad that's settled," I spat.

"So am I."

This time, I successfully managed to turn away from him before he could stop me, and I pushed my way into the crowd. I brushed past sweaty bodies and paused in gaps to scan the people all over the streets, but try as I might, I could not find the handsome man.

After a lengthy time had passed, I threw in the towel and returned to where I'd last been with Felix. He wasn't standing where I'd left him, but after glancing around, I spotted him sitting grumpily on the steps of a business a ways up the street. His arms were crossed as he puffed on one of his cigars, staring in front of him at what seemed like nothing in particular.

I rolled my eyes, but approached him. He turned to look at me with disdain.

"I thought you were dancing up a storm with twinkle toes," he grumbled at me.

"Couldn't find him."

"How tragic."

I looked around again. "Didn't I tell you to go dancing yourself?"

"I did," he replied snappily. "I danced with one of the most stunning women I've ever seen."

A little spark skimmed my chest, but it calmed when I studied the obvious lack of perspiration on his skin. "Really? And you didn't break a sweat?"

He puffed his cigar. "Piss off, Seraphine."

I made a face. "Glad to see you've only gotten more rotten in my absence."

"And you doing all this just to get a rise out of me isn't what you'd consider rotten?"

"Why the hell would you think me dancing with another guy has *anything* to do with you?"

Felix's eyes flared, but he didn't answer. He simply looked away from me, the smoke that escaped his lips becoming twisted in the humid air.

We were quiet for a moment before I smirked. "Besides, if I

wanted to piss you off, I could do way better than just dance with a guy."

He didn't respond, but a muscle feathered in his jaw – he was seething.

"Maybe I would have had him come back to the hotel with me," I suggested mischievously. "He could have spanked me until I was all red, or tied me up with ropes …maybe eaten me out while I was bent over a – "

Felix whirled upwards in the blink of an eye, flinging his cigar to the ground. He gripped me by the tops of my arms and lurched me closer to him, so close I could feel the heat of the fire crackling in his glare.

"Such wicked, heinous words, Seraphine," he hissed between clenched teeth. "Your lips are better than that."

I lifted my chin. "Still not jealous, hm?"

Those lavender irises churned relentlessly. "Not in the slightest," he snarled. "I'm only stopping you from disre-specting yourself."

"Liar," I claimed immediately.

He levelled my pompous stare with an emblazoned one of his own. "You are so…"

His words got lost somewhere, so I suggested some of my own. "Mean? Ridiculous? Evil?" I spat challengingly.

But something had shifted within those liquid pools of lavender fire – an admiration of sorts. I could hear the smirk in his words and feel it in his gaze as his eyes locked with mine.

"…Obvious," he finally admitted.

It was my turn to be caught off guard, but I tried not to let it show. He took a moment to straighten himself, his body moving deliberately slow, as if he were a lazy floe of ice wafting down an unhurried river. His frigid features melted slowly into cunning wisps of flame as he lifted his hands off me.

"All right, kindling. You have my undivided attention," he crooned. "Since you seem to be starving for it."

I gaped at him. "You've got to be joking."

60

"Oh, I'd never joke about such a thing."

"How many mental backflips did you have to do to come to that deranged conclusion?"

He chuckled to himself, angling his chin. "Something I've realized about you, Seraphine, is that you seem to enjoy maddening me. You particularly relish finding new limits to which you can push me. Naturally, I can only assume this stems from your innate desire for…well, my reaction."

He leaned in closer, his eyes transfixing my own. I could feel my breath quicken a bit at the scent of his cologne that now wafted into my nose – notes of rich cedarwood and inviting cardamom.

"I see the satisfaction in your eyes when you defy me, or anger me, or stun me," he went on, his breath falling on my skin. "You take pleasure in making me forget myself, in making me feel more than think."

I did not balk. "I have no idea what you're talking about," I said swiftly, raising my brows. "This all sounds as foolish as you are."

Immediately after the words left my mouth, I found myself pensive, wondering what they would garner, fishing for any hint of a clue on Felix's face…

I tried not to let the sudden awareness show in my features, but it was clear something faltered, for his smile simply widened into a grin.

"There it is," he mused. "You must find me just as intriguing as I find you."

He offered his palm out to me. My eyes flickered to his hand, then back up to his crafty face.

"Given you seem so keen to dance," he hummed, his lavender eyes alight, "allow me this chance to so foolishly indulge you, kindling."

My lips curled with amusement. "I think the one begging for attention here is you."

He flashed that Cheshire cat smile again. "Two people

begging each other for attention isn't the most farfetched theory in the world, is it?"

I arched a brow. "And if I don't want to dance with you?" I challenged.

"Oh, but you do," he purred with a wink.

I let my smirk crawl slowly across the width of my face. Then, I slyly slid my hand atop his.

He pulled me closer in a way that felt protective. I felt my heart thump in my chest at the sudden shift. The music still played on behind us, and we simply began moving with whatever Latin song filled the space. It was unpolished and far from the pristine execution of our ballroom dancing. But I appreciated the lighthearted airiness the music extracted from us – a liberating sensation, like nakedness of the body and mind. Something about it all seemed to wash away the remnants of any friction – and envy – we carried.

Within minutes, Felix was heartily smiling. Then grinning. Then laughing.

And so was I.

―――――

By the time we stumbled back into our room with numb, exhausted feet, the sun was just beginning to peer over the horizon.

"I'm just going to have a quick smoke," Felix said to me, motioning to the stairway. "Don't feel obliged to wait for me."

I nodded dazedly, throwing my shoes in a heap and waddling up the stairs. "Have a good sleep."

"You too, Seraphine."

I yawned loudly as I made it to the open doorway of my claimed bedroom, leaning against the frame as my body fully embraced the extent of my fatigue. But as I managed to reopen my eyes and the new breath filled my lungs, a nagging thought crept into my mind. A recollection of those cigars he'd bought while we were out – the excursion he'd suspiciously wanted to go on by himself to retrieve *snacks* – made me pause.

Those cigars weren't snacks at all.

Why would he bother lying about grabbing something, let alone insisting on doing so alone, if he had nothing to hide?

Though my body begged me to lay down, I slowly made my way back out of my bedroom and tiptoed to the top of the staircase. Given he'd been acting so strangely, I didn't think he would be so open to answering my questions – I'd likely need to seek them out myself.

The room was dark, but I could see the flicker of embers on the balcony. I squinted, realizing it was indeed a cigar he was smoking methodically as he sat at one of the recliners, gazing out at the horizon. It took a moment, but I finally was able to spot the box he'd purchased on the side table next to him.

I crouched down, trying to get a better view. For a while, he did nothing but smoke that cigar slower and slower – almost painstakingly slow. And just when I'd nearly accepted there wasn't anything abnormal going on, he turned and reached for the box, pulling out a little pouch.

My eyes became twice their size as he then spilled a bit of white powder on the table, used two credit cards to turn it into a thin line, and put his nose to the end.

CHAPTER 6

I COULD BARELY SLEEP that night. Every attempt at shutting off my mind only made me replay the moment that disturbed every ounce of peace I had. I tossed and turned like a manic insomniac.

I hadn't known the words for what I had witnessed, and so I had chosen not to try. I didn't even make a move to confront him. Instead, I'd stared in a flummoxed state of shock for several long minutes before finally retreating to my room on unsteady legs.

I'd never done drugs in my life. I had never smoked weed, let alone a cigarette. The idea of losing control, of losing myself, terrified me. And the sight of him being so reckless with his own life…

I grumbled as I finally threw in the towel on getting any sort of decent rest, sitting up in bed and rubbing my eyes. The sun had risen outside my window; normally the glow of natural light pleased me, but my discontent was too frigid for even the sun to melt. I made incomprehensible sounds of irritation as I splashed cold water on my face in the hopes that it would help me wake. It only contributed to my sour mood.

I dressed and left my room only to discover that Felix's was empty; he must have never come to bed. I peered over the staircase landing and found him in the same spot I'd last seen him on the balcony. Mumbling, I stomped down the stairs towards him.

He glanced over at me as I opened the balcony door; the pouch was noticeably absent from the side table, instead replaced with an assortment of fruits and pastries. "Morning. I ordered some breakfast," he said before bringing a cigar to his lips.

I grabbed a banana and a muffin, stuffing the latter in my mouth as I peeled the yellow fruit. "Thanks for remembering I eat food in the morning," I griped, my mouth full. "And not cigars."

His brows shook a bit. "That's a chintzy tone."

I was not in the mood; I ignored the comment, but could not ignore how frustrated I was with him. Despite that, I didn't even know what – if anything – I could say about what I witnessed without launching us into a heated discussion. "You didn't go to bed," I noted bluntly as I ate.

He shrugged nonchalantly, putting the cigar to his mouth once more. "I wasn't really sleepy."

I chomped on the banana before I'd finished swallowing the muffin, staring out over the balcony at nothing in particular. The only thing I was focusing on was keeping my mouth shut before it exploded with accusations and questions and anger.

"Is that billboard causing you distress?" I heard Felix ask.

My narrow eyes flickered to him, then back out to the spot I'd been staring at – it was, in fact, an advertisement for what seemed like a bank. Or perhaps an insurance company. Or an investing one. I couldn't be exactly sure, because it was written in Spanish. But there were dollar signs and an air of professionalism about it, so it must have had something to do with saving money, claiming money, or making money.

"No," I mumbled.

"Is your face aware of that?"

I stuffed my face with the last of the banana to prevent myself from snapping at him, reaching for an orange that I erratically – and aggressively – began to peel.

"Seraphine, are you okay?"

"*Oui.*"

"Why are you dismembering that orange?"

I huffed. "Why don't you stop asking so many questions and just let me eat in peace?"

I could feel his eyes on me as he sucked pensively on the cigar. "And while you're at it, could you please smoke that fucking thing somewhere else?"

He stared at me, his brows creasing. "Did I...do something?" he asked hesitantly.

I threw the orange back down on the plate in frustration. All I could think about was how furious I was about the drugs and how hard it was to keep that torrent of thoughts from rushing out of my mouth like a rapid river. "You didn't fucking sleep, you idiot!"

Felix blinked. I could only imagine this was one of the most confusing exchanges he'd ever had. "I'm not understanding why that's thrown you into a fit of rage."

I let out some animalistic screech of irritation as I stood, jabbing a finger towards him. "Because you did it to yourself!" I snapped, the words breaking free of their prison. "You snorted cocaine and you couldn't sleep because of it!"

He choked on his own breath, whipping the cigar from his mouth as he coughed. When his breath had returned, he looked at me with a bewildered expression. "What?"

My chest was heaving. "You bought a whole pouch of it yesterday. Don't try to play dumb. I saw it."

He opened his mouth, but no words came out. His stunned eyes remained fixed on me, the lavender whirling with a troubled glaze.

I shook my head as I exhaled harshly. "And I thought the smoking was bad," I muttered.

Felix cleared his throat, turning to look out beyond me at the cityscape. "Everyone has their vices."

I snorted. "Right. Some people partake in retail therapy, some eat a little too much food, and some people smoke meth. Please tell me they're all one in the same."

"They're all bad if not done in moderation. But done occasionally, none are a death sentence."

"Sure. But only one of those things is illegal."

"Prohibition doesn't necessarily align with moral values. Alcohol was once illegal, too."

"Right. And while we're on the topic, you drink a lot of that, too."

He cocked his head ever so slightly to the side. A small, silent challenge. "If you were the one doing drugs, is this the way you'd like me to react?"

I didn't balk. "I wouldn't be stupid enough to put my life at risk that way."

"Oh, but you were." His brows rose. "Didn't you run off to Alchnost's for the damn book that got us in this mess?"

My nostrils flared. "That's different."

"How so?" He frowned at me thoughtfully. "Wasn't your life at risk then?"

"This is not about me justifying my actions. I don't have to explain anything to you," I snarled between gritted teeth.

"Then I think I'm more than justified to not explain anything to *you*, aren't I?" Felix remarked.

The tension between us felt like a living thing, spilling over the edge of the balcony in a desperate attempt to find the space it needed as our tempers raged beyond its capacity. In the ensuing silence, I only held Felix's gaze with a barbed one of my own, my insides fuming like an overheated machine. Deflection and excuses aside, his tone and face had taken on something like that of the man I'd first met, that of the man I thought I'd left behind long ago. I did not like that man. I did not want to see him again. And the fact that he was here before me didn't do my ire any favours.

"Do whatever you want," I spat next. My dismissiveness and abrupt end to the conversation seemed to surprise him, for his brows shook as his eyes scanned my face. If he insisted on being a version of himself that I could not tolerate, I would not stand in his way.

Soon after the words left my mouth, I whipped myself around and made for the balcony door.

"Seraphine," I heard him say as the balcony door slammed shut behind me. I didn't look back as I quickly threw my shoes on and left the hotel room.

I clomped down to the elevator like a madwoman. The elevator plopped me down at the lobby, and I bustled out of the hotel in a blind rage. I didn't know where I was going. I didn't care. I just had to get away from the room, from him.

I marched angrily down a street in a different direction than the way we had walked the previous night. Cars whizzed by on the street as the low hum of people's chatter filled the sidewalks. I pushed past everyone and everything, feverishly making my way towards nothing in particular.

About half an hour or so after I'd begun stomping, I happened upon a park. There was a mother playing with her young child in the grass and a jogger running around the perimeter. At one end, by a little café, a busker played a guitar, sending sweet tunes of cumbia music whirling into the warm morning air. Compared to the crowd we'd seen the just hours before, the park seemed comparably still. But even in the absence of people, the lush greenery and twittering birds filled the space with a reminder of the sounds and senses of life.

I watched the busker playing the guitar for a moment, and eventually, he lulled me over to a nearby chair outside the café. I watched his fingers, scratched and marked from what appeared to be countless years of playing, smoothly glide up and down the strings of the instrument. I leaned back as I listened, letting my eyes fall closed as I tried to let my frustration waft away with the music. Minutes whisked away as my face, strained with tension, slowly loosened with the calming sounds.

And just as I was expelling a deep breath, disruption ravaged my tranquility. "There you are!"

I groaned, my frown reforming as I opened my eyes and furrowed my brows. Felix was hurrying over to me, his hair windswept and his breathing shallow.

"I see your days of following me haven't acquiesced," I groused at him with a disgruntled squint.

He came to a stop beside me and caught his breath. "Thank goodness I have a way of tracking you down," he noted. "You've proven to be quite the flight risk."

I scowled as my annoyance with his ability to sense my presence resurged from our initial unpleasant days. I folded my arms across my chest, avoiding eye contact with him as I nodded towards the busker. "You're ruining my peaceful morning harmony."

I could feel his eyes still on me. "We should talk."

"That sounds like even more destruction to my peaceful morning harmony."

He sighed. "I'll buy you a coffee."

"I can buy my – "

"I know you can buy your own coffee," he interjected with a bit of frustration. "You're very capable of doing everything on your own. I hear you loud and clear every bloody time you remind me."

I eyed him, to which he just gave me a frustrated, but pleading, expression. "Look, just let me get us some coffee and we'll sort this out."

I held his gaze, my scowl unmoving. Eventually, I simply motioned to the café entrance. He proceeded to disappear within it, returning minutes later with two large coffees and a plate full of what looked like small pastries.

"Arepas," he said as my eyes fell to the plate. "They're corn cakes. These ones have cheese in them. I think you'll like the taste."

I slowly took one of the arepas and bit into it. The sweetness of the cake mixed with the savoury cheese melted beautifully in my mouth. I could feel the muscles in my face relax a bit as I reached for another.

"Told you," he said with a small smile.

I threw a glare up at him, to which he cleared his throat. I did not deny, however, that he was indeed correct.

I finished my next arepa before leaning back in my chair and squaring my shoulders. "Well, you wanted to talk." I scanned him up and down – despite how much taller he was than me, he seemed so small sitting there in the shadows of my irritation. "So talk."

He took in a sharp breath, shutting his eyes briefly before refocusing them on me. "I went on the defensive earlier," he said. "I'm sorry."

I waited, but he only looked at me with inquisition, gauging my reaction.

"Is that all you've got?" I pressed tiredly.

He cleared his throat. "I was kind of hoping there might be…an exchange of apologies."

"You want me to apologize for me finding out you snort cocaine?" I asked incredulously.

He looked upwards in what seemed to be a prayer for patience before looking back at me. "More so for the way you reacted to the discovery."

I folded my arms against my chest, one of my legs crossing over the other so I could bounce my foot repeatedly in thought. I stared him down, chewing on my lips as I pondered the request, trying to decide whether it was absurd or reasonable.

He took notice of my body language, his jaw working a bit

as his own eyes took on a curious gleam. "Why *did* you react like that, anyways?" he asked casually, softly, as if we were talking about the weather and not about his perilous life choices.

I stilled, my foot coming to a halt. My eyes drifted to the table between us as I shifted my focus to the question.

A good question, indeed.

I frowned at my own garbled thoughts. The way I'd reacted to the discovery was if I had been possessed by my own rage. Surely, a reaction so robust must have had a clear, underlying motive – a reason for such virile emotions.

What could have possibly fuelled such an innate and impassioned reaction?

Care seemed like the best answer. I didn't want to see my friend hurt. It was a fair explanation, all things considered.

"I'm worried about your health," I explained matter-of-factly, meeting his gaze again.

His eyes flickered to our surroundings, then back to me. "So it wasn't because you think I'm a bad person?" he followed.

My frown deepened. "What? No. Why would – "

"You said some judgmental things," he explained before I could inquire. "About legality and the like."

I shifted in my seat. He was right. I had said it was illegal. And upon reflection, it was a weak argument.

I knew crimes were born when an action offended people. Murder was self-explanatory; anyone who purposefully took another life with intent and malice could be considered a bad person.

But what about killing someone in self-defence?

The end result was the same. Someone was dead by another's hands. But the intent behind it – that was the difference. A similar thread could be woven to the impoverished father who stole food to feed his family, or the woman who sold her body to pay rent.

Illegal actions, yes. But were they ill-intentioned?

No, I did not believe that just because something was illegal meant it was morally wrong. And, if that wasn't enough nuanced complexity, the illegality of drugs was more to do with producing it, possessing it, or using it in a public space. The consumption of it in private was certainly not the illegal part. And regardless of where he consumed it, I didn't think the fact he used drugs in and of itself made him – or anyone who did drugs – a bad person.

Someone who had moral disregard, who harmed others intentionally, who enjoyed the displeasure and the distress of others...*that* was a bad person. And that did not necessarily align with all things that were considered illegal.

I firmly believed good people could make bad choices, and likewise, bad people could make good choices. And most importantly, I didn't think those choices were necessarily always character-defining or redefining.

"I'm sorry," I replied. "I've never been faced with this situation before. I don't really know how to handle it."

He nodded slowly. "I get that." A half-smile flitted across his face. "I sort of did the same with the whole Phoenix adventure thing in the beginning."

My own smile was a little weaker than I would have liked. "Why do you do it?" I queried.

He swallowed. "I've...gone through some stuff in my life, Seraphine. And a lot of it hasn't been easy, especially when I've had to stow it all away for the sake of my family's reputation. Self-medicating isn't good. I know that. But...it's just been the way I've coped for a long time. Not regularly. It just helps take the edge off once in a while. I promise I'm careful with it." He took another deep breath in. "I'm sorry, Seraphine. I'm sorry I didn't tell you sooner. It's not very easy to talk about."

I studied him. I couldn't tear my eyes away from his. It was as if he'd latched on to me tighter and tighter with every word. I felt a mix of guilt and compassion pool into the depths of my heart with such unrelenting force that when I opened my mouth to respond, no words came out.

The corner of his mouth lifted with an apologetic smile. "I can't remember the last time you seemed at a loss for words," he said lightheartedly. "I know it's a bit much."

I shook myself out of my speechless stupor. "I'm…I just –"

I took a deep breath. "I went about this the wrong way," I finally managed to spit out, bringing my eyes to his once again. "I'm sorry. Again. That's all I can really say."

He chuckled a bit. "We're both apologizing too much. Let's just call it even."

I cracked my own smile for a fleeting moment, which faded as I cleared my throat. "Was it her leaving – the hard stuff, I mean?" I asked quietly.

Felix shifted, his eyes drifting down to the table. "The catalyst, yes," he finally replied. "And then I never really…dealt with it. Not properly, at least."

We were quiet for a moment. The liveliness of the park around us seemed to instill a humbling reminder that not all cares were free, rather than lift our spirits.

"Do you…want to deal with it differently?" I asked cautiously.

The seconds that ticked by felt like an eternity. At last, Felix sighed. "I don't intend to use drugs forever. So yes, I do want to fix this one day. With therapy, or a doctor, or an obscene amount of yoga and meditation…I don't really know." He gave me a half-hearted laugh, then stopped himself short when he realized I was still watching him intently. "I, um…it's always been easier to self-medicate, of course. It's a lot of work to sort through all my pain, rather than numb it. And I'm afraid of…I don't know. Failure, I suppose? Or making things worse? I guess I've never really had a good enough reason to risk more discomfort. But…"

He trailed off.

My eyes had not parted from his face for even a moment. "But?" I insisted.

He looked down for a moment, then back up at me through his lashes. Those lavender eyes were brimming with a sea of vulnerable sincerity – it was hard not to get lost in them. They were the brightest things on his weary face; they took so much attention away from the creases and tiredness in his skin that you would think he was as fresh as a daisy if you looked at nothing but them.

"But I do have a reason now," he finished. "A very good one."

I straightened, my heart squeezing. The statement was earnest, and as much as it relieved me to hear I could be his motivation, it also scared me.

What if I wasn't enough? What if I was the reason he didn't succeed?

"Can I do anything?" I offered.

He waited a moment, then shook his head. "This is my problem to solve," he said. "I'll bear the burden." There was a pause before he added. "Just…be patient with me. I've got a long road ahead, and I know it won't be something that changes overnight. It's…part of the reason I've put it off for so long."

"Of course," I immediately agreed. "Just…let me know if there's anything you need. Please."

He paused for a moment, then shifted in his seat. "Actually, there is one thing."

I nodded expectantly.

"Please don't tell my father," he asked, his voice solemn. "I don't want him to worry."

I studied his face, my lips rubbing against each other as I evaluated the request. "All right," I eventually said, though internally, I felt a bit hesitant to agree.

His smile and eyes were soft. "Thank you."

I nodded again, my eyes drifting to my cup of coffee.

Silence ensued between us, the busker's music filling the empty space. The sun had crawled high enough into the sky that its rays caressed my cheeks with a subtle warmth. There were a few more people in the park now, but overall, nature's gifts and the honeyed tunes from the guitar were still the overwhelming presence.

"We never do this," Felix noted, and I looked back up at him. He was watching me, his face as warm as the breath of sunshine on my skin, his lavender eyes a bit dozy. "We're always on the go, running around, doing something, moving on to the next thing as quickly as possible. We never take some time to just...be together."

I tried not to let the surprise show on my face. I was not expecting such an observation, however truthful it was. "You're right," I simply said, curious as to what he might add.

He leaned back a bit in his chair, his eyes stuck to mine. "We should do it more often," he suggested.

I let out a humoured breath. "I think you need some sleep," I joked.

He cocked his head to the side. "You don't think I enjoy spending time with you?" he questioned.

The humour left me as I fumbled a bit for words. "Well no, I – well, I know I can be a lot," I stammered.

His brows creased. "A lot?"

It was my turn to feel a bit vulnerable and exposed; I shrugged quickly. "I mean, I've got my quirks. I can be loud, and stubborn, and a bit...testy." I gave him a half-smile. "I know I frustrate you sometimes."

As my words drifted through the air, his eyes began churning. The lavender darkened, an intensity overtaking his entire being as he supported his chin with one hand and ran his fingers up the length of his jaw. He studied me as if I were a relic; I suddenly felt as if I were laid bare.

Finally, he shook his head slowly without breaking our

gaze. "I wouldn't change a single thing about you, Seraphine," he said, his voice low and thoughtful.

I blinked as he stood. "I don't take a moment with you for granted – especially not these still ones. I say we make the most of it," he said, nodding towards the busker. "His music spoke to you."

The way he said the words felt more like a statement of fact than a question, but I was so stunned at the sentiments he'd just surfaced that I simply nodded anyways.

Felix was quick on his feet, approaching the busker with a stride of confidence that mirrored that of a panther. "*Señor*," he began smoothly. "*Hablas inglés?*"

The middle-aged man stopped playing and looked up at Felix, his brown eyes as golden as his weathered skin. "*Sí*, a little," he replied.

Felix reached into his pocket. "How much would it cost to have you play for us privately?" he asked, motioning towards me.

The man seemed flustered. "Oh – well, I have never done this before," he fumbled.

"Hm," Felix simply replied nonchalantly as he opened his wallet. "Let this set a precedent, then."

He pulled out a thick wad of cash and outstretched it to the man. "Will you play for us for three thousand dollars?"

The man's eyes nearly fell out of his skull. "Oh, *señor!*" he exclaimed, his body trembling a bit. "No, I cannot accept this. It's too much!"

Felix nodded back at me again. "You brought her peace with your guitar after I upset her. You've proven your worth in gold already." He nudged the cash. "I would like to hire you for the rest of the day."

Tears welled in the man's eyes. "*Señor*," he breathed. "Oh, *señor*, you don't know how much this means…I just lost my job – I have been trying to keep from losing our house, and this?"

I was fighting my own tears as he shakily took the cash

from Felix's hands. "This…it will give us a few more months… *señor*, oh, *señor*, you are an angel! Truly! You are an angel sent from God himself!" He stood hastily. "Tell me, where you do you want me to play?"

Felix gave him a small smile. "Meet us at the Hotel Clarkson as soon as you are able. Let the concierge know you're there to play for Felix. They will know where to take you."

The busker nodded enthusiastically. "*Sí, gracias, señor!* I will be there right away!"

He began hurriedly packing his guitar, and as he did, Felix turned back to me. "Shall we?" he offered.

And I was still rendered speechless, so once again, all I did was nod.

CHAPTER 7

WHEN WE WALKED into the hotel, Felix made for the front desk. "There is a guitarist who will be coming to play for us shortly," he told the same concierge who had checked us in. "When he arrives, send him to our room. And when he leaves, have the manager offer him a job here playing music in the restaurant. If he accepts, tell the manager to pay him as he would Alejo Durán."

The young man simply nodded once. "Consider it done, *Señor* Clarkson. Anything else?"

"Yes. Send your best esthetician, nail artist, and masseuse to our room at their earliest convenience." He nodded towards me. "For the lady. And please send with them an assortment of your finest appetizers and champagne."

What in the world was this all about?

The young man smiled at me. "On my honor, you will have the best spa services and sensations for the taste buds this afternoon."

I felt as though I'd entered an entire new realm of shock, trailing behind Felix mindlessly in a sort of bewildered daze. Somehow, I managed to spit out a "*gracias*" before I carried on after him to our room.

The music was certainly beautiful, but not nearly as entrancing as she.

Her eyelids were heavy with the draw of a sweet, over-whelming serenity as she laid on the cushioned table, her naked body draped in luxurious towels save for the top of her back. One of her hands drew the towels in daintily to her chest, the other outstretched over her head, hanging like the petals of a delicate flower as the nail artist cared for and coloured them a deep red. That marking shaped like an eclipse on her forearm, the one she'd received from Alchnost's vicious attack, seemed softer in the evening light. It was as if she'd grown into it somehow.

The masseuse worked her shoulders, her warm skin moving softly as it was kneaded and stretched. The way she rested on the table as she faced me, with one leg slightly bent, pronounced the shape of her waist and the curves of her hips so bewitchingly, it was as if her body were a spell. And on her, the art she'd had inked into her skin seemed to glow with more definition, like they were under a spotlight; the tattooed eye of Horus on the back of her neck, the rose on her shoulder, the orca on her thigh, barely peeking out from underneath the towel. The busker played the perfect background music for her, the likes of Aphrodite and Hathor.

Seraphine had nearly been asleep when I strode into her vision, stepping into the pool across from her slowly with nothing but my shorts and my lit cigar. Her honey-brown eyes fluttered as she watched me settle into the corner, her gaze drifting from beneath her lashes as she tilted her head up a bit.

"I'm confused," she said, the first words she'd spoken in a couple hours.

I puffed on the cigar. "And why is that?" I replied.

She glanced around her, then back at me, her arched brows slightly bent. "Not saying I don't appreciate all this, but...why?"

I cocked my head to the side. "Weren't you saying I ruined your peace earlier?"

She considered. "Sure, but – "

"Well, consider it fixed," I interrupted. "I suggested we make the most out of our time together. What better way than by making peace?"

A smile tugged at those delicate lips. "And where's your peace, exactly?"

I'm looking at it, I thought. "Oh, don't worry about me," I answered. "Just enjoy yourself."

Her expression remained unchanged, but something in her eyes flickered. The warmth of the brown seemed to glow even brighter, as if she had been sated. The sensations of pampering seemed to have eased her enough that her mind opened, if even just a sliver, to something new and unfound.

She made to reach for one of the peaches she'd been brought with her free hand, letting the towel fall loose and exposing a bit more of her cleavage. It was hard not to stare as she brought the fruit to her mouth, shutting her eyes and biting tenderly into its sweet skin, as a siren bites into the sailor she's drowned. She brought the peach away from her as she chewed slowly, a drop of juice trickling down her lips. Sensually, she brought her thumb and deliberately pressed it to her mouth, dragging it over the juice temptingly to wipe it away. As she did, her almond-shaped eyes opened, fixing on mine with a lure I got entangled in.

It was a feat not to lunge for her there and then, to banish the workers and spread her legs passionately right there on the table. I had longed to bed her for what felt like an eternity, and every day, it felt as though I drew closer and closer to finally caving into those irresistible instincts.

But something always stopped me. Some days, it was the

focus on pursuing Sedaurea. Others, it was my personal struggles. Occasionally, I found myself grumbling at the existence of that goddamned bastard she seemed to care for – hopefully, that wouldn't be much of a barrier for much longer. Apparently, I had to be wary of exotic strangers, too. She'd nearly been swept away by one the previous night.

Ultimately, I suppose it was the complexity of our relationship that restrained me the most. This wasn't a woman I wanted to sleep with. This was a woman I wanted to love. But I didn't even know if I could love her the way she deserved, what with my...issues. And truthfully, I didn't know if she felt the same, especially now that she knew about my worst habits.

I shifted slightly, the water rippling around me as I thought. How angry she had become over the discovery of the drugs...it was passionate. But was it care born from love, or the care I'd pretended to have so poorly when my father confronted me about worrying for her? The kind that stemmed from preventing the preventable for logistics, and nothing more?

I was wary to approach her about it – for fear of rejection and for losing her altogether. If I couldn't have her as a lover, I still wanted – no, *needed* – her as a friend. She'd quickly become my confidant.

I had never been more motivated to face my demons than that moment. I watched her finish the peach and close her eyes, humming as she took in the last of its succulence and rested her head back on the table. A vision of true peace, and glory, and light.

Perhaps she could be the victory; perhaps she would be the one to draw me from the darkness, to lead me away from the shadows, to save me at long last...

My eyes drifted downwards as I swallowed.

Or perhaps not.

Because I liked me more when I used things that changed me. The drinking, the smoking, the cocaine...they made me more confident, a version of myself I longed to be every hour of every day. That was the entire reason I'd become hooked on it all. Even now, in the lingering effects of my last consumption, I commanded better than if I was sober. I had more chances at winning her over if I was assured and persuasive – a state I didn't naturally find myself in often. It was hard to compel myself to give it up entirely.

Confliction fuelled my thinking but, quite frankly, that is nothing new.

- S -

The sun was beginning to set when I woke.

I stirred dazedly as my eyes flickered open, blinking into focus the start of the glorious orange sunset that was crawling over the horizon. My mind felt so at ease that, for a moment, all I did was stare out into the distance, allowing myself to fully embrace the sight I beheld and the breaths I took. The guitarist and staff were gone, but the tranquility they'd instilled in me remained, along with the buzz of the champagne everyone I'd insisted I sip on.

"Welcome back, kindling."

His voice drew my eyes towards my right. He was sitting on one of the chaise lounges, a newspaper in one hand and a cigar in the other. His chest was still bare from his little swim in the pool, the last rays of daylight highlighting the definition of his pecs and abs as the final traces of water droplets across his skin caught in the soft light.

Felix's lavender eyes were illuminated when they met mine. "I thought I would catch up on the local news while you rested," he explained, holding up the newspaper. "And I found something you might want to look at."

I raised one eyebrow ever so slightly. "Oh?"

He outstretched the paper towards me. "See for yourself."

I slowly took the newspaper from his hand and examined the page he had folded over. It was an article detailing that satellite imagery had revealed the existence of a thriving, ancient civilization in the Amazon. This was apparently of significant discovery because the region the civilization had occupied was previously thought to have been uninhabited. I scanned the article and found a map of where the discovery was made – it was near the area we'd been in, and the writer noted there were several ongoing expeditions in the Amazon underway.

"One of these expeditions must have crossed paths with the temple," I noted.

"Mhm. Now look at this," Felix offered, and I looked back at him to see he was handing me his phone.

I took it and saw it was open to a search Felix had made for archaeological expeditions in the Amazon. There were a lot of articles on the recent civilization that had been discovered. Then there were a few on a pre-Incan mummy that had recently gone on display. But one article stood out to me, an article about a team from the National Major University of San Marcos in Lima and their recent excursions into the Amazon.

I scanned the article. The team had set out originally to look for what they believed was another ancient settlement in the forest, and had stumbled upon a temple – a very familiar-sounding, moss-covered temple, surrounded by birds of all shapes, colours, and sizes. My eyes widened as I read further; the team had deemed the closed structure too precarious to try and enter forcefully without a proper safety assessment and provisions. Instead, they'd decided to take back interesting finds for further research. Out of respect for what may have been a significant cultural discovery, the team had agreed not to remove too many artifacts from the site.

In fact, they had only physically removed three things – what the article described as three small bird figurines.

I clutched the towel to my chest as I sat up, the blood rushing from my head to my toes and back again. A photo of the figurines was in the article – they bore a striking resemblance to the Phoenix statues I'd seen on top of the temple. I had no doubt in my mind that these were the missing miniatures.

"Felix!" I exclaimed. "Those figurines must be the ones we're looking for!"

Felix chuckled, crossing his hands behind his head as he laid back in the lounger. "Not bad, huh?" he gloated.

"Not bad? This is great!" I raved, wrapping the towel tightly around myself and hopping off the massage table. "When do we head to Lima?"

Felix nodded towards the sunset. "Let's head out early tomorrow morning. I'm guessing it'll be easier to navigate a university campus during the day."

A part of me wanted to leave then and there, but another part of me was happy to indulge in a bit more rest and relaxation. Truthfully, it was the most revitalized I'd felt in a while.

"All right," I said.

Felix raised his eyebrows at me. "I think that's the first time I've ever suggested we wait a bit, and you haven't fought me on it."

I stuck my tongue out at him. "I'm trying to make the most of all this pampering I just got. Speaking of which, I'm assuming I owe you an apple crumble for all this?"

Felix cracked a smile, but shook his head firmly. "As much as I love your apple crumble, I don't expect anything in return for this." He hesitated, considering. "Although…"

When he didn't complete the sentence, I gave him an expectant look. "*Oui?*"

His eyes travelled back to mine, then traversed my face and body, before finally settling back on my gaze. He stood slowly, methodically, as if he wanted to ensure I could predict every movement before it was made. That smile he'd cracked was now more of a smirk. As he approached me, I felt something deep within me stir.

"Perhaps," he began leisurely, "when your little friend with the pathetic car asks why your skin is glowing, you can tell him it was thanks to me."

I lifted my chin a bit as I took this in, restraining the curiosity I felt from crossing my features. "And why would you want me to do that?"

He shrugged, not taking his eyes off me. "I just think it would be amusing."

I let out a breath. "Not that it's any of your business," I said teasingly, "but I'm not sure I'd care to have any further conversations with him."

It was his turn to feign disinterest – and he failed at it, for those lavender eyes came alive with a bewildered inquisitiveness. "Is that so?"

I nodded curtly. "I wouldn't pity him. He has another little friend to keep him busy."

Felix gave out a theatrical sigh as he puffed on the cigar. "It'd be a lie to say I'm surprised. And it conveniently explains his calamitous insecurities regarding me."

I studied Felix, the way gratification seeped into his features and broadened his stance at the discovery that Elijah and I were through. And something occurred to me, then, that I hadn't considered before.

"Interesting that you would want him to view you as competition when you're not," I noted poignantly.

He held his ground, but I saw a little flicker of faltering deep within those lavender irises. "I told you it was entertaining," he explained.

"And how far does Felix Clarkson go for his own entertainment?" I challenged.

He was on full alert now. "What are you insinuating?"

I folded my arms across my chest. "I was just thinking it was quite interesting that Elijah's car randomly caught fire the same day we ran into you on the beach."

His nostrils flared as something like shock glinted in the lavender irises I'd grown so accustomed to.

I stared him down. "Don't you agree?" I pushed.

A muscle feathered in his jaw. "Why bother seeking confirmation from me if you're so confident you've figured it out?"

I didn't let up on my staring or my tone. "Funny how you also happened to be there when that club went up in flames," I noted, lowering my gaze. "And when two chemicals that should not ignite caught on fire in my chemistry lab."

Felix's gaze broke; it flitted across and around me before returning to mine. And when it did, it was riddled with culpability.

I shook my head slowly. "Why, Felix?" I demanded. "People could have gotten hurt."

"I made sure people didn't," he muttered.

"That was a lot of property damage at the club. Somebody's livelihood."

"Insurance will cover it."

"And for what? Just so you can get a kick out of some arson?"

"No."

"Then why?"

He loosed a breath. "Because I am very, very bad with women."

It was my turn to exhale deeply as I lowered my arms. "Ah. So now you finally admit that this was all to sleep with me all along?"

He huffed, the cigar smoke forcefully exiting his mouth as his expression became exasperated. "For whatever reason, it seems you will not rest until you claw all of my secrets out of my chest, so if it's a confession you want, then it's a confession you'll get."

86

My intrigue set one brow to a peak.

"I'm willing to admit that the thought of tasting you is so irresistible that it makes me weak. Given the opportunity, I would jump at the chance to sleep with you, as would many, many others."

Both of my eyebrows were now raised.

"And yes, the delectable idea has crossed my mind many times since the moment I met you, which should not come as a surprise. Surely, you've looked in a mirror and recognized just how striking you are."

He puffed the cigar, avoiding my face as his stature stiffened. "But that was never the motivation behind my decision to offer you and your Phoenix my help. I never expected anything in return. I simply wanted to do the right thing." There was a pause as he cleared his throat. "Given your repeated interrogations into my motivations, I knew you wouldn't take kindly to any advances. So, I tried my best to keep my…desire for you somewhat reserved. Evidently, I haven't done a very good job, so there's no use in trying to deny it now."

I watched him shift a bit. "As for my drastic interferences… well, the only advantages I've ever really had are my money and my magic." He sounded almost…defeated. "I couldn't help myself. I needed to meddle – to have an excuse to talk to you, or to get you away from that clown. Call a spade a spade, I don't care. But –"

He finally met my gaze, swallowing as those lavender eyes were engulfed with a raging fire. "I only ever started those fires because you…fed the one in me."

I lifted my chin.

Kindling.

Not what starts the fire, but what keeps the fire going.

Something fluttered in my stomach, my chest. It made me pause, long enough for Felix to realize what exactly he had done – his admission seemed to have flowed off the tongue like a torrential downpour. I presumed he was not only gauging a reaction, but also coming to terms with the cat having been let out – or, rather, *thrown* – out of the bag.

The confession, although more detailed than I had expected, was not a surprise. We'd had our little exchanges; small, peculiar moments that could have been missed in the feigning of perceptiveness. I could pointedly remember that night in Heliopolis, his telling words. *I don't take other girls to my father's events.*

If anything was unforeseen regarding the matter, it was my reaction.

A flickering, devious satisfaction began flitting about my chest, like sneaky, little butterflies of vanity that twirled in his adulation. I normally didn't spend much time considering my accolades; though I certainly was content with myself, I didn't feel the need to be prideful, and I valued humility.

But to hear this reverence for me in his voice, to see the longing that had glazed his eyes…

It was riveting.

I couldn't help but indulge myself. A seductive, wicked smile tugged at the corner of my lips. "So hypothetically, if you had the opportunity, what would you do first?"

His eyebrows shook as he scanned my face, measuring my lips, the way my words were echoed in my facial features. "What do you mean?"

I took a step towards him. "Say you had your way with me. Tell me what you'd do."

My words woke something in him that had clearly been fighting to escape its slumber; it burst within his irises, washing them with that inferno I must have kindled all this time.

"I would…" he swallowed, shaking his head a bit before his eyes locked with mine so intimately, it was as if I could feel their grasp on my skin. "Why do you want to know, Seraphine?"

I considered my next move. "Perhaps all these adrenaline

rushes we've been facing together have made me look at you a bit differently," I suggested.

He lowered his gaze, taking a deliberate step towards me. The gap between us was mere inches.

So fascinating, the semantics of seduction.

They were just a few words, after all. A few choice words; a premise that just might make the delicacy he so badly wished to taste a reality, laid out on a silver platter before him. I'd coated the sentence with caramel, layered my eyes with saccharine promise. A fiend's work on a sweetened face.

I had his undivided attention; I could have robbed him then, and he wouldn't care. Maybe he wouldn't have even noticed.

His voice thrummed with his cravings. "Enlighten me, won't you?"

I felt my cheeks flush a bit, but I kept my chin high. "You've a keen interest in all things scientific," I stared, my words spinning him in webs of silk. "Is there any evidence to suggest that repeated, stimulating encounters in close proximity to another may induce strong feelings of…arousal?"

His lavender eyes were alight with something rapacious and lustful. "I would have to check, but your hypothesis strikes me as logically valid," he replied. "I've never been a fan of literature reviews myself, though. I much prefer experimentation to test the theory."

My lips danced on the thread that tugged them into the luscious smile I baited him with. "Wouldn't be the first experiment we've done together," I told him as I shrugged suggestively.

The fervour in his eyes intensified as he came even closer – I could feel his breath on my lips. "Is that an invitation, kindling?"

It was solidified, then, that my mischief had led us to the beginning of a dangerous game. By the look in his impassioned eyes, there was no going back. He had handed himself to me, and I had complete, unwavering control. Whatever I said or did next could completely change the dynamics of our relationship forever.

And in the heat of that moment, one that felt as though his very flames had encircled us, I looked up into those hungry, lavender eyes, and I surrendered.

"You decide," I whispered to him on a wind of ardour.

CHAPTER 8

IN MY GREEK MYTHOLOGY CLASS, I'd recently been taught about the story of the first human woman. Zeus ordered Hephaestus to create her as a form of vengeance against Prometheus for giving fire to humans. And so Pandora, the woman whose name means "all gifts," was created, having been given a gift from each of the Greek gods.

Zeus had given Pandora a jar and told her never to open it. Then he sent her to the brother of Prometheus, named Epimetheus, who had been warned not to accept any gifts from Zeus. But Epimetheus didn't listen and accepted Pandora, who gave into temptation and opened the jar. The jar released all evils upon the world, like hatred and war, sickness and death. Thus is the story of Pandora's Box.

I wondered if Felix realized he had opened our own version of Pandora's box as his lips collided with mine.

Perhaps not a form of evil, but a form of complexity, none-theless.

He dropped the cigar and stomped on it as he brought both hands to my lower back, pulling my body into his. He let out a muffled sound as we kissed, his lips moving and molding with mine, his breathing shallow and hastened. He tasted like earthy and rich tobacco, a mixture of danger and obsession, addiction and desire, an overwhelming flavour that filled my senses with a high of their own.

I felt his fingers trace my back, my sides, finding gratification in my skin, grabbing at my curves. My own fingers instinctively reached for his hair, rummaging through the strands as my heartbeat quickened. My tongue slipped through his lips, and he moaned quietly.

He grunted when he tore away, kissing my jawline, sucking on my collarbones. My eyes fluttered closed as I let out a shallow breath; he had ignited me.

In one swift motion, he then reached beneath my backside and lifted me up, holding me as if I weighed nothing. I wrapped my legs around his waist as he turned and placed me on the lounger, climbing on top of me, pinning me down as he kissed my neck. I clutched a fistful of his hair, my breathing staggered. I wanted no escape from him, from the feeling of his weight on top of me. I slipped into that primal state of senses, where I belonged only to him and that moment we were in.

I felt his fingers fidget with the towel, and soon it was loosened, and I wasted no time shrugging it off. He brought his lips to my breasts promptly, attentively, sucking on them in a way that sent me reeling. I gasped, needing him elsewhere and everywhere, desperately craving that tongue in other places.

"Down more," I begged, dragging my hands over that muscled chest.

He was obedient in his own way – he was teasing. His tongue traced down my torso slowly, flicking itself against my skin, swirling around my belly button. His fingers dug into my hips, then massaged my thighs. When his lips had reached the top of my legs, I thought I would go mad with longing.

He lifted slightly to look at me, those lavender eyes magnetic and whirling with desire and temptation. But I was raring for what he was so close to giving me – I wanted his face somewhere else *now*.

"Please," I whined.

He smirked, but he listened. I moaned, arching my back as I felt his tongue exactly where I wanted it, exactly where I needed him to be. The sensations he gave to me were euphoric – I couldn't lie still. Every flick felt like ecstasy. I lost control within minutes, one hand gripping his hair, the other grasping the edges of the lounger as I writhed and cried out. I couldn't control the sparks that escaped my skin, my magic dusting the edges of my body as it moved. My mind felt like it went to space, but still he didn't stop, so when I came back down to Earth, it was mere seconds before I shot back up again. I couldn't help my toes from curling, my body convulsing with the most pleasure a man had ever made me feel.

After it felt like he'd licked every fold and crevasse, he shrugged off his shorts. I should have been better prepared for what was waiting underneath, given how tall he was, but I still couldn't help but stare in awe, wondering how in the world he would fit in me. The fancy cars were certainly *not* an act of compensation.

He snatched his wallet off the table and fumbled inside it – I knew what he was looking for. He found it and put it on, and when he was ready, he grabbed me by both legs and yanked me forward.

"Fuck," he breathed as he entered me. He filled every inch of space I had, meshing our bodies so tightly into one that I gasped at his movement.

His lips found mine again, and I welcomed their reunion. "Does that feel good, kindling?" he exhaled against them.

I couldn't form a proper sentence. All I could do was moan, clawing my fingers in his back, hoping none of it would ever stop.

He chuckled breathlessly. "Good girl," he chaunted. "Enjoy yourself."

We moved our bodies together, slow at first, then faster, then rougher. The inhibition he'd maintained to be gentle quickly faded as he lost himself further inside me, and I felt ravished by it. It was feral, visceral, a rawness I'd never experienced before in my interactions with him. Little flames danced from his fingers, bringing the sensation of heat into the feast of the senses I was gorging in. Hidden under all those fancy clothes, this man's body was untamed and robust. I felt divinely feminine underneath him.

"Oh, fuck," he eventually groaned as he threw his head back. His movement staggered, and I knew he'd gone where I had earlier before.

He took several deep breaths before disconnecting us, yanking the protection off, and tossing it to the side. Then he collapsed beside me, both of us panting uncontrollably.

As my breathing slowed, I felt my eyelids grow heavy, and I began drifting off, my mind a tornado of feelings and sensations.

- F -

Seraphine did not wake when I carried her upstairs to bed.

She was still fast asleep as I laid beside her, an angel with soft breathing and softer skin. Watching her was like watching the amity I so badly wished to have. I swallowed, reaching out slowly, hesitantly, trying not to rouse her but unable to resist reminding myself how she felt. I brushed her cheek with the lightest touch I could muster, tucking a curl away from her smoothed face. She had been loved; she slept with harmony, the kind that comes from knowing sweet melodies will play in the morning.

My magic pounded through me like an unrelenting wind, strengthened and unbreakable. I assumed it was from the stimulation – in hindsight, I should have known better. But it was convincing enough in the moment.

She was the best I'd ever had. Her body was paradise, her movements invigorating. The way she kissed me felt more magical than the powers I had resting within my fingertips. The way she touched me felt like home. She had me wrapped around her finger unendingly, a helpless string of rope that only grew more twisted around the pillar it had been strung around; I could never escape her grasp on me. It was a pleasant certainty to be nestled feebly in the palm of her hand. To some, the thought of being so captive might be frightening, perhaps even insulting. But I trusted her to hold me better than I could ever hold myself, and in that faith, I found a feeling of contentment.

I sighed, turning away from her and facing the ceiling. Many nights I spent just like this – blinking at whatever lay above me. As if the view might change. As if it might affect me in some way. But it never did. Sleep evaded me like peace. I'd been like this since my mother left.

My father had told me that the first thing about my mother that he'd fallen in love with was her eyes. Those lavender eyes were the gateway to him loving her as a whole. And every day, I looked at my reflection and saw the pieces of something that had left me staring straight back into my soul. Maybe that was the draw to my self-destruction – tearing away the remnants of what she left behind, ruining any part of her that remained with me. But I couldn't abolish those pieces without obliterating the rest of me. I knew that, but the knowledge didn't make much of a difference. Combatting issues like mine took much more than understanding.

My eyes travelled to my backpack, where I'd hidden my journal. I thought about documenting how the night made me feel in there. Then I wondered if it would be creepy to do so. Then I decided I didn't really care. I reached over and grabbed the notebook I carried everywhere with me, as well as a pen. I dated the entry, and detailed what I felt I needed to, and then I replaced it in my backpack, right beside my new camera that hadn't been getting much use these days.

My fingers paused in my bag, lingering over the little pouch full of cocaine. I warily pulled it out, thumbing it in my palm. There was still plenty left in there.

I glanced at Seraphine, fast asleep beside me. I swallowed as I remembered her initial reaction to finding out my secret – how the worry had taken over her like a sickness. My gaze drifted back to the pouch, and I took the quietest, deepest breath I could muster.

I didn't want to do it.

But I didn't *not* want to do it, either.

I loitered upright in bed for a moment, my brain malfunctioning. It was such a stupid drug. A high you constantly had to chase, constantly had to resupply. And yet, for some reason, I couldn't talk myself out of it. I wondered if I got that from my mother, too – if she was so far gone in a state of selfishness that it overrode her consideration, or care, of what she may lose.

With a bit of defeat, I stood carefully from the bed. With the pouch firmly in hand, I made for the doorway on feather-light feet.

My father had also told me that my mother had been severely depressed, had spent many late nights drinking whatever she felt away.

I suppose the rotten apple truly doesn't fall far from the wretched tree.

- S -

When I awoke the next morning, I was alone in bed.

My rejuvenation was beyond words – I didn't feel the need

to wipe my eyes as I sat up, draping the covers over my naked body. The virility of my magic coursed through me, filling every inch of my body with a domineering power I hadn't experienced before. I felt…stronger, like I'd been filled with passionate fire. Perhaps there was something to be said about the efficacy of a day of respite.

I yawned as I checked my phone. I had a text from Emmanuella.

Emmanuella Rosa

Hey girl. Where you been? Haven't seen you since the weekend! Was wondering if you wanted to work out tonight?

I paused for a moment, thinking of a good enough lie.

Me

Hey Em! I'm visiting some family friends in San Francisco right now. Sorry, forgot to let you know. Should be back later this week!

Emmanuella Rosa

Oh fun! It's all good girl. See you when you get back!

I huffed with a bit of relief.

The sound of footsteps drew my attention to the doorway, and I watched Felix walk in, wearing nothing but his boxers and carrying a tray with coffee and pastries. The sight of his toned, bare chest reminded me of the events of the previous night. Now that I had a clear head, wistfully unaffected by any champagne, half of me couldn't help but wonder what the hell

I had done. The other half was devouring the sight of him; those remarkable lavender eyes glimmering in the new morning's glow only heightened an unwavering draw I felt yanking me towards him. It was as if I were suddenly tethered to him, and his presence alone was enough to make the threads quiver.

Felix's face was soft, maybe even a little embarrassed, as he nodded at me. "Morning," he said, clearing his throat. "I brought you some breakfast."

I smiled at him. "Thank you."

He placed the tray at my bedside. "You look like you slept well," he noted.

"I did," I replied, looking down at my hand. "The spa day must have done the trick. Even my magic feels different."

I could see him straighten in my peripheral vision. "Oh?"

I nodded. "I feel like it gained strength. Like something's been added to it."

I twisted my hand, studying my palm, then each of my fingers. Several long moments passed, my eyes eventually drifting back to Felix in search of the reply I hadn't received. To my surprise, he seemed at a loss for words. His brows were raised slightly to accommodate his rounded eyes, which blinked when mine fell upon them.

"Well, that's a good thing. You must be nearing the full bond with Aurora," he hurriedly answered, coming off a bit flustered as he began making for the doorway. Maybe it was bashfulness about our night together?

I studied him. "Is something wrong?"

"Hm? Oh, no, not at all. Just got a bit caught up in my planning." He gave me a trying smile. "I've been preparing a bit for Lima so we can head out as soon as you're ready."

I grinned. "You knew I would be eager, huh?"

He chuckled. "Goes without saying."

I grabbed the coffee and raised it to him. "I'll come help you in a minute."

"It's all right. Take your time and enjoy that coffee," he said. "We've got a big day ahead of us."

———

Lima was the most charming city I'd ever seen from above. Palm trees, bright yellow buildings, city squares made of stone and Peruvians on motorized bikes – all of it framed by a detailed, rocky coastline and the sparkling water of the Pacific. I fell in love with it as soon as I set eyes upon it.

The National Major University of San Marcos – or the *Universidad Nacional Mayor de San Marcos,* as the Peruvians would call it – was located in the area of San Miguel, opposite the street from the *Parque de las Leyendas,* which contained a zoo, some ancient ruins, and a botanical garden. The botanical garden housed some conveniently dense vegetation at its edge – dense enough that, combined with a lightning-quick descent, it was hidden enough for us all to land in.

"Sorry, Aurora," I told her as I disembarked, patting her on her neck. "More hiding for you two."

She nuzzled my cheek with the side of her face. The city perfectly complemented her plumage, what with all the yellow and warm tones.

"Stay safe," Felix told Fuego. His Phoenix nodded at him, and they both took off.

It was about midday in Lima. Once Felix and I traversed our way out of the trees and onto the path, I pulled out my phone and looked at my maps. From where we stood in the botanical gardens, it'd be a short walk to the university campus. Once we were there, we needed to get in and somehow find the archaeology department. But the university was massive – pretty much the size of UC San Diego. I still didn't quite know my way around the entirety of my own campus, so navigating a completely foreign one without any guidance may prove to be even more difficult. We'd need to ask for help, most likely, and we'd need to do that without making it obvious we were up to something.

"So, what's the plan?" I asked Felix, and I brought my eyes up from my phone to meet his curious lavender ones.

He blinked. "I'm in charge of the plan?"

I frowned. "Didn't you say you were planning for Lima this morning?"

"I managed to think the plan up until the arrival in Lima," he told me.

"You didn't plan past that part of the plan?"

"Well, the plan in my head after that point was to go to the university and get the statues," Felix said.

I looked at him expectantly. "So where do we start?"

He glanced around nervously. "I suppose we could start by going to the university."

"All right. And then…?"

"And then," he began theatrically. "We – wait for it – get the statues."

I narrowed my eyes. "*How* exactly do we do that?"

"That…is an excellent question."

"Do you have any idea where in the university they might be?"

"Another excellent question."

"What if they have security or something?"

"You are just on fire today with those questions, darling."

I gave him a look of incredulity. "So let me get this straight – we flew all the way out here with a half-ass plan and you expected it to just fall into place?"

"It's not a half-ass plan!" he exclaimed defensively. "It's just…half a plan," he added in a grumbled murmur.

I shut my eyes and brought one hand to my forehead, rubbing my temples. "Felix, it's quite difficult to come up with a response to this plan nonsense that properly conveys my feelings. But what I will say is that they are not good feelings."

He crossed his arms, sneering. "All right, Little Miss Adventure. Why don't you try and pick up where I left off planning, then? You know, since you're usually the woman with the plan and all."

I gave him a befuddled look. "Since when am I the woman with the plan?"

"You literally plan everything we do together."

"Not true. I don't plan the physics labs."

"This isn't the physics lab. This is Phoenix adventure stuff. And up until right now, *you've* usually been the big planner with Phoenix adventure stuff."

"And, clearly, it should remain that way."

He sighed loudly. "All right – going forward, we really ought to plan things out better between the two of us."

"Sure. Just remember that the next time you start planning without me," I replied.

He rolled his eyes and let out a breath of exasperation. "I was letting you sleep in."

"Sleeping in gets me nowhere if I'm following a half-ass plan."

"*Half a plan*," he corrected. "But duly noted. The next time I'm feeling generous, I'll make sure I disregard any consideration for your sleep in favor of your contributions to a plan, despite any effect it may have on the plan in question."

I squinted at him. "Are you saying I can't make a good plan when I'm tired?"

"Of course not." He paused. "But you're usually a little fussier on no sleep."

"Fuss*er*?"

"Yes. As in, more fussy than your average fussy." He thought for a moment. "Which is still pretty fussy."

"*Seriously?*" I retorted. "Have you met yourself?"

He scoffed. "I am many things, but fussy is not one of them."

"Pfft! Give me a break!" I snapped. "You're looking at fussy in the rear-view mirror. In fact, you're roaring down finnicky fucking avenue."

"Ugh!" he exclaimed, throwing his hands up and spinning on his heel. "Whatever! I can't deal with a spat right now. I just want to look at some penguins!"

I blinked. "Penguins?"

"I noticed they have penguins at the zoo here, and I'll be damned if I leave without seeing them!"

I stared after him in disbelief as he began marching out of the botanical garden. Then, after realizing he was serious, I kissed my teeth and trailed after him. How the hell was *I* the fussy one?

Felix was indeed correct – there were some Humboldt penguins not too far from where we'd been in the botanical gardens. He came to a halt outside their exhibit, and I stood beside him. We both watched the little flightless birds pitter-patter in and out of the water in silence.

"Look at them," he mumbled after a while. "They're fucking adorable."

I had my eye on one penguin who was wiggling his little tail. "They are," I said.

"Well, at least we can agree on something."

A small smile tugged on the corner of my lips as I glanced around at my surroundings. I spotted a small group of people, led by a young man in uniform – I assumed he must be working at the zoo. He stopped a little ways from us and motioned towards the penguins, speaking profoundly in Spanish. A tour, I assumed.

A tour…

"Felix," I said confidently, turning to smirk at him. "I have a plan."

CHAPTER 9

"Are you sure this is going to work?" Felix hissed at me as we rounded the street corner towards the National Major University of San Marcos. In his hands, he held the sunglasses and baseball cap we'd bought as a disguise for him from a nearby souvenir shop.

"You know, for a guy who barely did half of the planning legwork, you sure have no qualms about your audacity to question mine," I snarled back at him. He muttered something under his breath, but didn't make whatever argument he had audible to me.

The southern buildings of the university were visible to me now – covered in white plaster, some adorned with colourful murals in various art styles. The institution blended well with the Peruvian colours, almost like a canvas for its students.

After stopping at the intersection and waiting for the light to change, the indicator signalled we could cross over to the campus. We stepped foot on the cracking concrete paths, making our way towards a giant, white stone sign with the university's name plastered on it. Beyond it were several more buildings, bland in colour with their windows sealed by copper gates.

We stopped and glanced around. I could feel Felix looking expectantly at me as I scanned the surroundings. After a few moments, I spotted what I was looking for – a central administration building.

"Perfect," I said. "Come on, this way."

We walked up the little incline and into the building. There were many offices down a hall that split into more halls, and a woman with red-rimmed reading glasses was sitting behind a desk, typing away at her computer. I glanced at the clock. It read a quarter to two. We'd made it just in time.

I took a deep breath in, preparing myself. I'd rehearsed the lines multiple times in my head, researched the necessary information, and prepared the material I would need. I just needed to execute everything with a confidence that was credible. I glanced at Felix, who gave me a single nod as he put on his sunglasses and baseball cap. It was showtime.

We approached. "*Hola, señora. ¿Hablas inglés?*" I asked.

She smiled at us. "Yes. How may I help you?"

"We're interested in taking the campus tour at two," I said. "Do you know where we should go?"

"Ah, yes. You're in the right place. The campus tour starts in this building." She motioned behind her to a hallway. "Go left and you'll see a sign pointing out the meeting spot. I'm leading the tour, so I'll see you there in ten."

"Wonderful. Thank you so much," I replied, glancing at Felix. He gave me a single nod, and we followed her directions down the hallway.

When we arrived at the sign, there were two other girls waiting for the tour. I couldn't help but tap my foot impatiently, anxious for the tour to get underway so we could find the statues and get on with our adventure – that is, if the plan went accordingly. One other girl joined closer to two, and then the woman from the front desk finally approached us at the hour.

She spoke in Spanish first to the girls, and then turned to us. "Welcome to the *Universidad Nacional Mayor de San Marcos.*

My name is Fernanda, and I'll be giving the tour in Spanish and English today. We're starting here in the central building, where you'll find all your student services, admissions, and the bookstore. Now then, follow me."

Fernanda led us through several buildings; we passed a science and technology building, a business building, and a fine arts building. I grew exasperated as we continued to tour what seemed like every building but one that would contain an archaeology department. Felix had to nudge me a few times so I would remember to keep the irritation off my face.

Finally, as we neared the administration building once again, Fernanda stopped us in front of one just across from it. It was a couple of stories tall and had a faded, yellow tone washed over its old walls.

"This is the social sciences building," Fernanda announced to Felix and me after she'd spoken in Spanish. "Here is where students in sociology, anthropology, political science, and archaeology will spend most of their time."

I straightened, my heart pounding as I realized we now finally knew exactly where to look. It was ironically frustrating that it happened to be just across from where we started, but I became so eager that I managed to ignore that little joke from life.

"That brings us to the end of the tour," Fernanda went on, pointing to the administration building. "As you can see, we have arrived back to the start. If you have any further questions, please feel free to – "

"That's great, thanks!" I exclaimed to her, my impatience overcoming any self-control I'd managed to maintain. "Really great tour! Catch you later!"

My nails dug into Felix's skin as I grasped his forearm, and he yelped a little as I yanked him towards the door. I had flung it open and dragged him through it before Fernanda had a chance to reply.

"All right, all right, get those claws off me!" Felix hissed once we were inside, prying my hand from his arm. "Sheesh – is this the thanks I get for prettying your nails?"

"Shouldn't have let me get them nice and sharp," I retorted, but admittedly, I had to do a double take to ensure the red I saw by his skin was not blood I'd drawn, but rather the beautiful gel nails I'd gotten yesterday. "Come on – we need to find the archaeology department."

"And then?" Felix asked. "What, we sneak in, take the statues, and leave?"

I stared at him. "Sounds about right to me."

"What? Seriously?"

I frowned. "I don't understand your confusion."

"Well, we can't just *take* them!"

I raised my eyebrows at him. "Why not?"

"Because it's…it's stealing!" he cried in vexation.

I shrugged. "They stole the statues from the temple grounds," I told him. "We're just returning them where they belong."

He scoffed, rolling his eyes. "I doubt the university will see it that way," he mumbled.

"I'm sorry – do you have any better ideas?"

"Better than theft? Certainly!"

I crossed my arms. "All right, then. Let's hear it."

He cleared his throat as he began pacing. "Okay, okay… what if we…" he trailed off as he fell deeper in thought. "What if we ask someone if we can borrow them?"

I managed to scrunch out one long, tired blink in response.

"We could tell them we're…we're…oh! How about we tell them we're travelling photographers, and we heard about their big discovery, and we'd love to borrow them for a few shots for our magazine, and then return them in a couple of days?"

"Are you stupid or are you dumb?"

"Oh, pish posh, Seraphine," he replied rattily as he stopped pacing abruptly in front of me. "That's a good idea, and you know it."

106

"So what happens when they come looking for photographs?" I suggested. "Or the magazine? Better yet, what happens if they say no?"

He looked to his left, and then to his right. Then he sighed up at the ceiling. "Let's just steal them."

"Thank you kindly," I said smarmily as I turned on my heel. He muttered something under his breath, but I could feel his presence behind me as I started down a hallway.

There weren't many people in the halls of the building; some of the classes appeared populated, while many other rooms were darkened or empty. I scanned the doors as we walked, looking for signage that would guide us. Many classrooms just had room numbers, and smaller rooms had names of professors – I assumed they must have been their offices.

We eventually made our way to a stairwell and climbed it to the second floor. Immediately, I noticed a larger room set up like a lab to our right. The lights in the room were off, but the door was left ajar.

"That looks interesting," I noted, nodding towards the room.

Felix approached the doorway and peered in. "I can see some stones in trays," he said. "Might be an archaeology lab."

"That's what I like to hear," I said.

I reached into my bag and pulled the two sets of gloves we'd also bought, handing one set to Felix. We slipped them on before I pushed gently on the door and we stepped inside.

The room was a fair size, with benches and stools in the center while counters and cabinets lined the perimeter. There was barely any light coming from the large windows at the back of the room. I felt around on the side of the wall and found a light switch, flicking it. The lights buzzed a bit as they slowly, hesitantly, filled the room with a faint, yellow light.

I scanned the countertops. There were various rocks in trays, lab equipment left out, and papers and books strewn here and there on the polished surfaces. The benches in the center were relatively clear, with the occasional microscope ready for its next use. There were some cabinets with glass doors that Felix approached, while I made my way to the back of the room, where there was a large set of drawers.

I opened the top drawer. It was full of fragments – it looked like they may have been ceramics, with distinctive geometric patterns reminiscent of the Incan Empire's signature designs. I closed it and opened the next – there were textiles in this one, mainly tunics, with more patterned designs and bright colours. I closed that drawer and moved to the one beneath it – more fragments, but this time of bones. I raised my eyebrows. Were they human bones?

"Seraphine."

I turned to face Felix. He was motioning to the top of one of the cabinets with glass doors. The cabinet was full of carvings and statues, and sitting inconspicuously on the highest shelf, there they were.

The three Phoenix figurines.

My heart leapt inside my chest. "You found them!" I exclaimed excitedly, hurrying over to his side.

He had a small smile on his face as he went to open the cabinet door. It quickly faded when it wouldn't budge.

I frowned. "Is it locked?"

"It must be," he said, studying the cabinet. "Oh, yes – it needs a key," he then noted as he glanced under the handle. I looked, too, and saw the small keyhole.

"Let's look around," I said, studying the room. "Maybe it's around here somewhere."

We both began searching drawers and opening cabinets, rifling through various means of storage for any sign of a key. Eventually, I spotted a panel peeking from behind the door. I approached it and opened it, my eyes widening. There must have been about fifty different keys hanging inside, all unlabelled.

"Drat," I said.

Felix came over to me, sighing loudly. "Well, we better start somewhere," he said flatly.

So one by one, each of us would take a key and try it for the locked cabinet. And one by one, as they failed, we would replace them on their appropriate hook, taking our next attempt and repeating the cycle.

I was on the thirty-second key when it slid in, and the lock clicked. I grinned as I twisted it, swinging the cabinet door open. Felix and I exchanged glances before he reached for the figurines.

His fingers had barely curled around them when a male voice sharp with anger sliced through the musty air.

CHAPTER 10

"*¡DISCULPE! ¿QUÉ ESTÁS HACIENDO?*"

We froze, and I thought my heart had stopped beating.

Slowly, Felix and I turned. A middle-aged man was standing in the doorway, his arms crossed across his chest, and a look of antipathy plastered on his face. Judging by his age and the way he was dressed, with a nice, collared shirt and dress pants, I assumed he must have been a professor at the university.

I swallowed, looking at Felix. I was met with his gaze in return; while my eyes conveyed a look of surprise, though, his seemed astonishingly bored, as if he had expected this to happen. It took me a second to realize his look said "I told you so," and when I did, I could feel my stare turn into a glare.

"*¡Estoy hablando contigo!*" the man bellowed impatiently, drawing my attention back to him.

I cleared my throat. "What's he telling us?" I murmured to Felix.

"The hell would I know, Seraphine?" Felix hissed back.

"Don't you guys do Spanish in the American school system?"

"Not enough to understand angry Spanish!"

I gave him a weird look. "Isn't your brother Colombian? And fluent?"

"Do I look like my brother to you?"

"Didn't you ever want to learn to speak to him in Spanish?"

"Seraphine, I could barely keep my English studies straight – and I'm a bloody Englishman."

I sighed, smiling forcibly at the man. "Uh…*hola, amigo. ¿Hablas inglés?*"

The man's frown deepened. "*¿No español? Entonces no debéis ser estudiantes. ¿Quién eres? ¿Cómo llegaste aquí? ¿Y qué estás haciendo con esos artefactos?*"

Combined with the panic overwhelming my brain, the man was speaking so quickly and harshly that I couldn't even make out any similar words to those in French. "Um…"

"What the hell is he saying?" Felix whispered to me. "Something about our studies and the artifacts?"

"I think he's saying we can't be students here since we don't speak Spanish?"

Felix loosed a breath. "I should have watched more Dora the Explorer."

"*¡Dejen de hablar entre ustedes y respondan mis preguntas!*" the man bellowed, pointing a finger at us as he took a few threatening steps into the room. "*¡Y baja esas estatuas!*"

"*Señor!*" Felix replied, stepping in front of me a bit. "We no…understand…*understando*. We no *understando*! Please stop the *shouto*!"

"For fuck's sake, Felix, adding 'o' to the end of an English word doesn't make it Spanish," I mumbled behind the palm that immediately hit my face.

"I'm fucking trying, okay!" Felix exclaimed back.

The man's expression was now not only irate, but almost disgusted with us both. "*¡Dije que bajaras esas estatuas!*"

"The statues!" I snapped at Felix as I finally managed to catch one piece of what he was saying. "Put the statues down!"

Felix was a discombobulated mess almost instantaneously, fumbling the figurines around in his grasp until he finally managed to place them in one piece in the cabinet. He let out a huff as he turned back to face the man with a ridiculously fake smile.

"See?" he said, motioning to the artefacts. "No *stealo!*"

"Please stop talking," I groaned.

The man's scowl did not phase in the slightest as he reached for a wired phone on the wall. He punched in a few numbers, never taking his eyes off us for more than a breath at a time, before putting the receiver to his ear.

"*Seguridad, por favor venga al laboratorio de arqueología inmediatamente,*" he instructed sternly into the phone.

"Oh, fuck," I muttered.

It seems Felix had paid enough attention in Spanish class – or watched enough Dora – to also recognize that he had just called security. "Seraphine...this is bad," Felix rasped at me.

"I'm aware, Felix."

"What do we do?"

"I'm thinking."

"Well, think faster!"

"I can't think with all your yapping!"

He grumbled under his breath, but his yapping stopped. Admittedly, even with the newfound quiet, the eerie tension of waiting for whatever security would bring in aid of the boiling professor still hindered my planning abilities. I had no idea how we could talk our way out of this one, especially given we couldn't speak the same language.

As my mind drew blank after blank, the fright the entire encounter had doused me in morphed into an ocean of terrified horror. I threw a rattled glance at Felix, who had lowered his head, the sunglasses sitting a little further down on his nose. His lavender eyes were fixed on the floor, but they flickered in my direction when I moved. To my unabashed astonishment, they were light, airy, even amused. A little smile crept on his face, and he winked at me.

That's when the fire started.

The professor yelped as the flames erupted between us, engulfing much of the room. I shielded my face as best as I could, watching as the professor stumbled backwards, faltering in his movements. Felix seized the opportunity to make for the back of the room in a flash, clambering on top of the counter by the windows.

"Grab the figurines!" he yelled back at me. Immediately, I was bolting over to the open cabinet, coughing through the smoke that was quickly forming. I yanked the statues from the top shelf, the flames licking every corner of the lab except the immediate area surrounding me as the swell of the heat virtually wrenched the sweat out of my body.

I heard shattering glass and looked to see Felix had smashed through the windows. "Come on!" he shouted, waving his hand. A pathway parted through the fire directly to him.

The three statues in hand, I ran over to him and let him help me up on to the counter. As soon as I was there, I realized Fuego and Aurora were waiting for us on the other side of the broken glass. Felix must have called for Fuego telepathically.

"Go! Go! Go!" Felix hurried. I wasted no time ducking out of the window frame and on to Aurora's back. She flew upwards promptly, and a glance over my shoulder showed that Fuego and Felix were right behind us.

I watched Felix halt the fire he'd started as we escaped into the afternoon sun, magically invisible to those we flew above, like fleeting shooting stars you could never wish upon.

———

We decided it was safest to leave Peru entirely, but we were much too frazzled from the chaos to go straight to the temple.

We flew back to Baranquilla with a plan to sleep off the events of the afternoon and head back for the Amazon the next day.

We landed in a different patch of vegetation, closer to the Clarkson Hotel this time, and after the Phoenixes had gone back into hiding, we walked over to the elegant building. It was late afternoon by the time we strolled through the lobby and to the elevator.

Only when the door to the penthouse suite was shut did I let out a sigh of relief. "You really need to stop setting stuff on fire," I exhaled, patting my body up and down. Thankfully, it didn't seem I had any burns, despite the closeness of the flames.

He raised his arms theatrically with a wry grin. "Darling, I've no reason to be afraid of fire if my life is up in flames."

I rolled my eyes. "That lab is probably destroyed."

"I'm really struggling with your moral boundaries here," he noted, humoured. "So theft is okay, but property damage is where you cross the line? We'd be at the mercy of security right now if it weren't for me."

I shook my head. "Fine. I'll admit that was some great quick thinking."

He grinned at me. "You may be a great planner, but I'm a great improviser."

"More like a great arsonist."

His eyes flickered left and right slyly before he held up two fingers, a symbol for "just a little."

I let out an amused breath.

"It's easy to light things on fire when you don't need any kindling," he explained simply, flashing a smile. "Well, besides the little kindling that got you in the mess in the first place."

A little smile of my own crept across my lips as I looked him up and down. Now that we were safe, statuettes secured in hand, my mind was able to let my thoughts meander again. The magnetic pull I felt heaving me towards him began festering in the depths of every limb and bone; when our eyes met, I felt a need to get closer, to see that familiar shade of lavender within a breath's reach. They were the kind of eyes I could dip my soul in, that could keep me more embraced than the strongest of arms. That wasn't to say I didn't appreciate the feeling of his hands on the small of my back, of his body pressed against mine. If anything, I was craving that intimacy again...

The sunset was sending streaks of oranges and pinks across the sky as I sauntered over to the couch. "So, if I'm kindling, what exactly does that make you?" I questioned.

He studied my movement, the way I nestled my body into the comfort of the sofa. His eyes travelled across my face as he slowly came and sat beside me; I watched him make a conscious effort in the way he settled to maintain a proximity to me without letting us touch. Those lavender eyes began taking me in like a present they'd been hoping to unwrap.

"What do you think it makes me?" he replied.

I cocked my head to the side. "Last night, you made it sound like I was the kindling to your flame."

The way he looked at me, with a softness and a wildness all at the same time, was intoxicating. "That works." His eyes drifted to my forearm, where Alchnost had struck me with magic and given me a vivid scar; it had faded to look even more like a tattoo of an eclipse. "I'm starting to think that suits you more than I originally thought. Maybe there's some metaphor there, too."

I glanced at the marking myself. "My little souvenir from Alchnost?"

He nodded contemplatively.

I, in turn, found my gaze wandering to the small tattoo of a black star that sat between his thumb and forefinger. "I agree. It...compliments that."

Felix brought his hand up closer to his face. "In what way?"

I ran a gentle finger over my eclipse. "Well, no eclipse is possible – " my soft touch then grazed over the small star on his hand " – without a very important star."

His eyes met mine, the lavender twinkling as he let my words float in the air and my finger linger on his skin. I held his gaze; it was hard not to fall deep into that rare, spellbinding colour.

I let out a breathy laugh, suddenly a bit flustered. "Well, at least I didn't have to pay for this tattoo."

"You did…in a way."

I shrugged. "I guess. Not sure if it was more or less expensive than my other ones, though."

His gaze flickered over my body. "How many do you have?"

I eyed him. "You, with the eye for details, haven't already counted?"

"I was focused on other things the last opportunity I had."

I snorted. "Count them when you have the chance."

Immediately, his eyes were alight with interest. "Will I have another chance to count them?"

I measured him. "Is there a reason you wouldn't?"

He cleared his throat, hurriedly working to control the excitement on his face. "I, erm…I just…well, we didn't really talk much about last night," he eventually said.

The corner of my lips twitched. "You were busy half-ass planning this morning, and then the rest of the day happened."

He lowered his gaze. "Half a plan," he corrected quietly.

I traced his handsome features with my stare. He was enthralling. "Is there much you wanted to discuss about last night?"

He flexed his jaw. "Not much." His eyes glinted with an ember. "Just that…I enjoyed it."

I licked my lips. "I did, too."

His gaze fell to my mouth. "I enjoyed it enough that I… wouldn't mind if it happened again."

The idea of recurrence made my heart skip a beat, but the choice of words triggered my teasing nature. "Wouldn't mind dancing, wouldn't mind fucking…"

He cleared his throat at my touch, his eyes struggling to remain on my face and not travel to my body. "I'm using that phrase so I don't scare you with my real thoughts."

I levelled his stare. "I don't frighten easily."

A second passed. "Fine, then," he declared, leaning in so close that I could feel his next words waft into my ear. "All I can think about is riding you so hard– " he held up my hand " – that these pretty little nails leave their mark on my back."

The temptation was gnawing at me, and I could feel my cheeks growing flush as I leaned back to lock eyes with him again. "There's nothing stopping us."

The hold we had on each other through our stares was unbreakable. "Shall we go upstairs, then?" Felix suggested.

I smirked. "Why bother?" I hummed. "We have this entire place to ourselves, don't we?"

He grew curious. "I suppose…"

I giggled mischievously as I lifted myself up and over his lap, straddling him in a slow, delicate movement. The initial surprise in his eyes quickly morphed into something carnal, almost wicked. That lavender looked the same way I felt; ever since we'd joined last night, I felt inclined, maybe even a little desperate, to join again.

He brought his thumb to my bottom lip, stroking it softly. "Why do you enjoy playing with fire so much, kindling?" he murmured.

I bit down gently on the tip of his thumb. "Because it makes me feel alive," I cooed.

Instantly, his hand was at the back of my neck, and he brought my lips to his. The kiss was raring and eager, full of a longing we'd instilled in ourselves, one that couldn't be denied any longer. Once I had him this close to me, I didn't want to let him go.

I clung to him, wrapping my arms around his neck, my nails embedding themselves in his shirt. My hips dug into his body, moving sensually against him, building an excruciating tension that both of us couldn't wait to cut. He moaned against me as his tongue swirled around my mouth, giving me a lascivious gratification that only made me move faster, harsher.

It wasn't long before I felt him harden beneath me, and I couldn't help myself from reaching into the front of his pants and pulling him out. He groaned when I touched him, my thumb tracing deliberate circles around and over his most sensitive skin. The way he shuddered gave me pleasure, but I had bigger plans for him than just some simple strokes of the fingers.

I used my free hand to lower my shorts and slip my underwear from its place, parting my lips from his only momentarily so I could glance briefly at where to move.

"In my pocket," he breathed. "My wallet – "

I was tearing away at his wallet and had grabbed what I needed before he could finish his sentence. When I finally filled myself with him, I let out a gasp of both relief and yearning. It was satisfying to have him, yet it simultaneously made me demand even more of him.

He threw his head back with a moan as I moved with him, up and down, time and time again. His eyes fluttered open only to watch one of his hands slither around my neck, falling shut with the depth of his lust as I relished in the feeling the motion brought to me. It was as if he had claimed my neck as his own – powerful, possessive...

"I said that *I* wanted to ride *you*," he snarled roughly, his fingers digging into my skin.

"Is that a complaint?" I gasped out at him, clawing at his back with those pretty red nails.

He let out a breathy, provocative chuckle as his other hand slid down to where we were joined. "It's a promise, kindling," he growled as his other fingers began playing with me.

I let out a small sound as my light magic escaped me, my movements quickening with the anticipation of release. The sparks surged from every inch of my exposed skin when I found it, gasping for breath as I gripped his hair and arched my back. I let myself be ruined above him, sending every piece of me cascading around us to be immersed in him and only him.

"Fuck, Seraphine," he groaned. I felt warmth suddenly surround me, and I brought my gaze back down to see the flames that had burst from him as he thrust himself even further into me. Our magic twisted and turned around each other, engaging in an uncontrollable, tangled dance of their own as he finished, trembling beneath me with pleasure.

Just as quickly as we had started, our rhythm slowed to a stop. The magic that had escaped us began fading as we tried to catch our breath. When we finally looked at each other, I could see the reflection of my whirlwind thoughts in his eyes, however fleeting and frantic they were.

Despite the magnificence of how close we'd become, it wasn't enough.

It could never be enough.

We were insatiable.

- F -

A part of me knew I should confess then, come clean. Her eyes told me she felt what I was feeling; the gravity of us and our connection.

She valued honesty and transparency. But I was afraid;

telling her made it reality. And with reality came her reaction, which I couldn't predict, but that I feared would ruin everything I'd dreamt of.

She would find out one day, soon enough.

But today was not that day.

PART TWO
THE DUPLICITY

CHAPTER 11

- S -

WHEN I AWOKE, my powers were churning inside of me, invigorated.

I blinked, my eyes struggling to bring the darkened room into focus. I vaguely recalled falling asleep on the sofa shortly after my little romp with Felix, but I was now tucked snugly into bed, the silky sheets a welcome smoothness against my naked skin. I turned to see Felix lay sound asleep beside me; he must have brought me to bed with him. I checked my phone – it was three in the morning.

I rubbed my eyes a bit, sitting up. My magic was overwhelming me as it coursed through my veins, filling every inch of my being with unspeakable power. The lure I felt to Felix… despite having had him last night, the need to have him again was irresistible.

Felix stirred at my movement, his eyes parting wearily. "Seraphine?" he mumbled. "You okay?"

I nodded. "*Oui.* Just randomly woke up."

"Mhm." His eyes fluttered closed, his mouth twitching a

bit. "Strange. I thought you'd be more tired after all that…exercise."

I swallowed, studying his features. "Maybe you need to tire me out some more."

A crease formed in his brows. "Hm?"

"Take me."

His eyes popped open. "You want to have sex again?" he asked with a bit of incredulity.

I nodded.

He stared at me for a moment before his face shifted into a devilish smile. "Perhaps I should buy a lottery ticket if I'm getting this lucky," he mused before bringing my face to his with a strong, firm arm.

We kissed passionately for several minutes before he rolled on top of me. I felt his lips latch on to my neck, and as he sucked, I let out a sigh of pleasure.

"I told you it was a promise, didn't I, kindling?" he murmured into my skin.

"Shut up and fuck me already," I breathed.

"Demanding." He snickered as he reached for his wallet on the bedside table. "Put those nails to good use," he ordered as he dragged me by my legs towards him.

———

The next time I awoke, the room was bright, and I was alone. I still felt almost overwhelmed with magic, like it all had been set ablaze, but it was a bit more settled now. A silent yet persistent wildfire. Perhaps the bond nearing completion with Aurora was throwing my body for a loop, and it was taking some time to adapt. I wasn't entirely sure.

I stood as I rubbed my eyes, heading into the bathroom to wash my face. My eyes widened in horror as I glanced in the mirror – a significant hickey sat at the nape of my neck, where Felix's lips had been just hours ago.

"Shit," I muttered, touching it gingerly. That was going to need some disguising when I got back to the university.

I found my way out of the bedroom and out to the sitting area of the hotel room. Felix was standing at the doors to the balcony in his boxers, looking out over the morning sun.

That craving for him resounded through me, but it felt more under control than it had earlier that morning. "Hey," I said as I descended the staircase.

He turned, smiling at me – the air between us seemed surprisingly lacking in awkwardness, considering our late-night activities. "Morning. Breakfast is on the way." His eyes fell to the hickey on my neck, and his smile dropped. "Bloody hell. Was that me?"

"Either that, or there was a really horny ghost in our hotel room last night."

He nervously ran a hand through his hair. "Sorry about that."

"It's fine. I kind of asked for it, anyways."

His eyes scanned my body. "I suppose I tired you out enough that you slept well?"

"Very," I said as I approached him. "Sorry for waking you. I was feeling pretty…um…"

"Oh, trust me – an apology is not what I was looking for." He chuckled. "I could never get sick of that kind of disturbance in the night."

I rolled my eyes, but my lips struggled to hide my amusement. "We should head to the Amazon after breakfast."

His smile was wide and cheeky; he couldn't wipe the contentment off his face if he tried. "I could not agree more," he replied.

———

The flight to the blending temple was short, and it was early afternoon by the time we landed. We made our way through the jungle vegetation we'd traversed just days before, back into the clearing where the temple sat.

I wasted no time bolting to the pedestal, placing the tiny Phoenixes where they belonged as Felix made his way up the stairs. There was a satisfying click as the figurines slid into place, one by one, the way a puzzle comes together perfectly. When they were set, I began turning the wheel, and behind where Felix stood, the temple door began to rumble. Slowly, it lowered itself to its base.

As soon as the door was lowered, Aurora and Fuego bounded up the stairs and into the opening before we could stop them. They seemed magnetized to whatever lay ahead. Felix raised his eyebrows in surprise as he peered down where they'd gone before looking back at me.

"Well, better not keep those eager ones waiting," he said simply.

I nodded and began approaching the temple. But not more than a few steps later, I heard a loud, grumbling sound.

I turned to see the wheel slowly turning backwards, the figurines moving downwards in their respective spaces, further into the stone. And in front of me, I caught glimpse of movement – of the door slowly beginning to rise again. My eyes widened.

"Seraphine, hurry!" Felix exclaimed as he stepped over the rising door frantically.

I launched myself into the fastest run I could muster, racing against time as the door creepily, eerily, continued its ascent back to the top. Felix attempted to push it back down, but it appeared stronger than he was. As I finally ascended the temple steps, the door was just about halfway shut.

Without much thought, I leapt through the opening as a high jumper attempted to leap over a rod, with one foot rising over sideways before the other. Somehow, someway, Felix was able to catch me without too much reverberation, lowering me quickly to the ground. Behind us, the door continued to rumble upwards until finally, it sealed itself shut.

The sound of my heavy breathing filled the space as Felix and I glanced at each other. Then we both peered down the now revealed, torch-lit stone staircase that led deep inside the structure.

Aurora and Fuego were tiny specks at the bottom, ruffling their feathers and shifting uneasily where they stood. Their necks extended up towards us in a begging motion, almost as if they were pleading with us to follow.

Felix and I looked at each other once more, and when I nodded at him, we both began descending the staircase. Eventually, we stepped on to level ground in a torch-lit hallway that was very poorly lit.

Felix took a slight lead. I followed carefully in his footsteps, expressing the light and illuminating the stone corridor. I could hear the movement of Aurora and Fuego's feathers not too far behind me.

We walked slowly along the hallway until it opened into a bigger room, which I further brightened. After doing so, I could see that the walls and floors were made of the same stone we had seen on the outer face of the structure. In the center of the room stood a small column, and on top of it, a lone, silver key sat rather suspiciously. At the end of the room was a stone door with a matching silver lock clinging to its handles.

Felix glanced at the door, then at the key, and snorted as he approached the column. "Hmph. Nice hiding job."

"Felix, hold on –"

Before I could finish, there was a thundering boom on either side of the room, and holes were revealed in some of the stones. Without warning, a bunch of sharp objects shot out from each of the holes on both sides, aiming straight for the center of the room, where Felix stood. The Phoenixes both began squawking as my eyes widened.

"*Felix, duck!*" I screamed.

I had never seen anyone move so fast. Within a tenth of a second, Felix had brought himself all the way to the floor, his entire body becoming a rapid swoosh of movement as the objects flew to the opposite walls and fell to the ground. As quickly as all the motion and sound had started, it all then suddenly stopped.

Relieved that Felix wasn't hurt, I walked over to one of the objects and picked it up carefully. They had been darts with extremely pointed and hollow tips, which indicated that something would have been transferred from the dart into its target upon impact. I held the dart tip down, and just as I suspected, a thick liquid oozed out of the end, dripping slowly to the floor.

I turned to look at Felix, who was watching me as he breathed heavily with a shocked look.

"Poison darts," I said bluntly, showing the one I was holding to him.

He scoffed, shaking his head, his breathing still rapid. "What the hell is this – an Indiana Jones movie?" he gasped.

"We need to be more careful, especially around the obvious," I asserted, tossing the dart back with the others that had fallen and snatching the key out of his hand. "Come on, get up. I have a strange feeling that we're just getting started with the surprises in this temple."

He brought himself up to his feet as I used the key to unlock the door. It came undone easily, and I threw it aside before prying the large stone doors open. With Felix by my side and Aurora and Fuego behind me, we then entered the next darkened room, which I wasted no time lighting.

This room was similar in size and shape to the last, but had a few slight differences. The door opposite us had no handles this time, and in the middle of the room was a table-like structure supported by a single column beneath its center. In each of the four corners of the room, there stood a thin slab of stone with a shallow indent in its top, indicating that something should be placed inside it. There were some faded markings on the stone floor, but the contents of the table drew my attention the most. There were five Phoenix statuettes, much like the ones we had seen outside the temple, but they were coloured this time – one blue, one red, one yellow, one green, and one black. The black Phoenix statuette was placed in a shallow indent in the table's center, which led my intuition to tell me that the other Phoenix artifacts must each belong in one of the indents on the columns in the corners of the room.

"Seraphine, up there," Felix interrupted my thoughts, and when I turned to look at him, he was motioning to something upwards. I glanced over and saw there was writing just above the door that read:

"Five elements, five elements,
Five elements, no more
Bring my birds to their elements
To open the door."

"Sedaurea just loved riddles, didn't she," I said after reading it.

"Well, at least this one isn't too hard to decipher," Felix said, looking down at the statuettes. "The black statue seems to already be in its place. We just need to put the other four where they belong."

"But where *do* they belong?" I thought aloud.

Felix sighed and browsed around, seemingly unable to come up with an answer. His attention turned to something on the ground beneath us, and he frowned at it, taking a slow step back as he continued to analyze it.

I followed his gaze and found he was staring at some of the markings on the floor. After looking at them for a few seconds,

I realized that the artwork just beneath my feet were black orbs. Acknowledging this, I turned to look at the floor by the stone in the top right corner, which I found had green leaves strewn on it.

"Oh, I get it!" I said, picking up the green Phoenix statuette. "The markings on the ground tell us where they should be!"

"I was just coming to the same conclusion," Felix agreed.

I walked over and placed the green Phoenix in its indent on the slab of stone by the artwork of the leaves. It clicked into place.

"Green for Earth," I stated proudly.

"And blue for water," Felix added, and I turned to see he had set the blue Phoenix into its indent in the bottom left corner, where there were blue waves drawn on the floor.

I grabbed the yellow Phoenix and headed to the column in the top left corner, yellow suns had been painted on the floor. "Yellow for light," I said, lodging the Phoenix into its indent.

"And red for fire," Felix finished as he put the red Phoenix in the bottom right corner's column, where around it lay drawings of red flames.

There was a rumbling from the door, and slowly, it began lowering until it had completely opened.

"There we go," Felix said triumphantly, and with our Phoenixes trailing behind us once again, we marched through the open doorway.

After I had brightened the next room, it became apparent that it was the smallest of the three rooms so far. There was nothing in it – no columns, no pedestals, and no statuettes. The walls were the same as the ones we had seen previously, but the floor was no longer stone. Instead, it was made of dirt, the same kind found on the forest floor. In the center of the room, the dirt seemed to have formed some kind of conspicuous circle formation on the ground, and there was small, precise writing scrawled across the wall in front of us.

"Weird," I said, inching forward into the room so that I could read the writing better. Felix and the Phoenixes followed in my footsteps.

Upon further inspection, I managed to make out the words on the wall.

"Greetings, dear Keeper of my birds,
Thus far you have come, but unfortunately, in turn
I cannot yet present you with the wings you desire
Water, Earth, Light, Dark, and Fire
Each of the elements has a test to pass
Then, to you, my bird of Earth will hatch."

"Tests? I really don't like the sound of that," Felix stated slowly, his face close beside mine as he read the writing over my shoulder.

There was a reverberating boom that came from beneath us, a loud and taunting one, which caused us all to look down at the floor. Felix, Fuego, Aurora and I were all standing within that discreet circle formation in the ground, which was now forming distinct lines in and around itself as the dirt began breaking apart.

I looked at Felix. "Well, if it's any consolation, I don't like the sound of *that* either."

The dirt beneath us gave way, and we all began to fall.

CHAPTER 12

Screaming, I flailed my arms around, trying desperately to find Aurora and somehow get on her back. By some miracle, she found me in the dark expanse, scooping me up sloppily on her back. The descent we made was anything but smooth; within a matter of moments, we all tumbled onto a moist surface and rolled uncontrollably to a harsh stop.

I sat up and glanced upwards. To my horror, I couldn't see the hole through which we had fallen through. All I could see all around me was darkness. Panic began to ensue within me – had the floor covered itself back up magically? How would we get out?

I heard groaning coming from behind me, and I turned my head slightly to see that Felix was hoisting himself up as I had done just moments ago, rubbing the right side of his head. "Well, I could have done without that," he muttered.

Aurora and Fuego, who had remained quiet ever since we had landed on the ground, suddenly began freaking out, flapping their wings and wobbling back and forth while emitting ghastly squawking.

I glanced over at them with a frown, and it occurred to me then that there was another sound coming from their movements. Squinting at them, I realized that whenever they brought their legs to the ground, a splashing sound rang out in a sort of chorus with their frantic squeaking.

With my eyes wide, I looked down, and in the shadows of the hole we had fallen through, I could make out the distinct movement of water sloshing around my legs. The sensation of wetness began seeping into the fabric of my pants. Stunned, I stood up unsteadily.

Felix looked over at me worriedly. "What? Seraphine, what is it?"

Ignoring him, I quickly illuminated the space we were in. We'd fallen down a deep chasm, walled with packed dirt and rocks that were layered with tendrils of vines. A stuffy dampness hung in the air, contributing to the claustrophobia the space inspired. Sure enough, there was a thin layer of water on top of the moist floor that had not been there when we had first fallen on top of it.

"It's filling up with water!" I squealed hysterically.

Felix, who by now had gotten up and was observing the room in a flustered manner, nodded at something behind me. "Yes," he said, his voice wavering slightly. "From there."

I turned to look where he had motioned and saw that, in the dirt wall, there was a huge hole which was gushing water. It seemed to be flowing steadily, and since there was no way out from the top of this weird, dirt crevasse, it appeared to be our only means of escape.

I decisively looked at Felix. "We need to go down there."

"Go *towards* the source of the water? Are you crazy?" Felix exploded.

"What other way do we have out?" I snapped back angrily.

"The way we came, of course!"

"Felix, look up."

Felix glanced upwards and seemed to realize then that the hole we had fallen through was no longer visible. Frowning, he then brought his attention back to Fuego and snapped his fingers at him, causing his Phoenix to pause abruptly in his flurry of panic and pay attention to his Keeper. Felix mounted Fuego and flew him upwards towards where we had fallen. I watched as they reached the top and as Felix pushed upwards on the underside of the ground, producing no result. He then agitatedly flew Fuego back down, and they both splashed harshly against the water that was now up to our ankles.

"You're right," he muttered, and I couldn't tell if he was frustrated because I was right or because we were in what seemed like a very cruel trap. "It won't budge from underneath."

"I told you!" I shot back, scrambling over to Aurora and placing a firm hand on the base of her neck. She had a hysterical look in her eyes, but my touch made her pay attention to me and not the water surrounding her for just a second, which was all I needed.

"Hey, it's okay, girl," I told her as calmly as possible, pointing to the hole where the water was pouring out. "We're going that way now. Come on, follow me."

She still seemed quite uneasy, but obeyed, and I felt her follow me as I approached the entrance to the source of the water, where Felix and Fuego were already standing and peering curiously into it.

"Are you sure this is a way out?" Felix inquired as I stood beside him.

"No," I answered quickly, stepping into the hole. "But we don't have many other options at this point. Unless, of course, you want to sit here and wait for the water to fill up and drown us."

Felix looked at me for a brief second, shook his head, and then motioned down towards the source of the water. Without hesitation, Aurora and I began walking through it, followed close behind by Felix and Fuego.

The water source got progressively darker as we proceeded, but I continued to brighten it as we rushed through. All around the edges of the tunnel, I could see vines sprouting from the soil; I trampled the ones in my path on the tunnel bed. The water in the enclosed space was about halfway up my thighs, making movements tough, but we were so desperate and full of adrenaline at this point that it didn't seem to hinder us too much.

We walked for a few minutes, and the water level continued to increase as we went on, reaching the tops of my legs, then to the top of my abdomen, making its way up my midsection. I grew more and more panicked as we went on, my motions becoming clumsier and gawkier, as the Phoenixes had been when we had landed. It was completely out of my control, based purely on the primitive flight or fight response installed in my brain that kept telling me I was going to drown if I didn't keep moving.

The water was just below my chest when movement suddenly became very challenging.

You're going to drown, Seraphine.

I took a clumsy step forward and ended up falling forwards into the water, which was deep enough to swim in.

You're going to drown, Seraphine.

I began to flail my arms in some kind of swimming motion, but it was so uncoordinated and messy that it didn't help me get any further any faster. I gasped desperately and continued to violently crawl about in the water like an aquaphobe who had just been thrown in the middle of the ocean. It seemed as though, in such a dire situation, my mind had forgotten everything useful I'd ever learned about swimming and could only remind me of the fact that I was going to die.

You're going to drown, Seraphine.

I heard the Phoenixes suddenly squeal from behind me, and my attention was drawn backwards. Felix had stopped moving forwards, and was instead thrashing about. All the movement seemed to be a blur; I couldn't understand what he was doing.

"Felix?" I called.

He didn't look up at me. I frowned. What the hell was he doing?

"Felix, come on!" I exclaimed. "We don't have much time!"

He brought his frenzied eyes to mine, his movement stalling for only a split second. And that's when I realized.

The vines.

They were...alive. Moving.

I couldn't explain it – perhaps some cursed magic was in this temple. But the cause didn't matter; what mattered was that they had Felix. In the moment he stopped thrashing, I saw them twisting and curving all around him, tightening their grasp, keeping him from moving forward.

It was obvious the terror had taken over him and was using his body as a vessel to speak. The look in his eyes was distant and distraught. His mind had convinced him that he was hopelessly entangled, that death was imminent.

NO.

I hobbled over to him quickly, my own panic morphing into an enraged determination to get him out of there alive. I grabbed one of the vines and began yanking, summoning a strength I didn't even know I had. They were resistant, but they loosened.

"Just go," Felix exclaimed breathlessly. "You can still make it if there's a way out."

"No!" I shouted through gritted teeth as I pulled and pulled, clawing at the greenery, desperate to get him free.

As some of the vines peeled away, others began slithering around him like snakes. There were so many; it would be impossible to free him completely before others joined.

"Seraphine, it's pointless," he gasped. "You're better off without me."

I ignored him, teeth still clenched as I glanced around, searching for another strategy. I couldn't zap them with my magic – there was water, and I risked electrocuting the two of us. Felix's fire wouldn't work in the water, either. My eyes traced the vines back to where they protruded from the dirt.

The source. Pull them from the source.

I snarled as I gripped one of the vines from their roots and wrenched it from the wall. It fell limp as soon as it broke free of the dirt.

Success. Kill the rest.

"You shouldn't be doing this," I heard Felix say, his voice wobbling. "Seraphine, just – "

"I'm not leaving you behind, Felix!" I snapped angrily. He didn't retort with anything but a gasping sob.

The water was at my chest, but I was so full of adrenaline that my movements sliced through it like butter. Wherever the wretched vines came from, I heaved them free from their roots, tossing them all around.

I managed to kill one vine that released one of Felix's arms. The sudden freedom of movement seemed to startle him out of the panicked state; hope. He'd gotten a stroke of hope.

"Start pulling!" I demanded. He obeyed instantly, the two of us flailing the vines we uprooted all around the tunnel. Even the Phoenixes began to dismember the vines from their sources with their beaks.

Within moments, we'd pulled out enough that his other arm was free. The process hastened even faster; amidst the sea of floating vines we'd created, Felix and I mercilessly hauled more and more greenery from the tunnel walls until he could wriggle his torso and legs free.

"Finally!" I rejoiced when I saw the movement, and I grabbed a hold of both of his arms. "Come on!"

He practically collapsed forwards into the water as I pulled him towards me, and we both began floundering onwards again. The Phoenixes squealed as they trailed behind us; the water was up to my neck. Over the sound of the water sloshing as we tore through it, I could suddenly make out the familiar pitter-patter sound that was made when water fell on top of water, like when it rained over the ocean.

I paused. "Do you hear that?" I hissed.

Frowning, Felix stopped and perked his ears up. It seemed to take him a moment, but his fogged eyes began to clear slightly.

Almost instantaneously, relief began to fill me from top to bottom. We must have been nearing the portion of the hole where the water was falling from, which meant that there must have been a source of water from above that could also be our way out.

We took off in a graceless swim towards the sound, the Phoenixes following suit in their own bird-like swim behind me. The sound got closer and closer with each stroke.

Within a minute of us swimming, I could see the end of the tunnel; it appeared to open into another circular dirt room, bigger than the original chasm we had fallen through. There was a steady stream of water flowing downwards, almost like a small waterfall, that was filling the tunnel – but the area itself was larger and taller than the constricted space we were in, seemingly containing more air than water.

I became a faster swimmer than most Olympians, and so did Felix and the Phoenixes. We stumbled out of the tunnel and into the bigger area almost as quickly as we had spotted it, and I could see that the water was steadily pouring out of a much smaller hole – maybe a meter in diameter – that was situated on one part of the wall just slightly higher up than Felix was tall. And high above that, in the center of the ceiling, there was a gap – a large gap that led out. Our escape.

"There!" we both screamed simultaneously.

I ran over to Aurora, overflowing with a reprieve she must have sensed, because she lowered herself down into the water as I approached her. I hopped onto her back, and she didn't hesitate to take off towards the exit. Her soaked feathers made flight egregiously difficult, but she pushed onwards in desperation, her wings beating the air with loud thumps. She flung us all the way up and out of the gap, tumbling gratefully onto the dry, dirt floor above in a new, unknown room.

I stumbled off Aurora onto the dry ground, soaking wet, coughing as my inhalations tried to keep up with the remnants of my adrenaline. My powers were running marathons through me, aggravated and alert.

I heard the flapping of wings and looked up just in time to see Felix fly Fuego out of the hole and come crashing down beside us. He slumped off his Phoenix and onto all fours, his person just as soaked as I was. His now drenched gray shirt clung to every muscle on his chest, his leather jacket doing the same on his arms, and his hair dripping water. He shook violently, and he was panting loudly now, almost hacking. With an evident struggle, he somehow turned and sat with his back propped against the wall beside me.

We both remained there, inhaling and exhaling, trying to collect ourselves, for a while. It took several minutes before our breathing returned to a relatively regulated and calm state. The sound of the rushing water eventually subsided, the only noise heard being the occasional droplet falling quietly from the ceiling to the floor.

"I can't believe you did that."

I looked at him. He was watching me. The lavender in his eyes was solemn.

"You didn't leave me," he breathed almost incredulously.

I stared at him in disbelief. "You thought I would leave you?"

He swallowed, his gaze flitting over my face. "Anyone else would have."

My eyes were wide, my heart pained. "Felix…"

His irises swirled. "I wouldn't have faulted you for it," he whispered.

I shook my head. "We're a team. We made this commitment together," I stated. "I would never leave you behind."

There were new tears in his eyes. The traumatic event must have been running his emotions ragged. "But you could have killed yourself trying to save me," he said shakily.

I could have. If what I'd done hadn't worked, we could have both been as dead as those vines we discarded in the water. But despite my fears of death, that realization did not phase me nearly as much as it should have.

"I would rather die trying to save you than live knowing I could have been the difference between your life and death," I told him.

His tears fell, and he took a deep, trembled breath in. "You're really fucking stubborn, kindling," he whispered. "And I'm really fucking glad you are."

I sniffled, and as my own tears began to fall, I threw my arms around him in a hug. He embraced me back, and I could feel his cries seeping into my shirt as he buried his head in my shoulder.

As I clung to him in that moment, my powers whirled, and I faced an intimacy different than the way we'd shared our bodies. It felt like a blunt force that whacked me upside the head; a reality I didn't quite know how to process.

I feared death – this was true.

But I feared losing him even more.

CHAPTER 13

Eventually, Felix pulled away, rubbing away the remnants of his lament. "Okay," he said softly. "We should probably figure out what to do next."

I nodded as I rubbed my own eyes. "Agreed," I said after taking a deep breath.

I took this opportunity to brighten the dim area we were in. This new area was again a closed-in space, both walls and floor covered in dirt. Vines and greenery covered the walls and some portions of the ground, and towards the north end of the room, there was a thicket of thorny vines that surrounded a giant boulder; it seemed to be blocking some kind of entryway. There appeared to be no other way to exit the room except the gap in the floor from which we had escaped the water, and we sure as hell were not going back down through that.

Standing up, I walked over and inspected the thicket more closely. The thorns on the vines were barbed, and they had bright fuchsia tips, which gave warning signs that they might be poisonous. And, after what we'd been put through during our time in this temple so far, it was safer to heed that warning than not.

"I think we have to get through here and move that boulder," I stated simply. "It looks like there's some kind of passageway on the other side."

Felix stood and came up beside me. "Hmm. All right. Stand back."

I did as he told me. Moments later, he had ignited the vines in hungry flames, which ate away at the greenery with ease. The ashes fell to the floor, and within minutes, we could walk unharmed up to the large rock, which was a little bigger than Felix.

He made the fire disappear with the snap of a finger. "Can you help me push this thing?"

We both walked over to the left side of the boulder and placed two firm hands on its surface.

"Push on the count of three," Felix said. "One… two…*three!*"

I pushed against the rock with all my might, as did Felix, and slowly, it began to slide over to the right. Behind it, an opening was revealed, just as I had suspected. We continued to push the boulder until there was a big enough gap for the Phoenixes to fit through.

"Excellent," Felix panted, looking over at our two Phoenixes, who were both watching us curiously. I suspected he must have telepathically instructed Fuego to come over, because he instantly hurried over to us, followed by Aurora.

We entered the newly exposed passage. I led the way through the narrow, dirt tunnel, brightening it along the way. As I walked, water dripped from my hair, my clothes, my exposed skin. A shiver ran through me; the air in the temple was cool, and combined with my dampness, it felt like a breath of ice whenever I moved.

The sensation of heat suddenly surrounded me, replacing the whisper of cold I'd expected to feel with a welcome comfort. Despite my appreciation for the coziness, my confusion had me frowning, and I turned to look behind me.

Felix had left a little distance between us, his hand held up in front of him. At my back, he'd summoned a blanket of tranquil, radiant fire – it danced lazily, a much different blaze than the violent one I'd seen him summon in Peru. The slow, steady flames had been drawn with grace all around me, just beyond the reach of my skin to prevent a burn, but close enough that they'd kiss me gently with their heat. It was as if he'd encased my body in a halo of embers, the glow of oranges and reds flickering against me with the gift of heavenly reprieve.

My smile lifted with the flicker of the flames closest to me. "Thank you," I said.

He shrugged, the reflection of citrine and scarlet melting with the lavender in his eyes, like jewels that sat by a crackling wood stove in a cold, winter cabin. "Least I can do," he replied simply, his gaze glued to mine.

My turn away from him was delayed. I was drawn to the way the fire made him look, the way he was molded by the magic he made. It was hard giving my back to such fine generosity.

The fire remained behind me as I began moving forward again.

Within minutes, the tunnel led us out and into a wide, open area, which I wasted no time brightening.

There was nothing on the dirt walls of this room. At the opposite end, a long way away from where we stood now, there was another tunnel-like passageway that led out of this new area. Spread out randomly on the floor were odd, dark patches. I couldn't really tell what they were. All I could identify about them was that they seemed strange.

"Humph. Odd," Felix hummed, motioning towards the dark patches on the ground. I nodded in acknowledgement.

I felt the warmth of the fire fizzle away as Felix halted his magic and approached one of the dark patches. When he was within an inch of it, a sudden surge of fire shot out from its center. He yelped and fell backwards in surprise, and I somehow managed to push him upright just enough so that he wouldn't fall to the ground. I watched as the fire formed a sort of geyser, spewing flames before it suddenly vanished back down and sank once again beneath the dark patch.

"All right, then," I said. "The plan of action is to *avoid* the dark patches, thanks to our new observation."

Felix turned to look at me, and then decidedly offered me his hand. "Come on. I'll lead the way."

I glanced at his hand, then back up at him. "Are you sure?"

He nodded. "If I make a mistake, at least the fire won't hurt me."

I shrugged in response, and slowly, I placed my hand atop his. The large, masculine build of his made mine look dainty and feminine in comparison. He stared at our connected hands for a moment, and I saw something flicker across his face before he regained his original composure and enveloped my fingers amongst his gently, wrapping them in his grasp. Considering we'd both seen each other naked, I didn't quite understand the fascination at us holding hands, but I didn't question it aloud, either.

With our hands laced together, he began leading us through the maze of dark patches slowly and carefully. The Phoenixes scurried after us in our footsteps, and it took a while for us to reach the other side, but we did manage to without me burning to bits, and I would consider that a success.

Felix tightened his grasp on me, almost as if to prevent me from running away, as we strode through the next passageway.

The next room we entered was small, and the entrance to the next one was not too far from where we stood. The only things standing between us and the following passageway were hundreds of thin, bright beams of light. They spanned the width of the room perpendicular to us, each individual one starting at one wall and finishing at some point on the opposite wall, which altogether formed a sort of disfigured light trap. I hesitantly reached towards one with my free hand, and as it got near, the strength of the warmth increased. A burn seemed to await us if we walked through it, not to mention blindness if it hit our eyes.

I took a deep breath in as I brought my hand back to my side. "Okay, this seems manageable. I'll lead us through this time."

Felix nodded. "All right. Whenever you're ready."

I scanned the light beams, looking for a good start, and found a relatively large hole in the light beams to our left. Carefully, I led us through it, and then through another, and another. The Phoenixes understood what was going on and were cautious and successful as they followed. It took us a little while, but eventually, we all made it to the other end unharmed and proceeded to the next room.

This one was pitch black, and I immediately brightened it only to see it was the largest of all the rooms. At the other end of the room stood a pedestal, and on the pedestal was a shimmering, forest-green egg sitting amongst what looked like a nest of leaves. This would have been an instant relief had there not been one minor flaw, and that was that between the ground we stood on and the pedestal, there was no path. Instead, there was a deep, seemingly never-ending gap that got deeper and darker as I continued to stare down at it.

"Huh," I finally said, looking back up at the pedestal. The length of the hovel was immense – maybe a football field or two in length. It was definitely much too far to jump across. The only way was to fly our Phoenixes over to it.

I felt the grip on my hand loosen, and turned to see Felix had let go of me and was climbing on to Fuego's back. I didn't hesitate to hop on to Aurora's.

"I'll go first," I stated, looking sternly at him. "Just in case it's some kind of trap, at least both of us won't be lost."

He stared at me for a moment. Then he shook his head.

"No," he said. "I'll go first."

I blinked. "Are you sure?"

"Yes. Now don't let me change my mind." And that was all

he said before he tugged up on Fuego's neck, and the Phoenix took off over the gap.

I held my breath as they flew over to the pedestal, and time seemed to move very slowly. To my pleasant surprise, nothing bad happened to them, and they made it over to the other side in one piece. I let out a sigh of relief and promptly commanded Aurora to fly. She responded immediately, and we began to glide over the giant pit.

And just as we began to do so, I heard an unnerving rumble, and glanced up to see that parts of the stone ceiling were beginning to fall.

I gasped as one of the large rocks fell directly in front of me, and I jerked back on Aurora's neck, causing her to reel backwards and the stone to miss us by a few slight inches. Terrorized, I stared at the crumbling ceiling as we hovered in mid-air, suddenly unsure of what to do and where to go.

"*Seraphine!*"

Felix's voice snapped my attention over to him, and he yelled at me feverishly. "You need to fly to the spots a rock has already fallen, and wait until the next one falls! Watch the ceiling!"

Frenzied, my eyes shot back up to the ceiling. He was right. Yes, the ceiling was shaking, but only certain rocks were being dislocated, meaning they had to wriggle themselves free of the solid ones. If I timed it right, I'd be able to position Aurora and me in a safe space while we waited for the next one to open up.

I got a hold of my determination and confidence once again, tugged hard on Aurora's neck to the left, and had her hover in our new gap as the next round of rocks fell. I watched as the next space opened in front of us, and I had her fly there, a rock just breezing past us on its way to the abyss below. I flinched at the gust of wind it left in its wake, but tried my best to keep my composure. Quick glances in his direction showed that Felix watched every move we made with bated breath.

Over and over, I repeated this pattern of watching, planning the next move, getting us to safety, and waiting. Finally, a gap opened straight to the pedestal. I yanked on Aurora's neck, and we found ourselves shooting towards where Felix and Fuego stood.

We collapsed upon the jutted rock with such force that I lost my balance and tumbled off Aurora's back. She fell forward, and I struggled to regain my footing as I stumbled dangerously close to the edge. Felix rushed to my side and pulled me up so harshly that I plummeted forward against his chest with a squeal. He held me against him as we both recoiled from our abrupt movements, landing together on the floor alongside the pedestal.

I heard loud rumblings shortly after this happened and whipped my head around to see that all the remaining loose stones had dislodged and were now in the process of falling from the ceiling. Between the remaining stones and the gaps where there had been rocks, a giant hole in the shape of a crescent moon had formed in the ceiling. Through it, I could see the shadows of the towering trees in the early evening light, shading the Amazon Rainforest from the sun's fading glow.

Felix looked up at the pedestal and the egg that sat atop it. "We made it."

"Well, it's about damn time!" I exclaimed.

He chuckled and stood up, offering me his hand. I took it, and he helped me up before turning to me.

"Well," he said. "Have at it."

I met his gaze. "Are you sure?"

"I hatched the last one," he said. "It's your turn."

I smiled at him, and then turned back to the egg. Swiftly, my hand was over top of its surface.

Bright green light erupted from the egg as it broke apart and revealed my newest baby Phoenix. Its tiny body was covered in feathers the same forest-green colour as its eggshells, and its beautiful, little eyes were a striking lime green. Ecstatic, I carefully picked it up and brought it close in towards me, stroking its soft feathers reminiscent of the woodlands. It chirped and plopped a new pendant with an emerald-green stone in my hands, which I passed to Felix.

"Would you like to do the honours?" I inquired.

"My pleasure," he said, and he popped it open. "A boy – Suelo," he announced.

I giggled. "Hello, little Suelo," I cooed to him. The baby bird sang in response. Felix handed me the new pendant, which I strung around my neck, before he patted Suelo softly on the head with a chuckle.

Satisfied, I looked back at the pedestal, underneath where Suelo's egg had just been. There was a new inscription, which I read aloud:

> *"My feathers of Earth are now yours*
> *Onwards to my wings of fire you soar*
> *In the belly of the largest summit*
> *Is where, without fear, you must plummet*
> *Go where fire and water build land*
> *And there'll you find the bird you demand."*

"Hmph. A shorter one this time," Felix replied, taking a picture of the inscription with his phone. "We can look at that later. Let's get out of here."

I motioned up to the large moon-shaped hole in the ceiling. "We can fly the Phoenixes out through there."

I kept Suelo tucked tightly into my chest as we hopped on the back of our Phoenixes, and before long, we were soaring out of the temple's roof, past the tall trees, and away from the Amazon.

CHAPTER 14

By the time we had arrived back at the cellar, dawn had long opened its eyes over the horizon as I struggled to keep mine parted.

Felix opened the skylight and our Phoenixes darted through it, gratefully plopping themselves onto the ground as we hastily climbed off their backs. Fuego almost immediately shut his eyes and curled himself up into a sleeping position while Aurora rushed over to the water trough and drank desperately. Lumina, angelic white feathers shimmering in the morning light, wandered over to me, glancing at Suelo with a curious look in her eyes. I gently placed him on the floor beside her, stroking both of their heads as I let them get acquainted. Their series of chirps and peeps made me smile for a split second before my body's tiredness overcame me, and I let out an uncontrollable yawn.

"What time is it?" I wearily asked Felix.

Felix, who looked even more exhausted than I felt, pulled out his phone and turned it on. "It's just past six in the morning," he answered, shrugging his backpack off his shoulders and letting it fall to the floor.

I nodded, yawning again. It had certainly been one

eventful night, and now that the adrenaline rush from all the danger had faded, I was definitely feeling the need for a nice, long rest.

I watched as Felix hobbled over to the wall, leaning himself against it. His eyes shut, and he let out a series of groans as a frown wrote itself across his features. He brought his hand to his head, rubbing his eyes several times.

If I was struggling with the need to sleep, he was fighting a losing battle against it. I felt my stomach turn a bit. He looked horrible, maybe even sickly.

I walked over to him, outstretching my hand and placing it on his forehead. It wasn't exceedingly warm, per say, but he was perspiring. He was certainly in poor condition, perhaps from all the stress.

I brought my hand down, giving him a sympathetic gaze. "You should rest," I suggested.

His hand moved only enough so his dim eyes could meet mine. "I need to drive you home," he murmured.

"You're not driving right now."

"But – "

"Felix." I pressed firmly on his shoulder, and he peered at me again with those dreadful, weary eyes. "You need rest."

I didn't know if his lack of response was because he knew I wouldn't change my mind or because he was too tired to even try. Regardless, he simply let out a grunt and began walking dazedly towards the staircase. I placed my hand lightly on his back as we walked – he seemed so fragile and weak, which was a hard concept to wrap my head around, considering his height and build.

The sun was barely poking its way out from behind the clouds, making it a rather cool San Diego morning. We made our way into his villa and walked over to the front foyer.

"My room's upstairs, at the very end of the hall," Felix said. "On the left."

We ascended the glass stairs to the dark hardwood of the

second floor. We passed several other rooms on the way to his, some of which looked like they were guest rooms, as well as a collection of paintings by Rothko and Pollock in the hall before we arrived at a slightly parted door. He opened it further, and we walked in.

A large, corner desk made of blackened wood and complete with his textbooks, laptop, and other materials greeted me as I walked in. Behind it, through a doorway, I could see what looked like a pristine bathroom – I spotted a modern, square tub and rain shower. There was another doorway within it that led to a large walk-in closet.

Further into the room was a king-size bed, draped in a gray-ish blue comforter and complemented with light gray pillows. The bedside tables were also made of blackened wood and were topped with modern-looking light fixtures. A black sofa and armchair sat against the far corner, right beside the huge windows and glass doors that led out to the balcony and provided a spectacular view of the estate and the Pacific Ocean behind it. Between the sofa and armchair sat a white vase on another small table that matched the rest of the wood in the room. Across from the bed was a dark marble fireplace, above which hung a piece of abstract line art. There was a full-length mirror and a small bookshelf on the two sides of the other entryway to the closet.

It was into the bathroom and then the closet that he disappeared, reappearing with a pair of his sweatpants and a black sweater. "Here," he said, giving them to me. "You can wear them for the time being, until we can get you back to the university and into your own clothes."

"Thank you," I said, taking the loungewear.

He nodded once. "I'll be out in a few minutes."

"Okay," I said, and he went back into his bathroom, shutting the door behind him.

I slipped off my dirty clothing and put on the clothes he had handed me. I had never been more grateful for clean clothes, especially comfy menswear that was naturally quite oversized on me. Curious, I looked at the tags and found that they were Alexander McQueen articles of clothing. *Wow, even his loungewear is high-end,* I thought to myself, which, in retrospect, wasn't all that astonishing.

I walked around the room as I waited for him, glancing at its features. I suddenly noticed a picture frame I hadn't seen before; it was somewhat tucked behind the vase on the end table. Upon closer inspection, I realized it was a picture of a beautiful young woman holding what seemed to be a fairly young boy, no more than three or four years old. They seemed to be in some kind of entryway, which I soon recognized to be the foyer in Luther's mansion, and they were both eloquently dressed. The woman wore a sundress patterned with sunflowers, while the boy wore a black and blue argyle-patterned shirt with toddler-sized black jeans. Both the boy and the woman had the same dark brown hair as well as unmistakable, shining lavender eyes that glowed along with their bright smiles as they posed for the camera. It was instantly obvious due to their striking similarity that this must have been a picture of a very young, happy-looking Felix and his mom.

I pondered the photo, my eyes widening a bit. The sundress was all too familiar – it was the one I'd borrowed from Felix's closet the morning after he'd saved me from Alchnost.

So the dresses in the closet…they were his mother's.

I swallowed, my eyes darting over the frame. The way it was placed on the table almost seemed like an attempt to hide it, and yet, it still remained there. I found myself considering this peculiarity until Felix reappeared from the bathroom, wearing sweatpants and sporting his bare chest.

I watched as he meandered over to the bed and pulled back the comforter. He fluffed up his pillow a few times before crawling under the sheets. Then he pulled back the blanket on the other side of the bed, motioning to it as he looked at me.

"Come," he said.

I blinked at him. "I don't think either of us are in any condition for sex."

He shook his head. "I wasn't suggesting we have sex," he replied. "Just come and rest with me."

I studied him; the lavender in his eyes was pleading for me to stay. My heart thumped in my chest with a melancholic hum. I felt bad for how drained he was, and that there was a photo of him and his mother behind the vase, both hidden and present. A part of me was still reeling from everything we'd been through, too...

That depraved lust for him had quieted, though it was not completely silent, as I could feel it lingering somewhere deep within me. Even so, a part of me...it felt as though leaving him would be like turning away from the oasis I'd sought for days in a barren desert. Backing away from salvation, from sanctuary – the luminous hearth he'd nestled me in as we trudged through the temple, soaked to our bones. That feeling in his eyes, that need for him to be near me...I felt it, too. A craving to be around him, to not leave his side.

I decidedly climbed into bed next to him. He didn't touch me, didn't even make a move to get closer to me. He simply laid his head back against his pillow as I sank into mine, and we both shut our eyes. We were asleep within minutes.

———

I awoke when the sun was setting on Thursday.

I felt rested and relieved, much less worn than I'd been when we'd come back to San Diego. A glance to my right reminded me I'd agreed to sleep in Felix's bed, and he was still sound asleep.

I frowned. I wasn't sure if I could call him sound asleep, because really, he still seemed a bit restless. A frown had been faintly painted on his face, as if the artist wanted you to really look for the expression. His breathing was shallow and sometimes hitched, the pattern sometimes arrhythmic. Maybe that was the smoking. Maybe the frown was a nightmare.

I swallowed, my eyes scanning his features. He was undeniably handsome; he was chiseled like a Greek god. My mind wandered to our little trysts in Colombia once again, reminding me how much I enjoyed them. But then, my thoughts drifted to the temple, to him begging to leave me behind when he was tangled in the vines, and my refusal to do so. I remembered how he'd expected I'd leave him. And I remembered how the thought of him not making it out alive…

I found myself blinking back tears, suddenly choked at the possibility. It broke me. I couldn't picture it for fear that I would manifest it. He'd become a part of me – I couldn't fathom my life without him. Whether it be from drugs or a dangerous excursion, I suddenly felt this overwhelming need to…protect him. Where it had stemmed from, I didn't know. But it was now as much an innate response as the need to breathe and eat.

I sighed, carefully making my way out of bed and out of his room. He didn't stir. As I made my way to the top of the stairs, I heard familiar male voices. I descended to the first floor and strolled through the first archway to the sitting room, where Julius was talking to Francis.

Julius noticed me, and his face brightened. "Seraphine!" he exclaimed, coming over and giving me a hug. He wore dark jeans and a Gucci button-up that was more open than closed. "What a wonderful surprise!"

"Good to see you," I said, returning the hug with a smile. "What are you doing here?"

He motioned to Francis. "I was just returning the tie I borrowed from Felix." The butler held up the tie draped over his arm, almost as an acknowledgement, before he nodded at us and scurried off. "Say, where is Felix anyways?" Julius then asked me.

"He's still asleep," I replied.

"Still asleep?" he glanced at his watch. "It's seven in the evening." He returned a curious gaze up to me. "How long have you been here?"

I didn't respond right away, mainly because I'd not only lost track of time, because I also realized my being at Felix's villa for so long was nothing but unusual. A part of me was also a little hesitant for Julius to know about our little…shared experiences.

As I fumbled for an answer, Julius raised his eyebrows a bit, which made me fumble faster. "Since yesterday," I then lied, clearing my throat. "We were working on a lab report, and then it got really late, so he told me I could just crash in one of the guest rooms."

Julius looked me up and down. "In his clothing?" he continued, his expression becoming a bit humoured.

I swallowed. "My clothes were uncomfortable to sleep in."

"Were they?"

"…*Oui.*"

"My, my." His smile was twitching. "It's fortunate he lent you this comfortable set."

"Very considerate of him."

"Quite unlike Felix, if I'm honest." His smile now transformed to a grin. "There must be a good reason he did that."

My eyes became shifty. I tried to look anywhere else in the room but at him.

"Well, since I've run into you by such pleasant coincidence," Julius went on, "I can personally invite you to my upcoming Halloween party before I go."

I raised my eyebrows. "A Halloween party?"

"My favourite holiday." His grin was animated. "The theme this year is Playboy."

I rolled my eyes. "Why am I not surprised?"

"I think you'll make one fine Playboy bunny, if you ask me," he went on with a wink. "It's next Friday. You can drop by my place anytime after seven."

"All right. I'll probably get a ride with Felix."

Julius shrugged. "Felix never comes to my parties, but I'd be happy to send a car for you."

I frowned a bit. "Oh," was all I could really say. "Is he invited?"

"Of course he's invited. He just never shows."

The sibling rivalry was rearing its ugly head once again. I didn't know how I felt about going to a Clarkson event without Felix – especially one hosted by Julius.

"I'll have to let you know," I responded.

Julius gave me a sad look. "Oh, come on, now. It'll be a good time. You'll have plenty of fun, trust me." He motioned to himself. "I put on one hell of a party, you know."

I had to return a smile – his charm was magnetic. "I don't doubt it."

He gave me a quick pat on the shoulder and handed me a business card with his phone number. "I'll have someone come get you. A little VIP treatment. Just text me when you're ready."

I didn't object as he made his way to the archway. Before he left the room completely, though, he paused.

"Oh, and just a small tip for the future, Seraphine," he said, turning to smirk at me. "The next time you try to lie about fucking my brother, make sure you cover up the hickey on your neck."

My jaw fell open. I'd forgotten entirely about the hickey. Mortified, I clasped one hand over it instinctively, and the other over my open mouth.

Julius didn't say anything more, but I could hear him snickering as he made his way out of the room.

——————

I sat in the cellar, bundled against the Phoenixes with my lips pursed. I thought surrounding myself with them would make me feel better about what had occurred, but I found myself overthinking it all again and again in my head, no matter how much I stroked Suelo's little head.

"How crass can one guy be," I muttered in disgust, shaking my head to myself.

From her lounging perch in the corner of the room, Aurora cocked her head at me. She'd been watching me curiously since I'd entered the cellar, but I hadn't wanted to sour her relaxed mood, so I'd tried to keep my emotions to myself. Evidently, I hadn't done a very good job.

I sighed at her. "Men are just the worst, aren't they?"

The way her yellow eyes rolled and returned to me seemed to be her way of saying, "Don't even get me started."

Beside her, though, Fuego snapped his gaze at me in what could only be described as deep offense.

I snorted. "All right, all right. You're not so bad."

He squinted at me, then looked at Aurora. She flicked her head at him in annoyance, to which he simply scoffed and turned away.

My gaze lingered on my first Phoenix. It had been nearly a month since I'd hatched her, and we'd been through what felt like a lifetime of adventures already. Still, though, the bond we shared wasn't complete. How much longer could that possibly take?

"I can't wait to be able to actually talk to you," I thought aloud, my voice hinting at a need for reassurance.

Aurora looked back at me, her eyes sweetening as she nodded once. "Soon," she seemed to say.

The gesture, though subtle, was comforting. The way she was always in tune with me felt like a soothing harmony to a melody.

I heard movement and turned to see Felix make his way down the stairs. He looked much better than when I'd last seen him, and he was dressed as well as he normally was. At least that was a relief.

I must have worn my displeasure on my face, because he immediately frowned when he saw me. "What's wrong?"

I motioned to my neck. "Your brother saw," I said.

Felix's frown became more concerned. "Oh." He cleared his throat as he came and sat down across from me, his eyes wide with unease. "Did he say anything?"

"If I recall correctly, he said that the next time I try to hide the fact that I fucked you, I should be sure to cover up my hickey."

I could see the rage flicker instantly across his face. "What?" he snapped, shaking his head. "That's insolent."

I sighed and looked away, to which Felix placed a steady hand on my shoulder. "I'm really sorry," he continued. "I'll talk to him."

I shrugged. "Oh, not to worry. I'm perfectly capable of giving him a piece of my mind. Maybe I will at his party."

"What party?"

"His Halloween party next Friday," I said, eyeing him. "He said you were invited."

He seemed to recall the information. "You're going to that?" he asked incredulously.

"Well, he invited me, so I figured I would," I replied.

Felix rolled his eyes. "His parties are even worse than my father's. I never enjoy them, so I never go to them."

"That aligns with what he said," I remarked.

Felix kissed his teeth, glancing around the room. He appeared to be thinking things over. Then he brought his eyes back to mine.

"I'll come with you," he declared.

I blinked at him. "You don't have to go just for me."

But to this, he simply stood and offered me his hand. "It starts at seven, doesn't it?"

"I think that's what he said," I replied, taking his hand.

He pulled me up. "Good. I'll pick you up at six-thirty,

then." He motioned to the stairs. "I'm sure you'd like to go home now."

A part of me was dreading finding out about all the work I'd missed during our adventures. Another part of me was dreading leaving him – an overwhelming part of me, actually. But a small part of me did want to see my friends, and to get into my own clothes.

I nodded and followed him out of the cellar. When we'd made it to the foyer, he motioned for me to wait for him as he bounded up the staircase. He disappeared for a few moments, then reappeared carrying a plaid Burberry scarf.

He offered it to me with a bit of an apologetic smile. "This might help," he said quietly.

A small smile tickled my lips as I wrapped the scarf around my neck, and then we made for his garage and collection of cars.

———

"Good luck with your homework," Felix wished me as he pulled up to the university entrance.

"Thanks – I'll need it," I replied as I stepped out of the Lamborghini.

He bid me farewell and slowly began driving away. I turned to begin heading to my dorm. And I felt it, then, resounding through me as I walked, so much so that it halted me.

It was pain.

I frowned as I brought my hand to the base of my neck, swallowing as I tried to process the feeling. It wasn't physical pain, but it overtook my body as a blunt trauma would. My magic flickered sporadically beneath my skin in broken waves, as if it were aching, too. I felt as though I'd lost something near and dear to me; like I couldn't grab the edge of a cliff that would save me from my own demise, and down I fell into an endless abyss.

I turned and looked over my shoulder at where Felix's car had been. He was long gone, but in the distance, I could make out his vehicle getting smaller and smaller on the road leading to the Clarkson estate.

The sight of it strained something in me. Though my feet remained planted, I felt...need. A shiver ran down my back as I felt a sudden lack of warmth within me. That tether I'd felt after we'd first been intimate in Colombia...it was yanking me back towards him, as if we were shackled together. I felt as Felix had looked entangled in those living vines; hopelessly captive to a yearning that kept twisting and turning to bring me back to him. Two prisoners, jailed to each other.

But *what* had imprisoned us?

I shook my head as I tried to dismiss the feeling and continue onwards to my dorm. It didn't hinder me much in terms of capacity, but it was defiant. It wanted to make itself known. No matter how much I shoved the acknowledgement of its presence to the back of my mind, it sat with a distinct aura within me. A persistent lull, pulling me towards where I'd last seen that car, willing me towards it like I was in a game of tug-of-war.

Something indescribable was insistent that I return to Felix, and it would adamantly, unrelentingly beckon me until I did.

CHAPTER 15

Roscoe, Sajan, Emmanuella, and Keiffer were all sitting in the lounge, playing Monopoly, when I strolled in.

"Seraphine!" Roscoe exclaimed. "I haven't seen you in a few days!"

"I was visiting some family friends. I just got back," I said – that was the lie I'd told Emmanuella, right?

"Oh, cool," Sajan remarked.

"Want to join our game of Monopoly?" Keiffer offered.

I shook my head. "Thanks, but I've got so much work to catch up on," I replied. "And besides, that game ruins friendships."

"Our friendships are as unruinable as a pizza in the rain, though," Keiffer retorted with a cheesy grin.

Emmanuella scoffed. "Sheesh, Keiffer, you say the dumbest stuff sometimes," she grumbled at him. "That doesn't even make any sense. Who the fuck wants a wet pizza?"

Keiffer raised his hands defensively. "Well, forgive me for liking pizza no matter what it's been through."

I rolled my eyes, grabbing a granola bar from the lounge kitchen and heading back to my dorm. I turned on my desk light and got all my notebooks, textbooks, and writing supplies set up. Then I flicked on my laptop and logged into each of my courses.

Just as I was about to begin, my phone rang. It was a video call from my parents.

I sighed. It had been a while since I'd talked to them. Despite all the work, I couldn't bring myself to ignore the call.

"Hi, Mom," I said as soon as her lively face popped onscreen. "How are you guys?"

"Oh, it's so good to finally hear your voice, Seraphine!" she exclaimed cheerily. "You should call more often!"

"I know, I know…"

"Give me all the updates! How are your classes? How are your friends? Oh – wait. Before you start, let me go get your father! I think he's in the garage…"

I spent nearly an hour filling my parents in about all my studies, how my friends were doing, and conveniently left out any information about my rendezvouses with Felix – or the fact that I'd been to the Amazon, Colombia, and Peru. The moment I managed to hang up, I rolled my shoulders and cracked my neck, recentering my focus on the tasks before me.

To my dismay, the hill of work to be done rapidly grew into more of a steep mountain. I huffed to myself when I finally had all the things I needed to do written down on a piece of paper; I wasted as little time as possible prioritizing all the work by due dates, and then, I started to knock things off systematically.

By the time I'd submitted a few quick quizzes and assignments, midnight was flashing across my clock, and I'd only made a small dent in my pile of work. I let out a heaving breath as I rubbed my eyes. I was already feeling a headache coming on, and I hadn't even begun studying for the upcoming physics midterm – undoubtedly where most of my attention would need to go if I had any hope of passing.

I cupped my face in my hands as I bit my lip, thinking. Then I reached for my phone.

Me

What are you doing tomorrow after school?

I went to start on my next assignment, but before I could open a new document, I already had a response.

Felix Clarkson

Miss me already?

I rolled my eyes.

Me

I'm fucked. I need your help.

Felix Clarkson

I'm a little lost. Didn't you want to be fucked?

Me

Could you stop thinking about sex for three seconds?

Felix Clarkson

Truthfully, no. I haven't been able to stop thinking about you naked since…well, since I saw you naked.

I sighed.

Me

I need physics help. The midterm's next week and I haven't even started studying. You know better than anyone how great I am at physics, so the problem is kind of self-explanatory.

Felix Clarkson

Oh, you're bloody fucked, all right.

Me

Felix. Please. Can you help me?

Felix Clarkson

Of course I'll help you, kindling. Whether it be fucking you or unfucking you, I've got your back.

I felt my lips curl.

Me

Thank you…I think.

Felix Clarkson

Don't mention it. I could use a change of scenery, so I'll come to your building after I've finished classes. How about that?

Me

You're the best.

Felix Clarkson

The best you've ever had, right?

I snorted.

Me

Don't push it.

Felix Clarkson

I'll see you tomorrow. Try not to have too many wet dreams about me – don't want to wake up your roommate with those delicious moans of yours…

Me

I think you need a cold shower. See you tomorrow.

I put my phone to charge and went back to the blank document I had opened. I began trying to answer the assignment questions before me, but my intrusive thoughts began interrupting like little flies buzzing around my mind. I pushed back hard on them, willing myself to focus.

That gnawing sensation, the one that ate at me with hunger for him, and that overwhelmed me with the need to save him…it was stirring in me, distracting me. That invisible rope that bound me to him was writhing me around like an unruly captive. My body was screaming like an inconsolable child for me to go back to him, to be near him.

My normally inviting bed felt rather cold and empty when I crawled in later that night.

- F -

I stared at the rug sprawled on the floor of the cellar, my arms propped on my knees, my vision entirely focused on the mental images swirling through my head.

Her delicate, brown eyes. Her painted, soft lips. The small of her waist, the bend of her hips, the curve of her legs, the warmth of her skin…

I could not stop thinking about her. Not for a minute, not for a second. Not even for a breath.

"I knew the day you fell in love would be intense, but even I couldn't have predicted this level of obsession."

Fuego's teasing tone sliced through my mind, causing my eyes to flutter and turn to where he sat a little distance from me in the cellar. His eyes wore the smirk his lips would've, if he had them.

It was a peculiar thought – considering when, exactly, I'd fallen in love with Seraphine. I couldn't quite place the moment. It felt as though it had happened slowly, gradually, before abruptly consuming me like a merciless sinkhole in the earth. Something akin to a crab being placed in a pot of cold water, oblivious to the fact it is being cooked over a steady, rising heat until, suddenly, it is boiled alive.

Then again, it also felt like I'd loved her from the moment I set eyes on her. I remembered the rush of emotions I'd felt when we'd first met in the lab; it's hard to forget how it feels when you lay eyes on such magnificence. I imagine people who spent their entire lives searching for purpose or faith felt the same when they came across a deity upon which to devote both of those things to.

"*You still with us? Or have you gone to a lovesick planet of rainbows and fairies and sunshine?*" Fuego went on, reminding me I hadn't replied to his previous comment.

I took a deep inhalation, rubbing the sides of my face. "*I'm here, asshole.*"

"*Barely.*" I ignored the mocking tone. "*You will have to tell her eventually, you know.*"

I sighed, hanging my head between my hands. I knew he was right, but the reminder irked me. "*I'm aware.*"

"*When do you plan to do that?*"

"*On my deathbed sounds like a good time.*"

"*She will* make *your deathbed if she –* "

"*Fuego, I know.*" I huffed aloud, glancing at the other Phoenixes. Thank goodness they couldn't all talk to me. "*Just… give me some time to think on it.*"

Fuego rolled his eyes, but he let the matter drop. In return, I was left with the terrifying reality in my mind – the one I'd had to confront ever since my dreams had come true.

So many secrets, so little time.

- S -

Classes went by slowly and painfully the next day, adding a few more items to my growing pile of tasks. I tried my best to set myself up for success afterwards by rushing back to my dorm and feverishly preparing materials for our study session in the lounge. I'd managed to finish a quick quiz by the time the door to the lounge opened.

To my surprise, Hakeem accompanied Felix in the open doorway. "Hey, Seraphine," Hakeem said. "Ran into Felix on the way here. Apparently, he's saving your butt with physics or something."

I scowled at Felix, to which he simply smirked. "It was very kind of you to let me in," he said to Hakeem. "Thanks again."

"No problem." Hakeem turned back to me. "You haven't seen Elijah around, have you?"

I felt my insides twist and swirl with distaste. "Nope. Not for a while," I said with no indication that I was upset about the lack of his presence.

"I figured as much," Hakeem replied, shrugging. "Haven't been able to catch him for a few days. Maybe he's with family or something."

"They do live close by," I concurred. "He grew up here."

"Yeah, that's right." Hakeem smiled at Felix. "Anyways, I'll leave you to saving her butt."

Felix saluted him. "Much appreciated."

I rolled my eyes, but wished Hakeem farewell as he left the lounge.

"Was it really necessary to make him aware that I suck at physics?" I groaned at Felix.

He blinked at me with a bit of surprise. "I thought everyone was aware that you suck at physics."

I stared at him. Insult towards my physics capabilities aside, I couldn't help but feel a sense of reprieve that he was with me again. It wasn't just because I knew I'd get help with my studies – no, in truth, it had very little to do with that, and much more to do with the fact that his presence immediately brought me comfort.

The tether that squeezed and stirred when he was away, the magic that seemed unsettled…they seemed to diminish their straining and regain stability now that he was here. I could see him, *feel* him, well and whole before me. And something in the way he looked at me told me that he was doing the same. We were a sight for each other's sore eyes; the heat I'd lost somewhere in the dead of my body's winter returned graciously.

I couldn't make sense of it. Had that entire harrowing experience in the blending temple anchored us with trauma? What *was* this feeling of dependency?

I sighed, pushing my thoughts into a corner of my mind. "Whatever. Let's just get this over with."

Felix and I spent most of the afternoon studying together in the lounge. We made some flashcards and quizzed each other on formulas. Then we found some practice problems, solved them on our own, and compared answers. I was usually wrong, but I did manage to get a few right on the first try. That was some improvement, all things considered.

After a few hours, Felix stood and grabbed a cup from the cupboard. "What's this?" he asked, motioning to the mason jar with our grocery funds as he filled the cup with water.

"That's where my friends and I pool our money together for our weekly grocery run," I answered. "Speaking of which, it's Friday, so we're probably doing that tomorrow."

He held up the mason jar, which contained two five-dollar bills. Since we'd started at the university, Roscoe and Sajan had gotten a basketball coaching gig at the nearby elementary school, and Chenoa was working part-time at one of the cafés on campus. Some of our parents sent us allowances for food, too. Still, there wasn't usually a whole lot of money that was pouring into the jar.

Felix gave me a concerned look. "Um…it's looking a little…"

"Sad. *Oui.* I know. I'm hoping that's only because not everyone has made their contribution yet. Including me." I pulled out another five-dollar bill from my purse and walked over, plopping it into the jar. "There. We don't get anything super fancy, anyways. Usually bananas, some bread, peanut butter, maybe some instant noodles and frozen meals. But it's better than paying fifteen dollars for one lunch at the cafeteria."

Felix nodded slowly, replacing the jar on the counter. "I see."

I heard the door open then, and in strolled Keiffer, Emmanuella, Roscoe, and Sajan. Roscoe was carrying a few cue cards and a tripod in one hand.

"Hey there, Sera – what's up?" Emmanuella asked.

"Oh, not much. Just studying for our midterm," I answered, nodding towards Felix.

"Felix! My man!" Roscoe exclaimed, approaching him for a fist bump. "Long time, no see!"

Felix returned the fist bump a bit awkwardly – he clearly wasn't practiced with the gesture. "Hello, again. It looks like you're filming something."

"We're helping him shoot a campaign message for his political science class assignment," Sajan replied, nodding at Roscoe.

Roscoe flipped his dreads over his shoulder flamboyantly. "People pay more attention to politics when it's pretty, you feel?"

Felix let out a breath of amusement. "Quite a sound philosophy," he replied.

I could see Sajan nod in agreement behind him, his eyes appearing a bit dreamy as they considered Roscoe. The two usually did a fantastic job maintaining an air of platonic energy about them, so I was a bit intrigued to see Sajan slip. I couldn't blame him, though; Roscoe's looks were rich and impressive. Had he been playing for my team, I couldn't guarantee I wouldn't fall for him myself.

"That's a fun assignment," I noted. "More fun than physics."

"Right?" Em agreed, nodding at me. "And way more fun than practicums with whiny, snotty children."

My lips twitched a bit. "Is Keiffer a part of the whiny, snotty children in question?"

Keiffer stuck his tongue out at me. "Well, excuse *you.* I'm here because I was promised cheese sticks in exchange for my help," he replied. "Not because Emmanuella's supervising me or anything."

I snorted in response. "That answers my question better than I think Em ever could." Emmanuella cackled in response.

"Do you guys mind if we film in here? The lighting is way better than in my room. We shouldn't be too long, though," Roscoe asked me.

I nodded quickly as I stood, grabbing my things. "No worries, Roscoe. Felix and I can continue working in my dorm. Take all the time you need."

"You're a doll, Seraphine."

I motioned to the doorway with my head. "Let's go," I said to Felix.

He nodded, gathering his stuff swiftly and following me out of the lounge. We made it to my dorm and took some time resituating ourselves before we dove back into the dreaded land of physics.

A couple more hours and a slight mental breakdown later, I slammed the damned textbook shut and tossed it carelessly on my desk. "I don't want to do this anymore," I grumbled. "I need to work on other stuff – things that remind me I'm competent."

"You are competent," Felix retorted. "Just not at physics." When I shot him a glare, he quickly added, "But your perseverance is bloody admirable, I'll tell you that."

"Nice save." I huffed. "At least I got a few questions right. Maybe by next week I can get enough to pass."

He reached over to where I was sitting at the desk, placing a soft but steady hand on my knee. "I'll make sure you pass. Don't worry," he assured me in a low, soothing tone.

Something electric shot through me at his touch. My eyes

flickered down to his hand on my knee, then back up to his lavender eyes. By the way those specks of blue and gold whirled in those light, warm irises, I knew he'd felt it, too.

The way he spoke was genuine; he meant every word. It told me he could sense my concern, and that he truly intended to alleviate it. That accent was coated with the same conviction I'd heard when he'd told me he'd seek help for his mental health, for the drugs.

My eyes darted across his face as I recalled the afternoon I'd spent being pampered in Colombia; I'd glimpsed him watching me as I'd lain on the massage table in the purest form of tranquil ecstasy. He himself had seemed quite composed from where he'd sat in the pool, his gaze slow and intentional as it navigated me like a thoughtful traveller. Every exhalation of smoke from that cigar had shrouded his eyes in a cloak of surreptitious satisfaction. It was a similar look to the one they held now.

I remembered he had told me that royal treatment was for the sake of my peace. And when I'd asked him where his peace was, he had told me not to worry about him. At the time, I wondered why he thought my peace was the priority, and not his.

Now, I wondered if he knew that his peace was also mine.

Since we'd been intimate, I'd seen something in him come to life that hadn't been there before. The smoothing of his face, the little stars in his eyes. He seemed serene; it was as if the things that bothered him had been sent to the shadows, and he'd chosen to focus on brightness and blossoms. It made me feel at ease. I didn't want to assume that I was this newfound contentment I saw in him. But a part of me hoped I was – or, at least, a part of it.

I cleared my throat, bringing myself back from the venture I'd gone on in my thoughts. "Thank you," I told him quietly. "For all your help."

He nodded once. "Of course, Seraphine. We'll study again

tomorrow." He stood, removing his hand – I felt a little sad when the weight lifted off my leg. "For now, you should rest. Don't want to overwhelm your pretty little head."

"A little too late, but I appreciate the sentiment."

He let out a humoured breath. "I'll get going now. We can study at my place tomorrow, so text me when you want to get back to it. I've nothing planned this weekend but my own studies, so you're welcome to join whenever you'd like."

"You bet," I replied.

He grabbed his things quietly and gave me a lingering smile before wishing me goodbye and heading out the door.

The tugging that had begun ripping a crevasse in my chest every time he was gone started again; my magic immediately began wavering in protest. I couldn't help but think about his hand on my knee, how his touch was a reminder of his presence, his safety, his comfort – and mine.

As time passed, my mind wandered; suddenly, I was replaying all our most intimate moments, then fantasizing about how I wanted him. I tortured myself so much with the ideas that my desire became insurmountable. The reach for my vibrator in my bedside drawer was instinctual. The only thing I pictured was him and his body on mine, bringing myself to finish several times before I threw the toy back in the drawer with an expended sigh.

And as my eyes drooped shut, I only thought how the next day couldn't come soon enough.

- F -

I scrubbed the remnants of my release off my abdomen, gritting my teeth as I doused my skin in a hefty amount of soap. I'd always found the results of my self-pleasure a little…unappealing. But alas, it was the way it was. Such is life.

It had taken everything in me to prevent myself from trying to bed her on that tiny little mattress. The likelihood that the lack of space would have brought us even closer by necessity nearly drove me to insanity. Physics had been an afterthought the moment I'd seen her; it was an effort to keep myself focused on anything but her striking appearance and the knowledge of what her supple body felt like under mine.

I dried myself off and clambered back into my bed, disappointed she wasn't in it. We hadn't been intimate since we returned from Colombia. For some reason, the idea of asking her seemed far-fetched. I couldn't quite understand why. But I was aching for her again, primally.

I bent one arm underneath my head, shutting my eyes as I tried my best to shove any thoughts of her and her entrancing body aside. Try as I might, flitting images of our trysts began rolling like a reel of film aimed at testing the limits of self-control in my head. I made a face at myself and tossed a bit, forcing myself to think about anything else – calculus. The stars. Breakfast the next morning.

Nothing was mesmerizing enough to draw me away from the fancies of her. There she was, as intrusive and domineering as ever, with every bewitching feature I loved in a woman. It was as if she had been delivered to me straight from a realm of nymphomaniacs, wearing nothing but a pretty little bow on that head of luscious curls.

I grumbled as I felt myself stiffen. Again.

Huffing, I tossed away the covers and threw my hand back in my pants.

Whatever test of willpower she was, I was failing – miserably.

CHAPTER 16

- S -

I TEXTED Felix the moment I awoke at ten the next morning, asking him to pick me up at his earliest convenience. He immediately agreed to be at the university in an hour, which gave me enough time to dress and have a quick breakfast.

Excited chatter greeted me as I entered the lounge. Keiffer, Roscoe, Sajan, and Emmanuella were all gathered around the kitchen counter.

"Don't tell me you spent all night working on the film project," I said as I walked in.

"Nah, don't worry – we finished that all up," Roscoe said. "The four of us were just going to head out for groceries."

"We hit the jackpot this week!" Keiffer said excitedly, holding up our mason jar. "Look at this – we're eating like kings!"

I frowned when I realized the jar was nearly full.

Confused, I took it from Keiffer and shook out all the bills on the counter. In addition to the three fives, there were now a bunch of twenty-dollar bills. I counted the bills quickly.

I swallowed. "Eight hundred and fifteen dollars," I said in quiet astonishment.

I heard the boys hoot behind me, and they began buzzing about the items they were going to purchase that day. I, on the other hand, stared at the money for a few minutes, my frown slowly morphing into an expression of bewilderment that was impossible to hide as I processed what must have happened.

When I lifted my gaze, I was met with Emmanuella's perceptive eyes, and I knew from her sly smile that she had figured it out, too.

———

"Thank you for the grocery money, but you seriously didn't need to."

They were the first words I spoke to Felix as I sat down with my books in his Porsche. He was wearing a teal blue Balenciaga shirt with those signature black Armani jeans; the bright colour brought out the cool tones of his eyes. My pulse jumped a bit as soon as my eyes had locked with his – he truly was a marvel in the physical sense.

"Food is important," he said with a smile. "And expensive."

"I appreciate the gesture. I just –"

"I know you've got a thing about owing people," he interrupted before I could finish. "Trust me, I took that into consideration. But I also considered how you recently saved my life." He raised his eyebrows. "So consider me in your debt for as long as I live."

"You don't owe me anything for that, Felix."

He grinned, rubbing my shoulder. "And now you know just how much I mean it when I say the same thing to you."

I studied him, my lips pulling at the corners.

"It was nothing, Seraphine. All I hope for is that you and your friends enjoy some treats this week," he added.

My smile widened. "Thank you. We will."

"Just tell that one friend of yours not to spend it all on cheese sticks."

I snorted. "It'll be hard to convince him not to."

He winked at me as he started driving. "You're a pretty persuasive woman, kindling, so I wouldn't worry."

————

We decided there was no better way to study than surrounded by our Phoenixes. When we arrived in the cellar, I noticed Aurora and Suelo were cozied up amongst the pillows near the seating area. I approached and sat down beside them, giving each of them a kiss on their heads and stroking their feathers. Suelo looked nearly halfway grown – soon, I'd be taking on the skills of an Earth Phoenix Keeper.

Felix approached the water trough, and I watched him pass the whiteboard. I noticed he had written the riddle we'd collected after hatching Suelo.

> *"My feathers of Earth are now yours*
> *Onwards to my wings of fire you soar*
> *In the belly of the largest summit*
> *Is where, without fear, you must plummet*
> *Go where fire and water build land*
> *And there'll you find the bird you demand."*

"Were you working on this?" I asked, motioning to the board when he turned to look at me.

He shook his head a bit as he ran his fingers through Lumina's feathers. "I wrote it out to see if it would spark some inspiration. But I didn't get very far," he said. "All I've got is it's obviously got to be a mountain of sorts, given the 'largest summit' bit."

I nodded slowly, my eyes scanning the riddle. "Right, that makes sense. But this fire and water building land part…"

"I know. I don't understand it," he remarked. "I thought maybe it was in reference to Mars. That didn't make much sense, though."

I stared at him. "Mars?"

He cleared his throat, walking back over towards me. "Well, researchers have recently discovered parts of Mars where it appears there was water once, but they've now since dried. And I was thinking about Mars being the red planet, the god of war – you know, fiery symbolism and all that."

I blinked. When he saw my expression, he chuckled a bit nervously. "I get carried away when it comes to space. We learn new things about it almost every day." He shifted his gaze. "I suppose I was thinking a little too outside the box," he added, embarrassed.

Amused, I gave him a small smile. "Well, it's better than not thinking at all," I said. "But I don't think it's on Mars."

"It better not be," he replied. "It'll be really hard to get to Mars."

I turned back to look at the riddle. "I think you're on the right track, though," I said. "In regards to the whole relationship between the fire and water, I mean. Are there any places on Earth where there was once water, but that are now dry?"

"Oh, plenty. The oceans and bodies of water have shifted, too, as the continents moved over the years," Felix answered. "But I don't think any of that change happened on the summit of the largest mountain."

"That's Mount Everest, right?"

"Yes."

I considered what I knew about the tallest mountain in the world. Nothing about fire and water came to mind. I didn't think it was the solution.

"Are mountains the only things that have summits?" I then questioned.

Felix sat on the sofa, thinking. "Well, hills have summits. And volcanoes."

I cocked my head to the side. "Volcanoes have lava," I noted.

His eyes flickered to mine. "Yes," he agreed. "That's pretty fiery."

My heart began beating a little faster. "What's the largest volcano?"

He pulled out his phone and typed away at it. "There's some debate," he explained. "Looks like Tamu Massif was at one point. It's an underwater one, but now it's extinct, and I suppose a different chain of underwater volcanoes took its place."

"Hmm," I said. "There's no land built from an underwater volcano, though. It's under the ocean."

"Right," he said. "And so is the chain of volcanoes, so it's not them, either."

"What are the next highest volcanic peaks?"

He scrolled down his phone. "Mount Kilimanjaro is next," he said.

I shook my head. "There's no water around that to build land with."

"Popocatépetl Volcano in Mexico comes after that," he continued. "But judging from the pictures here, also no surrounding water."

"And after that?" I pressed.

He stopped scrolling, bringing his eyes to mine. "Mauna Loa."

I raised my eyebrows. "One of the volcanoes that make up the islands of Hawaii," I said, and as the words left my mouth, I already knew we had our answer. Hawaii had been built from the mixtures of lava and the ocean.

Felix was smiling. "We're getting pretty good at this."

"We should time ourselves with the next riddle," I said, standing up. "Shall we?"

"Oh, no you don't," Felix immediately interjected, coming over and forcing me back to sitting. "We're not leaving today."

"What?" I asked with a frown. "Why?"

He gave me an incredulous look. "Don't you remember why you even came over today? There are midterms next week, and we've barely got you passing your physics one thus far."

"I thought you told me you'd make sure I'd pass."

"Well, how do you expect me to help you study if you keep abandoning physics and fluttering off the continent?"

I huffed loudly. "We can be back before – "

"No, we can't guarantee we'll be back in time because we don't know what kind of bullshit we might find ourselves stepping in," Felix interjected. "May I remind you of the stolen statues we had to...erm...steal back? That was a significant setback."

I made a face at him and crossed my arms. "You really are the Fun Police."

He shook his head at me. "It's like you *want* to fail all your courses."

"I don't want to fail all my courses. I just find adventure time more fun."

He sighed. "We can leave next weekend, after we've written our midterms and caught up on our homework." He crinkled his nose. "Now that I think about it, we also need to go to my brother's party."

I looked at him expectantly. "So we leave after the party?"

"Yes."

"Promise?"

"I promise."

I conceded, uncrossing my arms. "You guys don't happen to have a hotel somewhere in the Hawaiian islands, do you?"

"We have several," he replied. "But why would we go to one when we can just go to our vacation home?"

I let out an amused breath. "Why am I not surprised that you have a vacation home in Hawaii?"

"Because it's not surprising." He smiled slightly. "It's on the island of Maui."

"That'll work," I said. "Won't take us long to fly from Maui to the other island."

"Not at all," he said, nodding. "But first, physics."

I groaned. "Physics is dumb."

He chuckled. "I know, kindling," he said, grabbing my text-book and sitting down next to me. "I know."

———

We studied physics until I thought my eyes would bleed. Then Felix insisted we work on other assignments – he grumbled something about me being insufferably cranky under his breath before shuffling to the sofa and starting on his calculus. I managed to check off a few more submissions from my list before we called it a day.

"Hungry?" Felix asked as we left the cellar.

"Is that even a question?" I replied.

He flashed a grin. "Let's see what the chef's prepared for supper."

The chef had prepared a glorious schnitzel dinner, complete with roasted vegetables and garlic butter perogies. I gobbled everything on my plate mercilessly, slouching back in my chair with a satisfied grunt when nothing was left. Felix watched me with a crooked, tickled smile, only pausing to take a sip of the water he'd opted to pair with his meal.

Footsteps sounded in the archway just as Felix was finishing his own food, and it was Luther who rounded the corner. "Ah, Seraphine!" he exclaimed. "I didn't know you were here!"

"You always seem to catch me when I've eaten my body

weight in gourmet food," I breathed, groaning as I went to give him a hug.

"It's good to hear you're being well fed," he said with a laugh as he looked towards his son. "I came to check in with you – see how things were going."

Felix exchanged a glance with me, then raised his eyebrows at his father with a mischievous smile. "Bloody hell, do we have a story for you."

We told him everything about our travels to Colombia, to Peru, and the horrific adventure we'd tumbled through in the blending temple. Well, not everything – we conveniently left out any mention of our intimacy, more for his sake than ours. He digested everything we told him with the giddiness of a kid in a candy store.

"My heavens," he breathed as he sat back, rubbing his head. "Thank goodness for your quick thinking, Seraphine – otherwise, my son might still be stuck in those magic vines!" He let out an exclamation of disbelief. "Who even knew there was such a thing?"

Felix's eyes had grown distant at the recollection; I'm assuming he hadn't fully managed to collect his thoughts around the near-death experience, and it evidently still unsettled him. "I suppose their existence is as likely as our Phoenixes, but with that said, I'll be happy if I never encounter them again," he remarked in a quiet voice. I nodded silently in agreement.

"I certainly can't say I blame you," Luther said, looking at me with a wide smile. "And now you each have two Phoenixes, with the next expected in Hawaii! My word, this journey grows more remarkable by the moment!"

I looked at Felix. "He hasn't met our new Phoenixes yet, has he?"

Felix shook his head, turning to his father. "Would you like to?"

He let out a breath of excitement. "Oh, would I ever!"

The three of us trekked back to the cellar, Luther's footsteps growing quickened with haste the nearer we came. When he finally beheld Lumina and Suelo as he entered the cellar, he let out an exhilarated gasp.

"Incredible," he breathed, his eyes glossy as he approached Lumina. He dragged his hand carefully through the feathers on her neck, prompting her to nudge him softly. Then he looked down at her feet, where Suelo stood, eyeing him curiously. Luther bent down, stroking the bird's neck and head. Suelo cooed in response, his eyes shutting with calmness at the touch.

I felt my eyes grow a bit misty; Luther loved these creatures as much as Felix and I did. He, too, found them magical beyond comprehension, gifts we couldn't imagine not being given. I felt wistful that his companion had been taken from him too early.

I looked over at Felix, a sad smile crossing my face. Felix was studying his father, but met my gaze when he noticed my movement. His replying smile was as reflective as mine.

"So Felix, you must be able to create light now too, hm?" Luther asked, bringing our attention back to him.

Felix nodded, creating a ball of light in one palm. Luther's eyes went wide with elation.

"How invigorating!" he exclaimed, looking at me. "And when your little Suelo is grown, you'll have the magic of the Earth." He shook his head with bewilderment. "It's outrageous to think that all my life, I never even knew it was possible. Not until you two discovered it was."

"We're all learning as we go," I said in an attempt to be supportive.

He chuckled a bit sadly. "Isn't that the truth," he said, turning back to the Phoenixes.

I saw how his eyes glistened at the feel of Lumina's feathers between his fingers again, how he watched her reactions carefully. He was so in tune with her that they could have played a harmonized melody; and yet, from the way his gaze held long-ing, I knew he deeply missed having his own Phoenix to bond with. Given how attached I felt to my own, I couldn't imagine losing either of them – especially in such a tragic and violent way. The grief must have been insoluble.

I swallowed. "Luther..."

My voice came out more sombre than I intended; I knew this because both Luther and Felix immediately turned to me with a look of concern.

I mustered a small smile. "Would you...want to join us to find the next Phoenix?"

In perfect sync, both men blinked at me in bewilderment. "Join you two?" Luther repeated in disbelief.

I motioned towards Lumina, whom he still stroked lovingly. "You could hatch one yourself."

Luther's eyes were as wide as cherry pies. He glanced at Felix, who met the expression with one of equal bafflement. Felix was the first to look back at me, his eyebrows upturned with puzzlement and his lips slightly parted. But somewhere in those irises, I could see a little glimmer of warmth – he, too, had seen how his father acted with the Phoenixes. And he knew why I had offered.

Luther let out a breath, shaking his head quickly. "Oh, Seraphine, I – well, thank you for your thoughtfulness," he stammered. "But I think my time as a Keeper has long come and gone."

I shrugged. "You just seem like you miss it. And now that you know it's possible..."

He smiled brightly at me. "I appreciate your insight. It would be a lie to say I don't look fondly upon that period of my life and wish it had lasted longer. But..."

His eyes flew between Felix and me. "I'm older now, you know. Not the same whippersnapper I used to be. And this journey....well, it's rightfully yours. I'm more than happy to bear witness to all of this – living vicariously through you two has been beyond rewarding for me."

I nodded once. "It's up to you. Just say the word if you ever change your mind."

His eyes were alight with gratitude. "Thank you, Seraphine. You are a very considerate young woman."

My smile widened in response. "Of course."

But Luther's countenance deepened even further with sincerity. "I truly mean that, you know," he reiterated, his gaze wandering to his son. "You didn't leave him behind. I will never forget that."

I felt myself falter with the sudden rush of emotions that washed over me, and my eyes fluttered down to the ground for a moment. "I would make the same choice again," were the only words I could muster. Truthfully, I myself was still reeling from that encounter with the vines – it made it hard to really delve deep into recollecting it. I could still hear the fear, the defeat in Felix's voice…

A fleeting glance at Felix showed his expression had completely transformed from one of confusion to one of indebtedness. And when his eyes met mine, they softened, melting into a shade of lavender so deep, I thought I could feel the fervour waft through the air and brush the surface of my skin like a paintbrush dipped in sun kissed flowers.

Part of me had wondered if his near-death had made him regret joining me in my quest for the Phoenixes. But from the way his smile drew lines at the edges of his lips and crinkles at the ends of his eyes, I knew that he also would make that same choice again. In a heartbeat.

This surprised me; it left me even more curious. It seemed not only improbable, but impossible. Why wasn't he deterred, especially since he'd been so concerned in the beginning?

Then I thought about me – was I averse to the adventure even after all we'd been through? Not in the slightest. Not as much as one should be, considering their fear of death.

Perhaps the two of us had come far enough to recognize the pursuit's bounty. The sight of something was even more alluring than its story. Or perhaps our minds were more alike than we'd originally thought; perhaps we both were attuned to the inner workings of a fair trade.

No risk, no reward. It was a law of the universe, one as old as time itself.

And though frightening…it was fair.

CHAPTER 17

WHEN FELIX DROPPED me off at the university that night, he stepped out of the Porsche with me.

I gave him a confused look as he walked around the car. "What are you – "

He pulled me into a tight hug before I could finish my sentence. My initial surprise faded into heartwarming refuge; I shut my eyes as I embraced him back. I didn't care why we were hugging. I didn't need to know. It was a blissful respite to simply hold him close to me.

When we held each other, I knew with certainty that he was safe. And so was I.

"What you offered my father was incredibly kind," I heard Felix mumble into the side of my head. "I know it warmed his heart."

He pulled away, and when I reopened my eyes, the smile in his gaze was flitting all over my face. "You are a real treasure for my family," he went on. "I hope you know that."

My heart glowed as I returned the smile. "If I'd known this would mean so much to both of you, I would have offered sooner. Seeing your father with the Phoenixes…it just felt so natural to ask in that moment."

He nodded as he pulled away. "I think, when your family is like mine, you get used to people wanting things from you," he noted. "As much as my father tries to maintain his cheerful disposition, I know he feels it, too." His smile fell to the floor. "We are not used to receiving compassion like yours. And I don't say that to pity us; I know we have privilege. But..."

He laughed a bit to himself as he shook his head and looked back up at me. "It is nice to be considered human every now and then." He shrugged. "It prevents our spirit from breaking."

I hadn't thought much about how the world treated the Clarksons; to be quite honest, part of me had assumed they couldn't care less what others thought of them. Why would someone who could buy the world care much about the world's opinion? But I recalled Felix had made reference a few times to the detriments and ugliness of his money, of his family's name. It seemed that forgetting a living, breathing being existed underneath all the wealth was another thing that happened to those who eyed the rich and successful.

I placed a hand on his shoulder. "I'm simply treating you lot as you've treated me," I replied.

His eyes twinkled. "We appreciate it," he remarked. "Now, get some rest. You'll need it for tomorrow."

"More physics?"

"Without a doubt. And – " he grinned. " – our favourite fitness trainer let me know she had a cancellation and is free tomorrow afternoon. I think it would be good for you to balance the mental exercise with some physical."

"I'm surprised you're not offering yourself up in that regard," I teased.

He cackled as he walked back to the driver's side. "Let's see how you feel after she's through with you tomorrow," he said with a wink.

I stuck my tongue out at him, to which he only smirked before he sat in the car and drove off. That tether started pulling, and my magic objected, but I knew it was only temporary.

———

I slept well that night, and I woke up early the next morning. Most of my floormates took Sundays as their rightful opportunity to sleep in, so I found myself alone in the lounge kitchen as I prepared myself a nice breakfast and called Felix.

"Morning. I'm ready whenever you are. Just grabbing a quick breakfast," I said when he picked up.

"My word – you're certainly eager," Felix remarked. "Are you growing fond of physics?"

"Absolutely not."

"Dare I say you're growing fond of me, then?"

I sighed. "We had such a nice moment yesterday. Can't you just let that be the reigning interaction instead of blowing smoke up your own ass?"

"You didn't deny it, kindling."

"Felix, we've slept together. Multiple times. I would sure hope I'm at least fond of you."

"Such pleasant memories," he sang into the phone. "I'll pick you up in half an hour, okay?"

"Thanks."

As soon as I hung up, the door to the lounge opened. It was Roscoe and Sajan.

"Hey, Seraphine," Sajan said. "Has Hakeem been in here?"

I shook my head. "No. The last time I saw Hakeem was a few days ago."

"Oh. Weird. He wanted to work out with us this morning – I thought we told him that we'd meet him here," Sajan replied.

"Maybe he went to the gym to get a head start or something," Roscoe suggested with a shrug.

"Could be," Sajan agreed, nodding at me. "If he drops by, could you let him know we're there?"

"Will do."

"Thanks, Seraphine."

They left promptly, and I finished my breakfast. Hakeem had not entered the lounge by the time I left to get a ride with Felix.

—————

When Felix and I were through with physics, I was – to my complete shock – confidently able to answer more questions than not. It was perhaps the most accurate I'd ever been at physics in my life.

"You're a miracle worker, you know," I told Felix as I shut the textbook. Uma had let him know she was on her way for a welcome training session.

Felix gave me a small smile. "It's a nice thought, but you're the one putting in the work."

"You are putting arguably more so." I paused. "At the very least, you're putting in all the patience."

He chuckled. "You've gotten more agreeable as you've gotten better, I'll give you that much."

I gave Aurora and Suelo each a kiss on their head before Felix and I made for the staircase. As we rounded the path to Felix's villa, I could see Uma and her workout gear set up in the same place it was last time. I waved at her when she looked over, to which she excitedly waved back.

"Glad I didn't scare you away with our last training session," she joked as we approached, outstretching her fist towards me.

I bumped it with my own. "It'll take more than a little soreness to scare me."

"That's what I like to hear," Uma said, nodding up at Felix.

"You training with us today? Give Seraphine some moving target practice?"

Felix laughed nervously, running a hand through his hair. "I think it would be best for Seraphine if she were the main focus today."

I snorted. "Best for me, or best for you?"

Felix crinkled his nose. "I'm just trying to make sure you get the most out of the lesson."

"Oh, I think you being a moving target for me would be most fulfilling." I smirked at Uma. "He's training with us."

Uma's grin was devious. "Don't worry, Felix. I brought the extra-thick boxing pads today."

He sighed. "Looks like this decision was made for me, so I'm not quite sure why you even asked."

"To give you the illusion of choice," I explained, strapping on the pair of boxing gloves Uma handed me. She then passed Felix a thick, black boxing pad, which he held up horizontally to me using a sturdy strap on its reverse side.

"All right. Show 'em what you're made of," Uma told me.

"Rage," Felix muttered. "I already know she's made of rage. I don't need much reminding."

She rolled her eyes at him. "Felix, nice wide stance on the brace, all right?"

"Right. Wide stance. That'll offset all the tiny woman wrath."

My jaw dropped. "*Tiny woman wrath?*"

"Seraphine, you're – what, five foot three?"

I scoffed. "Five foot *four*, which is the average height for a woman in North America, thank you very much."

He let out an amused breath. "That still gives me a full foot over you."

I sneered at him. "All right, all right, settle down there, big guy. You're talking a lot for someone who fears the anger of an average-height woman."

"Tiny woman."

"*Average.*"

"Tiny from *my* point of view."

"Fucking whatever!"

I let a punch fly towards the boxing pad, hitting it square in the center. Felix recoiled slightly from the impact, but held his ground firmly.

"Nice. Move around a bit, Felix," Uma instructed.

He shuffled a bit, and I aimed for the pad again. This one was off to the left, but still powerful enough to give off a satisfying whacking sound.

"That's it. Keep going. Felix, don't give her a still target."

We repeated this cycle several times, with me tracking Felix's movement and punching hard when I got the opportunity. Then, Uma had me practice some sequences instead of singular punches, which required a bit more footwork as Felix continued to shift positions. Within half an hour, I was panting heavily, my face dripping sweat.

"Time to switch to some kicks," Uma told me as I bent over, hands clasped over my knees as I tried to catch my breath.

"Oh, no," I heard Felix mutter between heavy breathing as he lowered the boxing pad.

Uma raised her eyebrow. "Problem?"

He rubbed his eyes with his free hand. "Women carry the bulk of their strength in their legs."

Uma snickered. "We sure do," she replied.

"*Especially* tiny women," I added with a smirk, even as my legs trembled a bit at the mere thought of kicking the boxing pad. Determined, I cracked my neck and rolled my shoulders as I prepared my muscles to work again.

Felix let out a huff as he steadied the boxing pad vertically this time. "All right. Hit me."

"Gladly," I said, and I began with a dropkick.

The amount of force Felix had to fight against greatly

increased; he took a step back with the impact, his arms recoiling a bit. "Bloody hell," he murmured.

My leer was a natural result of my gratification; suddenly, my legs felt more capable of kicking harder and faster. Much like the punches, we cycled through types of kicks and sequences. As we went on, Felix's reactions to the recoils became more and more strained.

By the time I was on my last round of kicks, Felix was groaning with each impact. "Finally," he huffed when my last kick had landed in the center of the pad. He hurriedly threw the pad on the ground before flopping down carelessly in the grass himself, rubbing his face with his hands.

I glanced at Uma, my chest rising and falling briskly. "How'd I do?"

She motioned to Felix. "Looks like success to me," she noted.

"Great," I said with a single nod towards Felix. "I should beat you up more often."

"Not a fucking chance," Felix whined, grunting as he sat up. "There is no way this is becoming a part of regularly scheduled programming."

I rolled my eyes. "Fun police strikes again," I grumbled.

Uma chuckled to herself as she began packing up her things. "Great work today, both of you. Now eat some protein and wash up – you've earned it."

"Thanks again for coming," I said to her.

"Not sure if I should thank you or not, to be honest," Felix added. She gave him the middle finger, to which he rolled his eyes.

We walked with Uma to the front of Felix's villa, where she promptly got in her truck and jetted off. When she'd disappeared down the driveway, I glanced at Felix.

"Shall we head back to the university?" I proposed.

He considered the question before giving me a curious look. "Why?"

I was taken aback. "Felix, I stink. I need a shower."

His eyes drank my body like it was a fine liquor, a thirst I'd seen before. "My shower's big enough for two," he proposed with a luscious coating to that English accent.

I raised my eyebrows as heat rose in my stomach. "I thought I gave you more than enough of a workout," I teased.

He chewed on his bottom lip. "Sure, sure…but seeing you all flushed, dripping sweat…my mind was going places I think I'd like to revisit." He cleared his throat. "Sooner rather than later."

I hummed suggestively, smirking. "Are you saying that me kicking your ass turned you on?"

He came closer to me, lifting his hand to my face and tilting my chin up towards him. The fire in my lower body erupted as his fingers traced down my neck carefully, intentionally.

A muscle feathered in his jaw as the corner of his lip tugged upwards. "Call it what you'd like. The point is that I've got other priorities besides rest right now," he said.

I bit my lip. "Consider me at the top of your to-do list, then."

———

The feeling of the luxurious, white towel Felix gently wrapped around my shoulders was soothing, like a comforting lullaby against my flesh. It contrasted nicely with the lingering steam from the hot shower he had just ravished me in.

The soft fabric carefully soaked the small droplets of water still dripping down my body; they'd cascaded down our skin like summer rain as he'd pressed me up against the tiled wall, my legs snugly entwined around his waist. He had handled me like I was delicate yet disarming; his fingers pressed slightly into my hips as he held me with a grip that struggled to find a consistent balance between soft and firm. It was obvious his intentions got muddled with his desire as he lost himself in me; I couldn't blame him. I found myself digging my nails harder and harder into his back as he moved within me, my fingers desperately running through it all as I let every inch of my body meld with his. The soft light that broke free of my grasp illuminated the little extra steam that resulted from Felix's escaping flames being immediately extinguished.

When we'd finally stilled, he brought me off the wall into a tight embrace. We didn't speak; we'd simply breathed into each other's flesh – him into the nape of my neck, and me into his chest. The water had continued to wash over us steadily, like little waterfalls that traced our skin from the tops of our heads all the way to the tips of our toes.

Holding him so close to me, feeling him squeeze my body tighter to his – the shelter of him was addictive. My skin ached to kiss his. My magic brimmed with power, rushing like white water rapids as I relished in every second my cravings were filled.

And as he draped me in some of the richest, plushest fabric I'd ever experienced, all I could think about was how it didn't compare to his touch in the slightest.

I turned to look at him, his lavender eyes glistening starkly in the steamy room as he wrapped a towel around his waist. "Thank you."

His smile overtook his lips and his eyes, a little droplet of remaining water trickling down his neck and into the hollow of his collarbone. "I should be the one thanking you," he joked.

"It was a mutual effort."

His gaze drifted over my body lazily, soaking me in. "It's sixteen, by the way."

"Hm?"

"I counted fifteen tattoos, plus the mark from Alchnost, for a total of sixteen." His fingers grazed the bottom of my right buttcheek. "Almost missed this cheeky little one on your arse, but it couldn't escape me in the end."

I grinned. "If I'm being honest, I lost track a long time ago, so I'll take your word for it."

He looked to the floor as he chuckled. "I must admit, I'm a little relieved. I was worried we were going to leave that in Colombia."

I glanced at him sideways. "Us having sex, you mean?"

He nodded.

"Why would we?"

Felix inhaled deeply, then just shook his head. "I don't know," he finally replied. "We were away from home, in the middle of things we don't normally experience. I thought maybe it was just going to be another one of those things. But perhaps I was overthinking it all."

I considered this. "There isn't much to overthink, I would say."

His eyes flickered to mine. "You don't think it's complicated?"

"At first, I might have. But I've realized it's only complicated if we make it so," I explained simply, wringing my hair out in the sink.

He watched me as I did this, his eyes tracing my movements like a hawk. I shook the last droplets of water out in the sink and let the ringlets fall back down to my shoulders as I stood up straight.

"Perhaps what concerns me is that we seem to dance around it," he noted when I turned back to face him.

"If I recall correctly, the last time we tried to talk about us fucking, we ended up fucking again."

His answering smile was a mix of sheepish and devious. "I can't really say I regret that."

"Neither can I." I motioned towards him gently. "But if you have more to say, then go on. I'm all ears."

He sighed, rubbing his face with his hand. "Maybe I'm just…too caught up in my own head, is all. I don't know what exactly I need or want to say."

I studied him. "Well, it concerned you that we wouldn't have sex again. Why don't we start with why that is?"

He didn't respond right away. "Probably because I was hoping it would happen again."

"And it did, so that alleviates that fear."

A smile tugged at his lip momentarily before it faded. "I think I was more worried, though, that I'd…ruined something."

My brows shook a bit. "Ruined what?"

He cleared his throat. "Well, we were friends. And now we're…I'm not sure."

I shrugged. "Friends who have sex?"

The sentence didn't seem to relieve him – if anything, I saw something like disappointment flash across his face for the briefest of moments before he forcibly nodded once. "I suppose so."

"You don't seem thrilled about the prospect."

He sighed, looking back down at the floor. "I have a hard time with that concept. I don't…"

When he trailed off, I gave him an expectant look. "I'm listening."

He chewed on his lip. "Before this, I've…only ever slept with people I didn't care about," he said with difficulty. "And because I had no intention of ever seeing them again, the entire experience was…different."

He looked back at me; his eyes were cautious. "I'm…struggling to adjust."

I gave him a soft smile. "There isn't a right or wrong way to navigate these things, so long as we're both comfortable. I have no expectations, Felix."

"But I do," he immediately countered, taking a step towards me. "Of myself. I…expect better of myself when it comes to you."

I held his gaze. "Why?"

He swallowed, his eyes ardent. "I...can't keep myself away

from you. It bothers me when you're not around. You're...very special to me, Seraphine. And you deserve to feel that."

He brought an unsteady hand to my face and tucked a strand of my curls behind my ear tenderly. I placed my own hand on top of his, pressing lightly on it as I let the words he spoke resonate with the thoughts I had. The likeness in what I had been experiencing since we'd been intimate and what he described...there was a strange relief to it.

"It bothers me to be away from you, too," I admitted to him. "Ever since Colombia, I can't stop feeling like I need to be near you." I could feel my eyes soften a bit. "I feel safer when you're with me. My magic feels stronger when you're close. And whenever we have sex...all I find myself thinking about is how soon we'll be like that again. I've never felt like this before."

As I spoke, I could see him fighting the urge to widen his eyes. It was as if he were trying to hide his true reaction to my words, rebelling against every muscle in his face to control his expression.

I watched him with a questioning glance. "Do you know why we feel this way?" I whispered to him. It was an honest question.

There was another struggle within him – maybe a thought process, maybe a fumble for the right words. Then, his jaw tightened as he stroked my cheek.

"I don't," he responded quietly. "But we'll figure it out. Together."

CHAPTER 18

IT WAS late in the afternoon when Felix pulled up beside the university entrance.

"You sure you don't want any more physics help today?" he asked as I undid my seatbelt. He'd offered to continue studying with me before we'd left.

"Thanks, but I've got some other assignments to finish and midterms to study for," I replied. "I really appreciate all the help, though. I feel like I actually have a shot at passing."

He nodded once. "You will pass, I'm sure of it."

I smiled slightly. "At least one of us is sure," I responded as I stepped out of the Aston Martin. The lilac sundress I was wearing billowed in the slight breeze; Felix insisted I borrow one to avoid changing back into my sweaty clothes. A small part of me wondered if he knew that I'd discovered they were his mother's...

"You've worked very hard, not to worry," he assured me. "Let me know if you feel you need any more practice."

"I will. Thank you, Felix."

He smiled at me. "Of course."

I shut the door to the car gently, waving goodbye to him as he drove off, and my magic began wallowing within me.

I sighed to myself and whirled on my feet, ignoring my body's all-too-familiar demurral at our separation as I headed to my room. Commotion coming from Everly's open dorm drew my attention as soon as I had made it to my floor.

I stepped around into the open doorway and saw her in the middle of her room, sorting through…everything and anything possible, it seemed. Perhaps a tornado had touched down in only her room and disappeared into a void after. I was taken aback at the mess.

"You okay?" I asked blankly.

Everly whipped around to face me, an embarrassed smile on her face. "Oh, hey!" she exclaimed. "Just doing some cleaning!"

"I can see that," I noted, stepping over some plastic bags filled with…something. "You need some help?"

"No, no, it's okay," she said, laughing a bit nervously. "I've been putting off tidying up for a while – it's my bad it got this way. I can deal with it, no problem."

"Deal with what?" Emmanuella's voice came from around the corner, and she appeared in the doorway seconds later. Immediately, her eyes bugged out of her head. "What the fuck? Were you robbed by a herd of rabid goats or something?"

I frowned. "Can goats catch rabies?"

She shrugged. "Not sure. But if they can, I can guarantee that this – " she motioned to the disaster in the room " – would be the aftermath."

Everly rolled her eyes. "Come on, it's not *that* bad."

I blinked, then exchanged a glance with Emmanuella. The look on her face mimicked the same dubious one I had on mine.

Everly sighed. "Thanks for offering to help, but I can take care of it."

"If you're sure," I replied, nodding towards Emmanuella. "We should let her focus."

Em turned to make her way out of the room, and just as I was about to follow, something caught my eye.

On one of Everly's bedside tables, scattered amongst some headphones and loose papers, was a little blue lighter. And all over the lighter, there were little cartoon images of cheese.

I squinted at it. "Um, Everly?"

"Yeah?"

My eyes flickered over to her. "Isn't that Keiffer's lighter?"

Everly turned immediately to where I was looking. Behind me, I could hear Emmanuella hurriedly shuffle back into the room.

"Oh," Everly said after blinking at the lighter for a few moments. "Yeah. Uh…he must have forgotten it here when he…"

She trailed off, and a cheeky smile flew across her face as she began giggling.

I stared at her, then looked at Emmanuella. She was befuddled as she watched Everly chortle.

"Don't tell me you hooked up with Keiffer," she said bluntly.

Everly bit her lip, shrugging up at us. She was as giddy as a schoolgirl. I raised my eyebrows.

"What?" Em exclaimed. "Why? When?" She shook her head. "…But most importantly, why?"

"Oh, I don't know," Everly chimed between laughter. "We were out at a party a couple weeks ago, and we got a little tipsy and just…you know. One thing led to another."

Em looked like she was having an existential crisis. "There is no universe in which banging Keiffer makes sense."

"You're being too hard on him!" Everly insisted. "He's funny and sweet if you give him a chance to be, you know."

Emmanuella made a face and looked over at me, clearly searching for some reinforcement. I hesitated for a moment as I decided what to say.

"I mean, everyone has their own preferences," I noted. "What about Hakeem, though?"

Everly snorted, shrugging. "What about him?"

My brows shook a bit. "Was he upset about it?"

She laughed loudly. "Oh, gosh, Seraphine, I would never tell him!"

"You wouldn't?"

"No!" she said. "Why would I?"

I sucked my lips in a bit. "Well, I mean, he really likes you. And he's a good guy, too. Maybe you should just let him know you're not interested. You know, to avoid hurting his feelings."

She scoffed at me. "How is that my problem?"

"It's...not your problem, per se. But I just think – "

"You just think I'm a heartless slut, is that it?" Everly cut me off.

I frowned, surprised at how pissed she'd suddenly gotten. "What? No! I was trying to say – "

"You're just perfect, right? And you think you're better than me because you've got all your shit together. That's what it's all about, huh?" she went on, her snappy tone insufferable. "Standing there and judging me must be so damn easy for you."

I blinked, flabbergasted. "Everly, I have no idea what you're going on about."

"Of course not. Probably because you think I'm crazy."

It was hard not to think she was crazy at that point, but I immediately shook my head. "My intention wasn't to hurt your feelings. I was just trying to give you some advice."

"Yeah, well, your unsolicited advice came off as very critical of me. Not to mention your unhelpful comments about my room."

I wasn't sure if I was being punked or not. "Everly, I only offered to help clean your room."

"Right – because you think I can't manage it on my own."

202

She sneered at me. "Just like you think you're better than me when it comes to directing my life."

"Look, I'm sorry you feel that way, but that's not what I meant by offering to help. I seriously was just – "

"But *I* didn't feel that way."

"I get that. But I can't control the fact you misunderstood me."

"You *can* think before you speak, though." She waved an insulting finger at me. "You can control your actions."

I opened my mouth to respond, but my utter bewilderment at the situation had my tongue remain wordless for much longer than I anticipated. Was this some kind of joke?

"Everly, with all due respect, the fact that you felt one way about what I said doesn't make the true intentions behind them inherently malicious," I explained calmly.

"Oh, that's awesome, Seraphine." She laughed with no trace of humour. "Be even more condescending, will you?"

"This is ridiculous," Emmanuella cut in, stepping closer to Everly. "You're blowing this way out of proportion, and really, you're the one stepping out of line here. Seraphine's done nothing wrong."

Everly rolled her eyes. "Right, right – suck up to your roommate. Besides, I know you're jealous I hooked up with Keiffer."

Em's face became a contorted mess of shock and disgust. "Are you fucking for real?"

"I saw the two of you going out for a smoke the other day. Don't pretend you don't like him."

Emmanuella shook her head rapidly and turned to me. "Is she okay?"

I was just watching Everly with concern and confusion. "I don't know. I think it's best if maybe we just leave."

"That would be fucking fantastic, actually." Everly scoffed, turning away from us. "Don't let the door hit you on the way out."

Emmanuella opened her mouth to respond, but I nudged her quickly and shook my head. I mouthed the words 'not worth it' to her. She rolled her eyes and sighed, but followed me quickly out of Everly's room. Seconds after we'd left, I heard the door slam behind us.

Emmanuella and I were quiet as we made our way back to our dorms. As soon as we were inside Em's room, she let out a holler.

"What in the fucking shitbitch motherfuck was that all about?" she exclaimed loudly.

I was still in a bit of denial – I couldn't believe what had just happened. "Your guess is as good as mine."

"Is she insane?" Em went on, waving her hands in the air. "Like, literally – is she fucking crazy? What did you even do?"

"I don't know."

"Has anything ever happened between you two before?"

I shook my head slowly, staring at a spot on the wall, still processing everything that had occurred. "I don't think so."

"Sheesh ka-bibbles!" she yelled, staring at her own crazed face in her mirror. "You would have thought you'd told her she was a worthless sewer rat, the way she was acting!"

I sat on the edge of her bed, rubbing my eyes with my palm. The entire confrontation had left me feeling drained.

"Seriously, should we, like, call a wellness check for her?" Emmanuella asked me. "That was not rational human behaviour."

I let out a breath. "No, it wasn't. But when have the cops ever made a mental breakdown any better?"

Emmanuella considered this. "Fair point, my friend." She paused. "So maybe an exorcism?"

I gave her a trying smile. "Let's just leave her be. Maybe she's just really stressed about something else, and she's projecting it on me. Hopefully, she'll come around." I reached out to pat her on the arm. "Thanks for having my back, by the way."

Emmanuella snorted. "Wasn't very hard, given what you were dealing with. But no problem."

I stood, stretching a bit. "Don't worry about what she said to you, either."

"What do you mean?"

"The whole Keiffer thing."

Emmanuella made a hissing sound. "No skin off my back. She's wrong, anyways." She made a face. "I mean, come on – Keiffer? Yuck."

I stifled a laugh. "Glad you're in good spirits. I've got some homework to do, though, so can't say the same about me."

"Oh, girl, same. Midterms next week."

"I know."

She sighed. "I should study, too. Good luck."

I saluted her in response as I made for the doorway through our bathroom to my own dorm.

———

My studies were unexciting, but it was relieving to check more and more things off the homework task list. By the time I went to bed, I nearly had a clear slate.

Monday morning brought the first in my series of midterms. As the week went on, so did the studying and the completion of all my assignments. Felix and I took our physics midterm on Tuesday, which I didn't feel horrible about. The rest of the week passed by quickly, with my last midterm finally being written on Friday at noon.

It was a nice, early start to the weekend to be out of classes so early. San Diego didn't understand the concept of seasons, so even though it was near the end of October, it was still bright and warm. I felt my skin flourish underneath the heat of the sun as I walked back to my dorm. A nap was much needed before Felix and I headed to Julius' party later that night, and our trip to Hawaii the next day.

When I woke up, I packed everything I would need into a small backpack – the usual wallet and phone among other essentials, the scarf and dress Felix had leant me, a strapless black bodysuit, black heels, two garters, a bow hair accessory that I repurposed into a black bowtie, and knee-high tights for the Playboy bunny costume…

I frowned at my bag. Bunny ears. I didn't have bunny ears. How was I supposed to be a Playboy bunny without bunny ears?

I pursed my lips, looking over at Emmanuella's closed door through the bathroom.

I approached it and knocked, asking, "Em? Are you in there?"

"Yeah, girl. Come on in," I heard her call back.

I opened the door to her room. She was propped up in bed, reading one of her books for class. "What's up?" she asked me.

"You don't happen to have any bunny ears, do you?"

She raised her eyebrows at me. "Sexy bunny for Halloween or something?"

"Playboy bunny."

"Same thing," she said, stifling a laugh and walking to her dresser. "Lucky for you, I have been sexy bunny, zombie bunny, and sexy zombie bunny in years past," she said, reaching in and pulling out a headband with black bunny ears.

"You're a lifesaver," I told her, taking them. "Thank you. I'll give it back after the party."

"It's tonight?"

"Yeah." I paused. "Speaking of which, I might not be back for a few days. Don't worry about me if I'm not."

Her face became curious as she eyed me. "Someone special at this Halloween party?"

I thought about my answer – honestly, it was a better excuse than any one I could come up with, so I went along with it. "Maybe," I said with a small smile.

A smirk pulled on her lips. "Is that special someone…Felix?"

I gave her a bewildered expression. "What? No. Felix and I are just friends." It wasn't a complete lie – we were friends who saw each other naked, but friends, nonetheless. Explaining the reality of the situation, though, seemed a bit strange to me. I wasn't entirely sure I wanted everyone to know Felix and I were…well, whatever we were.

Still, I could feel the heat in my cheeks, though, and I knew she saw the redness that ensued when she snorted. "You want to tell that to your face?"

I sighed, turning away. "I wouldn't want to jeopardise our friendship," I said unconvincingly.

"Ah, there they are. The famous last words we all use as an excuse." She snickered. "Well, have fun with whoever it is."

I rolled my eyes. "Thanks again," I said as I went back to my room. I finished doing my makeup and stuffed the bunny ears in my backpack before slinging it over my shoulder and making for my door.

———

Felix was waiting for me in the Ferrari. "Hey," he said, watching me as I sat down in the passenger seat. "That's some drama on the eyes there."

I smiled. "It'll look better with the rest of the costume," I said.

"Right," he replied as he started driving. "Makes sense."

"Are you dressing up?"

He sighed. "I suppose I should if I'm attending a Halloween party," he said.

"There's the Halloween spirit."

"What's the theme again?"

"Playboy."

Felix rolled his eyes. "Classic of him. Makes it easy for me, though. I just have to dress like Hefner."

I gave him a smirk. "You're not going to be a Playboy bunny?"

He returned an amused gaze. "I'm not committed to this holiday enough for that," he remarked. "I'll leave that to you."

"Got it," I said, reaching into my backpack and pulling out his scarf and the dress. "Thanks for letting me borrow these, by the way."

"Of course," he said, glancing at my neck. "Oh, yeah. It is all gone now." He said it so bluntly, so blandly. It was almost as if he were disappointed by it.

"Thankfully," I noted, turning to look at the window. The La Jolla neighbourhood whizzed past us, and soon enough, we were at the estate.

We entered Felix's home and went upstairs, him disappearing into his room as I ventured into a guest bathroom. I changed into my costume, admiring my handiwork in the mirror when I'd finished. It was probably a little sluttier – sexier? – than I normally went for. But this was a Halloween party at Julius Clarkson's house, and my parents weren't around to see my costume choice like they had when I lived with them, so what the hell? It was the one holiday where I could be as sexy – okay, no, it was definitely slutty – as I wanted with no real societal consequences. I fluffed my curls one last time and exited the bathroom, just as Felix was leaving his room.

"I'm not sure if this is – " Felix stopped short the second his eyes fell upon me. "Fucking hell," he blurted. "Look at you."

Immediately, I became flustered. I went to tuck a strand of my hair behind my ear as a whirlpool formed in my stomach, the wind turbulent, the lightning striking my nerves. The fact that I'd caught him off guard gratified me, and admittedly, he had stunned me a little himself. He wore a pair of black slacks that sat low on his hips, drawing more attention to his toned, bare chest. Over his shoulders, he'd thrown an oversized Versace coat in the signature black, white, and gold pattern, and a slim, black tie hung from around his neck. It certainly resembled what the creator of Playboy would wear. But the wafting of his cologne combined with the way his body was so nicely framed by the clothes…

A part of me wanted to abandon the party altogether and play into whatever personal fantasy Felix desired. The fire I felt for him was raging. But I suppose there was time for that after the party, too – and I needed to have a little chat with Julius.

I sucked in my lips. "You look good," I said as I finally managed to tear my eyes away from his abs.

He chuckled nervously. "Oh, uh, thanks," he stammered before clearing his throat. "But I mean, you – " he nodded at me, fidgeting a bit as he stuffed his hands in his pockets " – you look…"

I swallowed, glancing down at myself. "Is it too much?"

"No," he said hurriedly. "No, not at all. It's – " he gulped " – it's what commitment to the holiday looks like, that's for sure."

"In a good way or a bad way?"

"Good," he answered without thinking, his eyes glued to my body. "A very, very good way." He was scanning me up and down repeatedly, shifting a bit in place. "If Hefner were alive, I'd be shocked if he didn't make you Playmate of the Year."

I bit my lip slightly. "Thanks," I said quietly. I wasn't sure if it was exactly the best compliment, but I knew he had good intentions with it, anyways.

I must have been metal, and Felix must have been a magnet, for his gaze was fixated on me and showed little intent of moving away. I eventually had to raise my eyebrows a bit at him to draw his attention back to my face.

He promptly shook his head. "Sorry. We should go. After you," he proposed, motioning to the stairs. I nodded and began descending, knowing full well why he'd wanted me to go first, and not minding regardless.

"I should warn you," he said as we left the house for the garage, "that my brother might try and get at you if he sees you looking like that."

I snorted. "Nothing I can't handle. Wouldn't be the first Clarkson brother, after all," I teased, throwing a sly glance back at him.

He hid his face from me, but not before I could catch the corners of his mouth twitching upwards and his cheeks going beet red.

CHAPTER 19

I HAD DECIDED to call Felix's home a display of new money, while Luther's mansion was reminiscent of old. Bearing that in mind, I could only classify Julius' villa as a clusterfuck of money, neither old, nor new, nor anything in between.

From the exterior, it showed some promise. It definitely had some Latino flair – the walls were stucco in a bright yellow colour, one that reminded me of some of the buildings in Colombia and Peru. There were several archways that lined a sort of wraparound porch, and the concept seemed very open, with little barrier from the inside to the outside.

But when we knocked and Julius opened the massive, iron door, he revealed behind him a headache-inducing mix of vibrant colours, loud music, and vulgar imagery, as well as all the scantily clad partygoers. Right in the center of the foyer was an exuberant indoor fountain, the water of which was spurting from between the sculpture of a woman's parted legs. Protruding from the curved stairway behind it were three stucco busts of – well, busts. They were ridiculously large, disproportionate busts with their nipples taut and perky. The walls were bright orange in the foyer, and I could see glimpses of walls in the other rooms that were a pink-red and lime green. I held the philosophy of 'to each their own,' but this was a royal fucking disaster.

Julius wore a red silk robe with black pants, along with that signature grin that could easily get him into more trouble than out of it. "Seraphine, you sexy little thing, you made it! I was worried when I didn't get a text from you that you'd decided not to come. And you somehow convinced Felix to – "

Before he could finish, Felix slapped him across the face.

I gasped as Julius reeled, rubbing his cheek with his hand. "*Oye!* What the fuck was that for?" he exclaimed at Felix.

Felix stared at him coldly. "That's for trying to humiliate her the other day," he stated briskly.

"What the hell are you even talking about?"

He snagged him by his robe's collar. "You know what you did – don't play stupid. What happens between me and her is none of your business."

"For fuck's sake, *hermano*," Julius said, raising his hands defensively. "I was just – "

Felix tightened his grip, cutting Julius off. "Don't you ever make her uncomfortable again."

"All right, all right." Julius let out a little muffled choking sound. "Message received."

"It better have been," Felix sniped, releasing his grip. "Where are the drinks?"

Drinks? Should he even be drinking if he wanted to quit his bad habits?

Well, it wasn't cocaine, which I felt was the main problem. Though he did drink alcohol quite a bit...

I figured he wouldn't appreciate me grilling him on his choices, especially when he specifically asked for my support in that way – giving him time and trust. I needed to trust his judgment, and he needed to feel that he was trusted so he wouldn't lose motivation.

I also wasn't a doctor, or a rehabilitation specialist, or a therapist, or any sort of qualified expert on the matter.

So whatever my feelings were about it, I decided to just keep my mouth shut.

"The bar's by the pool," Julius answered simply. To this, Felix only responded by easily brushing past him into the house.

I watched him in a bit of shock as he stormed away.

Julius turned to me, his eyes apologetic. "Seraphine, *chiquita*, I thought we were just having a little fun – you know, joking around. I didn't know you were offended," he told me. "You should have said something."

I shrugged. "It's done now. I just like to keep my personal life private, that's all," I replied simply.

"Aww, *hermosa*, come here," he said, offering me a hug. I smiled slightly and accepted it, embracing him for a moment before he pulled away. "You know you're like a step-sister to me – I thought it was all in jest. I'm sorry it hurt your feelings."

"Apology accepted," I said, before frowning. "Also – *step-sister?*"

He grinned. "You know, close enough to act like siblings, but not illegal to play with each other in a different way." He winked, giving me a once-over. "Wouldn't ever want to rule out the possibility of seeing you naked, now would I?"

I rolled my eyes, scoffing as I whacked him on the arm. "This isn't porn," I snapped at him. "Now, where's the food?"

He chuckled. "Come on in. I'll lead the way."

I followed him inside, past the staircase. Beyond it was a huge, central courtyard, flourishing with greenery and featuring a turquoise-blue pool and hot tub, along with many sitting areas and firepits. The courtyard was framed by archways and left unroofed, meaning nearly the entire main floor was technically outdoors – the second floor, though, boasted a balcony that wrapped around the courtyard from above, and there I could see doors that led into other, enclosed rooms. It reminded me of a Spanish casa, and I actually didn't mind the design, save for the hyperbolic statues of naked women and references to female genitalia in almost every nook and cranny. There were some ghosts and ghouls that hung from the railings, and some zombie bunnies placed on the stairways and amongst the plants, but they weren't really enough to detract from the obvious sexual themes that ran throughout the house. But considering everyone in attendance seemed to have a severe lack of clothing, I supposed we all fit right in.

We descended a small flight of stairs into the courtyard, and before us, there was a spread featuring some Halloween-themed treats – candy apples that looked as if they were dripping blood, cupcakes that looked like brains, candies and chocolates, the whole works. I grabbed some of the goodies and glanced around. I could see the bar near the center, accessible from in the pool and outside of it. Try as I might, though, I could not spot the Versace coat.

"So, what do you think?" Julius asked me, grinning as he motioned around us. "Pretty great setup, huh?"

"Could never expect anything less from you," I remarked, eating some of my candy corn. "The food is great."

"You really are a foodie, aren't you?" he joked.

I shrugged, biting into my brain-cupcake. "I like to eat."

"Good," he said, smiling. "You should."

I heard a woman's voice then amongst the crowd, and it seemed to be aimed towards us. "Julius! There you are!"

I turned. She was about my height with a thin frame, complete with well-proportioned curves that were highlighted by a costume very similar to my own. Her long, brown hair fell to one side of her beautiful, pale face, and her big, brown eyes were fluttering as she smiled widely towards Julius. Her smile was perfect, her cheeks plump, but her jaw and neck defined. She must have been a model of some sort – she was stunning.

"*Hola, mamacita*," Julius greeted her, bringing her in for a quick embrace and kiss on the cheek. "Seraphine, this is Nina," he then said, motioning to me. "Nina, this is Felix's friend, Seraphine."

"Seraphine, so nice to meet you!" she exclaimed giddily, offering me her hand. I was a bit taken aback – were these two dating? Could Julius even be in a committed relationship?

She seemed lovely, though, so I shook her hand and returned her smile. "Nice to meet you, too," I said. "You look great."

"I was just thinking the same about you!" she said cheerily. "Nice bodysuit!"

"Thank you," I said. "Figured it would work with the theme."

"It absolutely does!" she agreed, turning back to Julius. "Can I steal you for a couple minutes? I want some photos."

"Of course," Julius replied, grinning at me. "Enjoy the party. Let me know if you need anything."

"Will do," I said, and I watched them walk away together. He placed his hand low on her back, almost on her butt, as they walked. There was no way they weren't romantically involved, but I found it hard to believe that Julius had a girlfriend.

I turned back to the food, grabbing a few more things for my plate, and then walked to the bar. I ordered a blood-red sangria, and when it was in my hand, I glanced around for a place to sit.

There were people everywhere, laughing amongst each other, engaged in conversation. Some were wading drunkenly in the pool, and others clearly had no qualms about making out in front of everyone else. There were significantly fewer men than women scattered about, which didn't surprise me, considering the host. I finally spotted a calmer seating area – two curved, outdoor couches, upon one of which sat a woman who was watching me.

I paused on her face. I didn't recognize her, but she was striking in her own way – jet-black hair that cascaded around her gaunt shoulders, an augmented chest that was hoisted to sit unnaturally high on her frame. Her stomach was flat as a board, but her hips appeared as if they had been pumped with air. Her long, thin fingers, topped with red stiletto nails, waved at me with slight, barely-there motions.

Seeing as it seemed to be an invitation, I approached her. "Hello," I said as I sat down across from her.

Upon closer inspection, I could better see the details of her sharpened face, like her sunken cheekbones and defined jawline, which made her look incisive and daring. Her lips had to have been plumped because they didn't seem to match the rest of her face – I wondered if her cheeks had been, too. Something about the shape of her blue-green eyes and how they were elongated by her eyebrows gave her this barbed look that spoke of secrecy and sin. The black lingerie she wore was partly see-through, her black heels boasting signature Louboutin red bottoms.

"I've never seen you before," she purred. Her voice was smooth and sharp, the type of voice that says she'll be back and never returns. It was both intimidating and enticing.

"I'm sort of new to all these events," I explained. "I'm Seraphine."

She crossed one long leg over the other, reaching for a martini on the nearby table. "Valentina," she said simply, sipping her drink. "So tell me, what brings a new face to this daring little soiree?"

I was confused by the question. "Julius invited me."

"Mhm." She reached into her bra, pulling out a cigarette and a lighter. "And you brought Felix with you?" she questioned.

I studied her, but before I could ask, she held up a hand. "I saw you at the door with him," she explained, lighting the cigarette and putting it to her ruby red lips.

I watched her puff it slowly and sensually, letting the tuft of smoke dance from her mouth and into the surrounding air. The way she moved was feline, like a panther, and she had the cat eyes to match. "Felix had to talk to Julius about something," I said slowly.

Valentina nodded, clicking the floor with her heel. "And then he wandered into the party when he could have gone straight home," she noted, bringing her eyes back to mine. "I haven't seen Felix stay long at Julius' parties much before."

I didn't really know why she was pestering me about this. Something about the way she stared at me sent a chill down my spine. What was that poison buried in her glare?

She lifted her chin. "Humour me with how you know the Clarksons, will you?" she said.

I swallowed. "They're my friends."

She raised an eyebrow – this seemed to pique her interest. "Oh?"

"I met Felix in my physics lab this semester," I went on.

Her face relaxed, a smirk crawling on those scarlet lips. "How cute. A college girl. I understand now why you're so naïve," she hummed, puffing out another cloud of smoke. "You must have made quite the impression on Felix."

I couldn't understand what she was talking about, so I simply frowned. "How do you know the Clarksons?" I spun to her.

She grinned at me. "Do you want the honest answer, or the answer that will feel the most righteous to you?"

I held her gaze. "I think honesty is the best policy."

She gave off an amused breath, twirling the cigarette in her fingers. "The Clarksons don't have many friends. Felix doesn't get along with anyone – apart from you, for some reason. It must be your innocent charm." She looked me up and down, the words ensnaring me like a rabbit's foot in a trap. "As for Julius, well – " she tossed her hair " – he pays well for most of our company."

I stared at her. "Are you saying – "

"That I'm an escort?" she snorted. "Look at me, honey. I was built to be gawked at, and then the doctors made me even more so. If the dogs like to chew bones, I might as well get paid for it."

I blinked, then glanced around. "And these women are also…?"

"Most of them." She cocked her head to the side. "I would assume the majority have slept with him, either past or present. Some of them are socialites. You know, to make him look good." She shrugged at my confused expression. "The more desirable he looks, the more the public is drawn to him. And the more they're drawn to him, the more likely they are to buy whatever he's selling."

I shook my head. "I don't understand. There was a girl – "

"Nina. Yes." She rolled her eyes, scoffing. "She isn't an escort, just some stupid little lovestruck fawn. I guess she met Julius at an event and has been drooling over him ever since." She cackled a bit cruelly to herself. "She's either unaware that she's sharing him with everyone else he wants to fuck, or completely in denial. Maybe she's on some kind of impossible mission to change him. Who knows."

I thought about that sweet face, that beautiful smile. "You're telling me that he cheats on her on a regular basis with the same women he brings around her, and not one of them has said anything?"

Valentina winked at me slyly. "We're paid pretty good to keep our mouths shut and legs open, you know. If asked, we're just his friends."

I squinted slightly at her. "And for what reason would you be sharing such a big secret with me?"

She hummed in amusement. "Oh, I like you, Seraphine. That intuition is something else." She gave me a look. "You and I – we're a lot more alike than you might think."

I stared at her. "I'm not sure I agree."

She laughed again, a wicked sound vastly devoid of humour. "There's no need to be ashamed of our secrets, is there? I think it's better if we bond over them – let loose a little.

It's hard carrying that weight around all the time, hm?" Her eyes fluttered towards me. "And I know you wouldn't want your secret spilled, so you wouldn't dare spill mine."

My chest tightened. "I haven't told you a secret."

"You didn't need to," she explained wryly. "I've never seen Felix look at a woman the way he looks at you." She lowered her gaze. "You must be a pretty good lay."

I couldn't believe what I was hearing. Not only was Julius even more of a sleaze than I could ever have imagined, but this woman had observed one interaction and somehow managed to deduce its hidden meaning. And the worst part was that she wasn't entirely off. I didn't know how great I was in bed, but she knew we'd been to bed together, nonetheless. I instantly felt even more out of place than I had when I walked in – there was something twisted about her, and about the world the Clarksons dwelled in. I didn't even want to think about what other dirty little secrets might be hidden within their wealthy pockets.

The astonishment must have been written on my face, for she cackled. "Hasn't this been fun?" she teased, raising an eyebrow. "He's waiting for you, you know."

I was still blindsided. "What?"

She nodded upwards in my direction. I turned to look, and there he was on the second floor, leaning against a pillar with a drink in one hand and a cigarette in the other. The vapor from his cigarette twirled and twisted in the air around him, the shadows from the overhang of the balcony shrouding him in darkness. Even from a distance, I could see a glint in his eyes, those irises whose colour I knew so well fixed directly upon me.

"My, that wolf is famished," Valentina chaunted, and I turned to see she had stood. "Months upon months in the woods, trudging through mud and cold, all alone with no pack to love and only a moon to howl with. But after all this time, to stumble upon such a lovely, little doe…"

She chuckled a bit as she came and sat down beside me,

her eyes venomous. "Of course, to the hungry wolf, a doe is satisfactory. But two, playing innocently together as the grass dances beneath them – now *that* is irresistible."

Before I could process what was happening, she leaned in and kissed me, those crimson lips dancing around my own. I stiffened, but made no effort to stop her. Instead, I shut my eyes and let it happen – let her run her tongue over my teeth, let her move my lips beneath hers, until finally, she pulled away. It was more of a prey response than I would have liked, regrettably. But I didn't quite know what else to do.

I blinked my eyes open and found her grinning as she rose. "Better not keep the wolf waiting," she crooned, and with a devious wink, Valentina then turned and sauntered away.

I stared at the spot where she'd been, trying to understand what the hell had just happened. Slowly, almost shamefully, I then turned to look back up at Felix. My chest turned in knots when I saw the way he was looking at me – his chin lifted, his eyes feverish, his eyebrow peaked. There was no mistaking the look on that face, an obvious mixture of jealous intrigue and a desperate, bloodthirsty desire. A jolt of electricity arrested my spine, buzzing throughout my entire being.

Better not keep the wolf waiting.

I lifted myself out of my seat and made for the staircase. My steps were slow and methodical, but my mind was rapid and whirling. When I rounded the corner to approach him, he turned to face me. I stopped in front of him, my eyes never once parting from those fields of lavender.

"You looked like you were having fun down there," he said to me, the eyebrow still lifted. His voice was low and brash, and though the scent of alcohol wafted from him, he didn't appear inebriated.

I held his stare. "Depends on your definition of fun. But if you're feeling left out, I can go find her, too."

"Oh, please don't," he replied instantly, without thinking.

"No person in their right mind plants a weed with their favourite flower."

It was my turn to lift an eyebrow.

"You should be careful of the company you keep," he added quietly.

I threw a glance out at the party down below, the barbaric people gathered in a dark world only they understood.

Wolves. A pack of wolves.

Secrets masked by glamour, skeletons in closets hidden by dresses and fur coats.

I spotted Nina, the fawn – the prey. And then I saw the women who glared at her with such evil, vile looks. For wolves, they sure seemed threatened by such an innocent fawn. But undoubtedly, Nina seemed blissfully unaware.

I refused to be so aloof.

I was livid at the dark secrets unveiled, shocked by the people who surrounded me. I was frustrated that I hadn't pinned Julius as the cheater he was, nevertheless one who had no qualms with fooling a girl who cared for him. And if that was who he was, the mark of which I hadn't quite managed to hit on my own, did I know for certain Felix wasn't up to similar mischief?

The thoughts were boiling me as I stood before him, clenching and unclenching my fingers. I began to overthink and question things I hadn't before. He'd mentioned he'd slept with people he hadn't cared about. Had Felix hired escorts? Were they the same escorts that roamed beneath us?

Was I no better than an escort myself?

Maybe Felix hadn't paid me directly for our nights – but he had treated me in Colombia, given me money for groceries, helped me study. The sudden revision of meaning to the gestures felt like a fan to the fire within me.

All these people didn't know I was any different than one of them. How would they know? I was dressed like them, drifting amongst them. They all looked at me and assumed the same things about me that I now knew about them. The men in the room – the men knew they were surrounded by toys. To them, I was nothing but a *toy*.

I met Felix's gaze again, and I could feel the ire in my own. "Are you the company in question?" I challenged.

He studied me, his eyes narrowing and widening several times. "What did she tell you?" he asked me in a hush.

I motioned to the crowd below. "This place is filled with women who are hired or hireable. And here I am amongst them, no better, no worse." I bristled. "This is your brother's whorehouse, and I fit right in, because anyone who sees us thinks I'm just your stupid whore."

His features became displeased. "But you're not my whore. Or anyone's whore."

"Am I not?" I straightened my shoulders, the tension magnifying in my muscles, my bones. "You pamper me. Spoil me. You've done so ever since we met. A place for Aurora, money for food or clothes, luxurious treats. Countless favors. And in return…"

I let my sentence finish itself.

He shook his head slowly, his eyes never leaving mine. "I do those things for you because I care about you," he assured me. "Not because I want anything in return."

I pursed my lips, but I didn't find any argument to the contrary.

He came a bit closer, his gaze searching my features. "Do you not think you deserve it?" he asked, his voice laden with concern.

The question made me pause. I realized my reactions stemmed less from what I believed I was worth and more from how people had treated me. I generally expected the worst, especially from men – but Felix was not a man of my past. And I should not have been treating him as such.

I lowered my chin with a bit of a sigh. "I think I'm just not used to a man who isn't a total piece of shit," I replied.

This drew a snort from him. "Don't set the bar too high. I do have a tendency to set things on fire, after all," he admitted, to which I cracked a small smile. "But…you saved my life, Seraphine. No amount of favours could ever repay you for that, let alone make me expect anything from you. I just want to care for you as you've cared for me, to better your life the way you've bettered mine."

His lavender eyes were magnetic. "Let me be clear – I've never paid for a woman in my life, and I have no intention of ever doing so." He gestured to where Valentina and I had been. "She's made many offers to me in the past, all of which I've refused."

My brows twitched. The context made things click. That stare she'd given me – it was riddled with an envy that I'd gotten what she couldn't, and I hadn't had to sell myself for it. And it was the same venom she'd spoken about Nina with.

"It's a matter of principle for me. I despise the way my brother acts, and I try my hardest not to remotely resemble him in any way," Felix declared intently.

I looked out over the party, the people here, wondering if their crookedness had somehow seeped into the air. I believed him. Those quarrels I'd witnessed between him and Julius – I understood now. It was not a sibling rivalry, and it never had been. It was a difference of morals and lifestyles. Whatever hell these wolves were born from was not the hell Felix chose to endure.

When I looked back at him, gone was the wolf, and in had roared a lion before me. Strong. Dignified. Defiant of the reputation assigned to him, and determined not to be his brother's shadow.

And just as he could rise above whatever people thought he was…so could I.

Why should I care about their opinions of me?

I knew the truth.

I defined my worth. Not them.

I turned back to look at Felix. "I suppose a lioness has no reason to fear wolves," I replied simply. "Or a snake."

He studied me for a few moments. Slowly, a smirk crept upon his face. "That is true," he said.

I nodded firmly. "Let's go."

He cocked his head questioningly. "Go where?"

"I'm tired of all this racket." I motioned gracefully down the hall, my smile sultry. "Take me somewhere quiet. Somewhere we can be alone."

His eyes danced under the spell I'd charmed him with. He obediently took my hand in his and began leading me further into the casa.

Away from the wolves.

Towards a lion's den.

CHAPTER 20

THE ROOM I followed Felix to was far from the party, and the noise and the chatter were drowned out as we shut the door behind us.

I thought he would take me to a bedroom, but I quickly realized that was not the case. The best descriptor I could muster was a game room or a lounge. The room was dark, painted maroon red, and floored with dark wood. There was a small bar in one corner, a dartboard against another wall, and black leather seating – a dive bar sofa across the length of one wall, above which were wall-length mirrors, as well as armchairs and stools at the bar itself. The only seating that wasn't leather was the huge chaise lounge by the large open window, whose sleek curves were plastered in black velvet. In the center of the room was a red-fabric pool table, above which hung a decorative, neon light in the shape of two playing cards – the two of hearts and the ace of spades.

I paused and watched Felix stroll over to the bar, ducking down beneath it. He resurfaced with a bottle of whiskey, a glass, and a box of Colombian cigars. He poured himself a hefty amount and then looked up at me.

"Would you like a drink?" he asked. "There may be cider

in the fridge down here. I'm sure there's also some wine – you like white, right?"

I looked at his glass of whiskey, then back up at him. "I'll have what you're having."

He stared at me. "You want whiskey?"

I nodded.

"But you hate whiskey."

"I used to hate you," I told him. "Things change."

He didn't move right away. But when he did eventually reach down and grab another glass, I watched the corners of his mouth twitch upwards into a small smile. He poured me a smaller glass than his own and pushed it gently towards one of the stools. I walked over and sat down across from him.

We clinked glasses, and in one, swift chug, I downed the horrific alcohol. As I placed the glass back down on the bar, Felix raised his eyebrows at me, to which I only nodded towards the empty glass.

"One more, please," I asked.

He never took his eyes off me, but he slowly reopened the bottle of whiskey and poured me another small glass. When he had finished, I took it and downed it also in one go. The taste of the liquid made me cringe internally, but it made it easier if you got it over with quicker.

I nearly slammed the empty glass back on the bar and decidedly slid it back towards him. "Now I'm good."

He watched as I folded my arms across the counter and rested my head on the back of my hands, sipping his own drink slowly. "You're in a curious mood tonight," he noted quietly.

I shrugged. "I like the look on people's faces when I do something unexpected."

Again, this humoured him. As he reached for one of the cigars, the smile pricked at his lips again.

I hurriedly beat his hand to the box. The motion surprised him, and he watched with a slight frown as my fingers curled around one of the cigars and brought it up towards me. I extended it to him, lifting my eyebrows in expectation.

He let out an amused breath, but he was done asking questions. He brought his fingertip to the end and produced a small flame, lighting the cigar. When the smoke was wafting, I brought it to my lips and sucked.

Again, it tasted disgusting, but I'd already committed. His eyes were glued to mine as I inhaled slowly, filling my mouth with tobacco and smoke. Then I removed the cigar and leaned forward, towards him. Slowly, sensually, I let the smoke drift from my lips out towards him. I watched it wrap his features in mystery, shroud his eyes that were magnetized. It wafted around us with the twists and turns of an exotic dancer.

When it had cleared, he propped his arms on the counter, leaning towards me. Those lavender eyes were churning.

"Do it again," he told me, his face so close that I could feel the breath from his words as they escaped his parted lips.

I sucked on the cigar again and breathed its contents out onto him, surrounding us in smoke. When the clouded air cleared, I could see his breath had quickened.

His eyes fell to my lips, and he brought a fingertip to them, tracing them with a light touch. "Again," he breathed.

I continued breathing in the tobacco and breathing it out onto him, watching his reaction and savouring it. With each clearing, it revealed one more layer of desire in his eyes that awakened more of it in mine. His fingers found their way to my chin, lifting it up towards him, becoming a tighter and tighter grip with each smoky breath. When I neared the end of the cigar, he brought my lips to his as I exhaled, the smoke billowing from both our mouths as they met and meshed together.

I could taste his breath – a mix of bad habits that smelled outlandishly inviting. Something about his kiss made me realize I'd developed a vice of my own. I found myself, time and time again, lusting after mysteries. My game of choice was a game of chance. There was a thrill to letting myself fall from a Phoenix's back, or chasing a power I wasn't familiar with, knowing full well it could destroy me. It was a thrill I supposed would be similar to the one people got from betting their life's earnings at a casino. I wouldn't be caught dead gambling my money, but I was very adept at gambling my heart.

My grandmother had always told me, "Seraphine, never trust the man who carries a rose between his teeth. He knows how to hide the thorns behind a flower, how to blend the blood with his lips, how to only show you the beauty and mask its risks." And it made sense to me, until it didn't. Why is he bearing the pain from the pricks? Why hide the thorns behind a flower? Are the risks for me, or for him? Could she not see how striking he made danger look?

It was in this moment that Felix Vaughn Clarkson became my Achilles' heel. Something about him drove me insane in a terrifyingly enchanting way. I needed to open all his doors if it meant smashing them repeatedly until my arms were bruised and broken. I did not care if it collapsed into pieces, lock unopened, key unfound.

I could read my own thoughts in his eyes as we pulled apart for only a brief second, an awareness that really, it was only a matter of time. Nobody connected with him like I did. We are not magnets; we are drawn together when we are alike. It's an unwritten law of solidarity.

He kissed me softly again and again, then more passionately. At last, he swallowed profusely, and he pulled away almost hesitantly. "I need to go get something," he said in a raspy voice. "Wait for me here."

I nodded. I could only assume what it was. He pulled his hand from my face and hurried out of the room.

The anticipation I'd built up had my heart thundering in my chest. I stood and wandered around, pacing with expectancy. The crescent moon hung outside the window, the only potential witness to whatever would happen in this room.

228

It took about ten excruciatingly long minutes for Felix to return, and when he did, he brought with him a feverish look in his eyes and a devilish smile on his lips. I turned to face him immediately, my heartbeat rapid.

"All right," he crooned, locking the door behind him. "Where were we?"

In a pride of lions, the lioness does the hunting, so I beckoned him over with my finger. "I want to play a game," I replied.

He approached me smoothly. "A game?" he queried, bringing one hand around my waist, the other lifting my chin. "What's the game?"

I lowered my gaze so that I looked up at him through my lashes. "Chess."

He raised an eyebrow. "Chess?"

I nodded slowly, swallowing as I brought my hand up to where his fingers held my chin and gently lifted them off. "*Oui*. And in this game of chess, I want to be the queen," I told him as I replaced his hand around my neck, my breath faltering slightly at the feel of his fingers winding around it. "The queen is the most powerful piece on the board. She can move up or down, left or right, diagonally one way or the other. You can push her in any direction you choose, for as many spaces as you please, and still she carries on, because she is limitless in the game."

A grin worked its way across his lips as I felt his fingers tighten slightly around my neck. "And are you the white side, or the black?"

The white pieces make the first move. "White," I answered firmly.

He cocked his head to one side. "Very well. You start, then."

I smirked, prying his fingers off my neck and pointing at the pool table. "Lean against that," I instructed.

He seemed intrigued by my demand, but listened, leaning

with his back against the pool table. I came to a stop before him and tugged gently on his tie, loosening it. I then brought it up and over his neck, straightening it with both hands before bringing it over the top of his eyes. Then I wrapped it around his head like a blindfold, tying a knot at the back.

"Mhm," he grunted. "I like this game already."

When the tie was secure, I lifted both of his hands with both of mine and put them on either side of my waist. He clung to me quickly, rubbing his hands up and down my sides. And as I let his hands wander, I brought one of mine to the front of his pants forcefully.

He jolted. "Hey – careful with that," he warned gruffly.

I sneered, amused. I took one finger and traced up and down him with the faintest touch I could muster, gratified in the quick reaction I felt taking place beneath the fabric. He stiffened, his fingers digging into my hips as I retraced the same path, over and over. On my last trip upwards, I grabbed the zipper and pulled it down.

His fingers were kneading my backside as I wrapped my fingers around him and pulled him out. He exhaled as I worked with my hand, keeping my movements tantalizing and slow. I could feel him tremor a bit as I then removed his hands from around me and lowered myself to my knees.

The second my tongue grazed against him, he moaned, "Oh, fuck."

I had to keep from smirking to avoid skinning him with my teeth. I enveloped as much of him as I could with my mouth, sucking him like I had the cigar. Meticulously, I drove my tongue around him as his legs tensed and relaxed, one of his hands gripping the pool table as he brought the other to my hair.

"Fuck, Seraphine," he hissed, bunching my hair in his grip and using it to guide my head. I felt the heat from the moment rush through my body, a pulsing sensation beginning between my legs.

After a few minutes, I felt him tremble slightly, and immediately, he gasped, "Stop, stop! Seraphine, stop!"

I instantly obeyed, looking up at him as he removed the blindfold and gawked down at me. "Shit," he huffed, shaking his head as his chest heaved. "This was almost a very short encounter."

I bit my lip as I grinned, watching as he braced himself against the table and attempted to catch his breath. "It's your move," I teased.

He brought his eyes back down to mine, looking my body up and down. "Mhm…what to do with you," he thought aloud, glancing around the room. "There," he then demanded, pointing at the chaise lounge.

I rose from my knees and conformed, lying down on it. But when Felix moved towards me, he began shaking his head.

"Not like that," he said. "Turn around and bend over."

The command excited me. I flipped myself around, following the curve of the chaise lounge as I extended my arms forward and arched my back.

"Good girl," he purred, and I glanced over my shoulder to watch what would happen next. He removed his coat, letting it fall to the floor as he came to stand behind me. The anticipation was driving me wild.

I felt one of his hands rub my posterior slowly, and then brace me. Swiftly, he then slapped it with the other, not too hard, and not too soft – just enough for that stinging sensation.

I moaned, to which he chuckled. "I thought you might like that," he murmured. And then he smacked me again, and again. My body quaked with each slap in pleasure.

I felt his finger then travel between my legs, where the clasp to fasten the bodysuit was. Every inch of me pounded with exhilaration as he popped the clasp open with ease and ran a finger over me. The touch sent a tremble up and down my spine, and my eyes fluttered closed.

He didn't keep me waiting for his tongue. When I felt that

first flick against the place I craved it most, I gasped, reeling from the elation. I gripped the velvet between my fingers as he licked and kissed and brushed, my teeth digging into the skin of my forearm.

The pleasure built and built, but just before I was about to release, he suddenly stopped and pulled away.

I gasped, my body shaking. "No, please," I pleaded.

He chuckled. "Patience is a virtue," he murmured in my ear, nibbling on it a bit.

I nearly ripped the velvet off the chair. "Felix, don't make me beg," I breathed.

"You sound nice when you beg," he noted. "And besides, do you know how many health benefits there are to being in that phase, so close to release? Increased immune function, large boosts of endorphins, a more intense sensation…as a pre-med student, I feel it's my responsibility to recommend only the best course of action for health in every aspect of life."

I was not in the mood for a science lesson. Frantic and desperate, I reached down to try and touch myself. Felix caught my hand and forced it back upwards, tutting as I felt fabric wrap both my hands together – the tie.

"Naughty girl," he baited. "It isn't your move."

It was so overwhelmingly torturous, but so irresistibly erotic at the same time. "You're a cruel king," I huffed at him, digging my fingernails into the fabric.

"You'll thank me later," he assured me. His finger traced around me, heightening me back to the edge, and again, he retracted before I could release. I gasped as he did this to me again, and again, over and over. The intensity of the sensations amplified to a point where I thought I wouldn't be able to take anymore. And then, I heard the familiar sound of an opening packet, and I felt his length rush inside me.

My body shuddered as I plummeted off the deep end, swathed and overcome with the most powerful feelings of pleasure I'd ever experienced in my life. I screamed out his name uncontrollably as I shook, his hardened body never faltering as he moved over top and within me. The indulgence seemed never-ending, waning slowly with the sounds of my cries and moans as my head fell to the velvet on the chair. Our movements in the mirror caught my eye, and I watched how he moved us, how he overtook me, what the smoothness and power of every thrust I felt inside me looked like. It was the most invigorating sexual experience a woman could ask for. We looked and felt like poetry.

I had the satisfaction of watching him lose control and moan my name when he eventually finished inside me. He untied my hands before he stumbled backwards, removing the protection and wandering over to the trash at the bar. I was still quivering as I flipped myself over onto my back, the only sound in the room our heavy breathing.

I struggled to keep my eyes open as I blinked at the ceiling, the fulfillment seeping through my body and washing me in a wave of fatigue. I caught glimpses of Felix returning to the chaise lounge and felt him lift me up with ease. He lay down and placed me gently over top of him. Instinctively, I curled myself up against him, his heartbeat quick and steady beneath the palm I rested on his chest. I was wrapped in the warmth of the Versace coat as he covered us both in it, and felt the gentle touch of his lips as he pressed them to my forehead.

"Well, I don't know about you, but that was the most fun I've ever had playing chess," he whispered into my skin.

A smile pulled at my lips. "Mhm," I agreed.

He didn't reply to this except by running his fingers through my hair and kissing my forehead again. My breathing had calmed, and so had his, and the heavenly warmth I felt by being enclosed with him effortlessly lulled me to sleep.

CHAPTER 21

- F -

As the angel rested beside me, I fought the devils in my mind. The hatred for that bitch who'd tried to hurt her. The despise for my brother and his actions. The unending depression I wrestled with daily, and the guilt from the secrets I was hiding.

They were different secrets, different from the abhorrence that riddled my brother's infidelity, different from the manipulation the escort had tried to pull. But Seraphine was the person I valued most, with whom I was vulnerable enough to share things I'd never shared before. It felt wrong to hide things from her - especially the ones that affected her.

I glanced down at her as she slept, running my fingers again through those curls. Her face was amity and harmony, her hand a pillar of strength on my chest. I wanted her to rest her fingers atop my skin forever. I wanted her next to me for every additional night I lived through.

There are some things in life that make you want to live, not just survive. Seraphine was one of those things worth living for.

But I was withholding information that could kill the image

of me in her eyes. I was living a lie by omission, fuelled by my own insecurities.

I sniffed. My nose was dry and cracked from the last remnants of cocaine I'd snorted before she'd found me. I still hadn't stopped. I was as obsessed with it as I was with her.

And I didn't know how to surrender to either.

- S -

When I awoke, Felix was gone, but he'd left the Versace coat draped over me. I sat up and readjusted myself, clasping my bodysuit closed and throwing the coat over my shoulders. Then I stood and exited the room, wandering down the balcony hallway in search of a bathroom.

I eventually found one and freshened up, examining myself in the mirror. No hickeys this time, which was a relief. I felt sore though – in a good way. The remnants of sensation from the night made me replay it in my mind, and I found myself biting my lip. That unrelenting, winding tether that kept us fastened to one another was fiercer, stiffer. And the way it wound around my being, around my bones, felt like the way Felix wrapped himself up in me. My magic was unwavering and relentless within me – it almost felt as if it had become me. I swallowed, having to shake my head out of my own overpowering thoughts, and left the bathroom.

I paused outside, listening to my surroundings. The sound of morning birdsong echoed in the courtyard as the sun brought light to where the life of the party had been. It was jarringly quiet compared to the night before, and empty, save for the litter and trash strewn about, as well as the poor maid with a trash picker mulling over it all.

The faint sound of music drew my attention to my left. It sounded like it was coming from the main story of the casa. Decidedly, I began making my way towards the staircase.

As I descended the stairs, a shooting pain slashed across my right palm. I gasped as I stumbled, turning my hand upwards. There was no wound, but the pain carried on – it felt as though I'd sliced my hand. I clenched my teeth, grimacing as I pressed into my palm, trying to understand the agony that came from nowhere. It pulsated and throbbed, and then slowly, it began fading. I frowned as it dissipated, leaving my palm unscarred and untouched. There was no rhyme or reason; I couldn't understand what had happened. It was much too severe to be a muscle spasm.

When I'd studied my hand long enough to determine the pain wasn't going to be returning, I continued my descent of the staircase and made for the growing sound of the music. I found myself walking through several vibrant, nauseating rooms until the music led me to Julius' kitchen. There were lime green and yellow walls, and geometric tiles that made no sense to me. At the counter island sat Julius in a barstool designed to look like a peach, with a beer and a steaming plate of breakfast food. And standing over the sink at a cutting board was Felix, who was shirtless and dressed only in the pants he'd worn the night before. I discovered the music was coming from a vintage jukebox in the corner.

Julius noticed me enter and grinned at me. "Well, look who it is. *Buenos días, senorita.*"

I yawned, covering my mouth. "Good morning," I replied.

Felix turned to look at me and gave me a slight smile. "Morning, Seraphine," he said with a wave.

My eyes widened when I saw it. "Your hand!" I exclaimed. His entire right hand had been bandaged in the center of his palm, and even through the bandages, I could see the blood from a pretty hefty gash. "Are you okay?"

"He's fine. He just sliced it open while chopping up some fruit for you guys a few minutes ago," Julius explained, snorting. "A noble sacrifice by a noble idiot."

"Shut up," Felix told him.

But I wasn't paying attention to their quibbling. Instead, my eyes fell to my right palm, where the pain had resounded just moments before. The exact same spot where the bandages covered Felix's wound on his hand, an injury that had also apparently occurred at the same time. The chains seemed to twist further within me, locking my joints in place. A strange rush of magic overcame me as I frowned at my own palm, flexing my fingers as I let the power flow through me.

Had I…sensed Felix's pain? But…*how?*

I swallowed, trying not to make it obvious that I was questioning potential magic I didn't understand as I brought my eyes back up to Felix. But he'd seen my pause and confusion, and he frowned slightly at me, as if to say, "What?"

I shook my head and shrugged, as if to say, "Nothing."

He looked me up and down, and then turned back to the plate of fruit he'd been working on, setting the knife down on the counter as he lifted the plate to the kitchen island. "Here, help yourself," he instructed me.

"Thank you," I told him, approaching the plate of fruit and picking up a slice of melon. As I popped it in my mouth, I caught sight of Julius watching me with a sneer.

"So, you bone *my* brother in *my* house, and I'm seriously not supposed to tease you about it?" he taunted.

As I chewed, I tried my best not to bite my own cheeks in anger. But it was hard to keep a straight face when confronted with that smug smile and crude allusions in his vulgar, sickening home – especially after learning what I had about him.

I could feel Felix immediately by my side, and I heard him open his mouth. But before he could speak, I raised my hand. I was going to handle this.

In the most blunt, stagnant voice I could muster, I replied to him simply, "Not unless you want me to tell Nina the truth about all those escorts you call friends."

Immediately, Julius' face dropped. He stared at me in

bewilderment as he lowered his fork to his plate. I raised my eyebrows slightly at him. I meant every word.

When Julius didn't know how to respond to me, he turned to Felix instead. "Why would you tell her?" he hissed.

I could see Felix shrug. "I didn't."

"Then how – "

"Some of your escorts are keeping their mouths as open as their legs," I warned. "Maybe they're a little confused by the instructions you give them when they're working. I can't be sure."

I saw Felix's lips twitch, but I hadn't even intended for the statement to be humorous. I didn't find anything funny about the situation. Maybe it was hitting too close to home, given the recent happenings with Elijah and my past with noncommittal men. Or maybe it was because I couldn't stop thinking about that poor doe and her lovely smile, just words away from being broken. Regardless, I had no qualms about being ruthless to Julius.

It became obvious that Julius was not only taken aback by my boldness but also upset by it. "Why does any of this even concern you?" he sniped at me with a bit of bite.

"Because it's gross, and creepy, and wrong," I responded evenly. "What you're doing to that poor girl is wrong. Imagine how it's going to feel for her if she ever finds out. Imagine how it looks to everyone watching. Don't you care that you're making her out to be a laughingstock, and yourself to be a degenerate?"

He rolled his eyes. "You're not my mom," he recanted.

The fact that he knew he was going to break this girl's heart and didn't seem to mind sent me into a fury. "Right. And from what I understand, you probably learned to be this way from her," I snapped at him.

He recoiled, sitting back in an angered shock. "Excuse me?"

238

"You know what she did to your father," I said with a seething brusqueness.

The laugh Julius let out was more concerned than humourous. "She was a very doting and supportive wife."

"Oh, sure. And that's why he divorced her."

Julius squinted at me. "My mother and father mutually agreed to split."

I snorted. "Right. And I'm the Queen of England." I cackled. "That must be what she told you to say so her little cheating scandal wouldn't get out."

Julius let out a huff of bewildered exasperation, looking at Felix with the deepest creases I'd ever seen on a man's face. "What the fuck is she talking about?"

I turned to Felix, expecting to see some semblance of the vengeful spite encasing my expression. Perhaps he knew more than even I did.

But to my surprise, he seemed...troubled.

His eyes were wide, his face blank, with no trace of a sneer or smirk to be seen. When he met my gaze, he swallowed shallowly. The alarmed glaze over his lavender irises immediately halted me.

My brows furrowed at his response, my anger mixing with a sudden perplexity. "Isn't that the truth?" I asked him.

Felix just continued staring at me. His eyes flickered once to his brother, and then – in the most adverse of events – he looked shamefully down at the floor. I caught a glimpse of pity in his eyes; not for himself, or for me, but for his half-brother.

And suddenly, I understood.

It *was* the truth – the truth that had been concealed from Julius himself. He had no idea the true reason behind his parents' divorce.

And I had just...blurted it. With malice.

I could feel my throat constrict with instantaneous regret. I struggled to settle on a Clarkson brother to face – my eyes darted between Julius and Felix in a panic. Eventually, it became clear that neither was receptive. Julius still glared at me with an incensed confusion, while Felix's eyes remained fixed on the floor.

My voice was a bit hoarse when I next spoke. "I-I should go," I stammered.

Before either could object, I hurried out of the kitchen, out of the casa, out of their sight.

———

When I rushed my way down into the cellar, all of the Phoenixes looked up at me in surprise. Aurora and Lumina had been playing with one of their toys, and Fuego had been eating in the corner, but they all instantly froze as I huffed my way over to the sofa and plopped myself down. Near it sat Suelo, preening, and noticeably fully grown.

Seeing his size, with proportionate emerald-green feathers lining his body, made me pause in my repentance over what I'd said to Julius. I noted the strange events of the morning, the gash on Felix's hand I'd somehow detected before seeing it. Maybe having two fully grown Phoenixes, one of which I was nearly fully bonded to, allowed me to feel Felix's pain?

I searched deep within myself, trying to locate the light from Aurora. When I found it, I held it within my mind, shutting my eyes as I further let myself fall within my own being. There, buried underneath the strength of the light, was the faint glow of an earthen connection. I harnessed it, opening my eyes as I forced an expression of it into my open hand. Slowly, steadily, a stem began to emerge from my skin, growing and growing until it reached the end of the curve. And from that end, the receptacle formed, and two sepals on either side, before petals slowly appeared around what eventually took shape as a yellow chrysanthemum.

I stared at the flower for a moment before gently plucking it from my palm, twirling it in between two of my fingers like a ballerina. Then I turned to my palm again, and as I took hold of the magic, I expressed it to form a white lily. I plucked that flower and held it with the chrysanthemum as I made a gardenia with the magic. I continued building myself a bouquet, admiring the colours of the flowers I created.

When I was finished, I brought the bunch of flowers to my nostrils, shutting my eyes as I breathed in their scents. They were very real, and they smelled like it, too. Their fragrance wafted through my nose and into my mind, a combination of scents that felt like heaven. When I reopened my eyes, I focused immediately on Suelo, who was watching me with an air of conviction.

I smiled at those confident, lime-green eyes. "This is a beautiful gift. Thank you," I told him.

He nodded once at me, his gaze falling to our surroundings. I followed their path, taking in the cellar around us. The wooden floors, the furniture and rug – a part of me deflated. This was not a sanctuary for birds. It was created with human purposes in mind. But the ones who lived here, who spent a great deal of their lives here, were our Phoenixes. It should have been designed for them.

Decidedly, I stood from the sofa, my eyes scanning the human features about the room. Then, without really processing my thoughts, I began pushing the couch towards the bookshelf, in the corner. Then I moved the armchairs and the coffee table, and covered them with the rug. When it was all out of my way, I turned to the rest of the cellar – a blank canvas.

I swallowed, extending my hands facing upwards in front of me. I gripped my powers, and felt the world around me, latching on to the soil beneath the wooden flooring. Then, with all the power I could muster, I forced it upwards.

The wood cracked and crumpled as the earth beneath it rose. The other Phoenixes bustled out of the way, towards me, as the soil overtook the processed wood. When the ground resembled the forest floor, I turned my attention to the walls. I pressed my powers to the air with one hand, letting flora grow slowly from the ceiling and walls. With the other, I began raising trees and ferns and other foliage, running my magic over the space and sprouting a forest along with it.

I grabbed hold of the water trough with my powers, twisting and molding until the metal fell to the floor and melted into stones, within which a pond set itself in the soil. I grew lotus flowers and lily pads amongst the sparkling water, and began placing fallen leaves and other flora in scattered patterns across the woodland I created. In some of the trees, I placed various fruits, and in a few of the bushes, I expressed berries. I lined one corner of the room with a vegetable garden, filled with leafy greens and tubers and roots. An indoor, self-sufficient jungle – a place fit for a family of myth-ical creatures.

When the surroundings were perfected, I turned my attention to the furniture. I latched on to them with my magic, breaking their craftsmanship, building them into forest occupants. The shelves on the bookshelf became uneven and slanted as the wood reformed into its raw, logged state. The armchairs became toadstools, the sofa morphing into a giant log bench padded with soft, lush greenery. The tables and chairs became more gnarled as the wood was encouraged to look as though it were fresh from the tree, and I wrapped them in green moss for comfort. Every single lamp on the wall became a glowing, luminescent mushroom. With one, final breath, I masterfully crafted the rug into a bed of woven wild-flowers, arranged the new woodland furniture to my liking, and at last, the work was complete.

As I stared at my handiwork, stabilizing myself after all the power I'd expended, the Phoenixes slowly began wandering into their new home. Aurora picked a mango off one of the trees. Fuego peered at his reflection in the pond. Lumina began scratching her head on a log, and Suelo sat amongst the bed of flowers, gazing at their petals as they glistened underneath the skylight. I grew gratified with myself and my surroundings, empty of the anger I'd manifested into productivity. Everything felt more natural, more unpolluted.

The sound of footsteps echoed into the space, and I turned to see Felix appear from the wooden staircase I'd left untouched. "Seraphine? Are you – "

His eyes widened as he realized the space he'd entered. "My word," he breathed, his eyes following the foliage across the ceiling, tracing the shape of the trees. When they eventually landed on me, standing in the corner with the forest furniture, it seemed he could only blink in shock. "You've done some redecorating."

I couldn't tell if it was good surprise or bad surprise, so I just gave him a small smile. "Sorry. I probably should have asked you first. I just got a little too invested in my new powers." I looked around. "It didn't seem like a place for birds before. But I think it does now."

His eyes began wandering again around the jungle surrounding us. "No apology needed," he said in a bit of a trance. "This is the most magnificent thing I've ever seen."

His feet carried him to the pond, beside where Fuego stood. He shook his head in a bit of disbelief. "Wow," he whispered. "Just...wow. This is incredible." He looked at me. "Those are some wonderful powers."

My smile widened, my heart glowing. "Show me your hand," I told him as I approached.

He outstretched it towards me, and I took it in mine, studying the gash down the middle of his palm. With a gentle finger's touch, as light as a single feather, I ran down the length of the wound and shut my eyes. I brought forward the powers within me, the wish for curing, the determination to soothe. And as my eyes fluttered open and I ran my finger back up the cut, I found healed skin replacing my touch. The special gift of an Earth Phoenix.

When the superficiality of the wound had dissipated, I clasped my other hand over the top of it gently, kneading tenderly into his palm. I felt the sensation of the skin, deducing that it had truly healed both on the surface and deep beneath. It was as if it were never there. I removed my top hand and gazed down again at his as I held it steadily in my other, my eyes darting over its features. Larger than mine, but a touch softer than my own skin, a touch I knew well. The same hand I trusted with my body, my face, my breasts – the same fingers that had felt the most vulnerable parts of me. The hand of a man with a magic touch, healed by magic of my own.

I realized I was spending far too long staring at his hand and snapped myself out of my own thoughts, glancing up at him. He was watching me curiously, and he faltered a bit when I finally released my grip.

"The Earth heals," I noted quietly, watching as he brought his hand closer to his face. He shook his head with a bit of bewilderment as he admired the work I'd done.

"Indeed," he murmured, eventually lowering his hand back to his side and meeting my gaze. Those lavender eyes were alive with wonder.

I swallowed. "I felt your pain," I said to him. "When I was walking down the stairs – I felt it when you cut yourself."

His eyes twinkled, but he didn't reply to this.

My eyebrows met slightly. "Why could I feel your pain?" I pushed. "Because of my new powers?"

I felt his eyes scan my face, as if they could plant a field of lavender flowers within my skin. Something about his eyes was secretive. He cleared his throat quietly, before his eyebrows raised minimally. "Perhaps," was all he said. "I'm not entirely sure. But that makes sense."

I took a deep breath and glanced around. "I was too harsh on your brother."

I could see Felix shrugging out of my peripheral. "You didn't say anything untruthful."

"But my delivery was spiteful," I went on, bringing my eyes back to him. "I shouldn't have said anything about it. I didn't know that *he* didn't know."

"How did you even find out?"

"Your father told me."

Felix considered this. "I personally don't understand why they never told him," he mused. "So many tabloids spread the rumour, but they continuously denied it to him. They would always tell us the tabloids were not the truth – which, in most cases, they aren't. But in this case…he was bound to find out eventually."

I shook my head slowly. "I wish it hadn't been me. Or in that circumstance."

Felix put a comforting hand on my shoulder. "He'll get over it. Don't worry. If you're particularly bothered, you can apologize when you see him next."

"I should apologize now."

He shook his head. "I didn't deny the information before I left him with his own thoughts. He'll need some time to sort through that." He paused. "And to cool down a bit."

I sighed, but simply nodded and looked towards the Phoenixes among the forest. "We should probably get a move on," he then proposed. "Make the most of the rest of the weekend. Let's grab our things from the house." He studied Lumina and Suelo, who were both munching on some berries. "Should we bring them along?"

I thought for a moment. "We won't be able to use their powers if we don't take them," I finally responded.

He nodded slowly. "Right. That's settled, then."

And so it was. When we had changed and grabbed everything we would need, we returned to the cellar, where we all took off into the early afternoon sky.

CHAPTER 22

THE COOL OCEAN breeze blew a refreshing mist gently over our faces as we soared underneath the sun. We flew for several hours until the Big Island came into view. Felix and Fuego flew in front of me as Felix yelled back, "I'll lead the way!"

Lumina, Suelo, Aurora, and I followed him as we banked towards the left side of the island. As we neared the ground, I glimpsed a large estate spread out along the coastline. We approached the highly secluded property, built to overlook the ocean from atop a slightly raised slope. Its obvious extravagance, even from the air, was nothing short of what I would expect from a Clarkson vacation home. A massive, aqua-blue pool accented with natural rocks and a tennis court caught my eye, and if you followed a beautiful pathway through palm trees and bushes of flowers, you eventually made your way down to the white-sand beach and the beckoning ocean.

Felix led us down, and we landed in the middle of the thriving gardens. The bushes and trees provided a beautiful mix of vegetation, and the Phoenixes nestled in comfortably amongst the private greenery.

Felix turned to me. "Let's head in."

We walked along a stone pathway, past where the pool and

a gorgeous water feature were, towards the home. It was massive, and on either side of the steps to the back porch were huge yellow hibiscus plants.

We approached the back French doors of the house. There was a keypad built into the right handle. Felix grabbed hold of it and then stopped.

"Shit," he muttered.

I frowned at him. "What?"

He looked at me with a sheepish expression. "The password," he said.

I raised my eyebrows. "You don't remember?"

"No."

"Well, you're looking at the wrong person."

He thought for a moment, then pulled out his phone and dialed a number before putting it on speaker.

"Erm…umph…hello?" came Luther's gruff, muffled voice.

"Father, hi. It's me. What's the passcode for our vacation home in Hawaii?" Felix asked.

"Felix, I'm in the middle of my workday," Luther groaned in agitation.

"Yes, and I'm the pride and joy that is your second-born son."

"Not in the middle of my workday."

"It's Saturday, Father. Can't you just embrace the weekend like the rest of us?"

"Son, there's no such thing as a weekend in this line of work." A pause. "Now just a minute. Why the hell are you at the vacation house in Hawaii?"

"We think one of the Phoenix sanctuaries is in Mauna Loa we told you about it over supper a week ago, remember?"

"My boy, I can hardly remember what I ate for breakfast this morning." I heard him chuckle a bit, which made Felix roll his eyes and me bite my humoured lip. "So Seraphine's there with you?"

"*Oui*, hello, sir," I chimed in. "Sorry to bother you."

"Oh, nonsense, dear. Have you been to Hawaii before?"

"No," I replied. "First time."

"Ah! Wonderful. Well, I hope you enjoy staying at the vacation home. It's one of my favourite places to be, if you ask me."

"Thank you, sir. A passcode so that we could go inside would be helpful, though."

"Right, right, just a moment…erm…" Another pause. "Felix, is it not March third?"

Felix stared at the phone. "I beg your pardon?"

"That's your birthday."

Felix gave me a look of disbelief. I stifled a laugh.

"Father, I *know* when my *birthday* is."

"Ah, well, I'm glad to hear that. It is your birthday after all." He chuckled again. "Would be rather troublesome if you forgot that."

"Father, the passcode. *Please.*"

"I just gave it to you, son."

Felix frowned. "Is the passcode my birthday?"

"Zero-three-zero-three…that's what I thought it was."

Felix inputted the numbers, and then pressed an 'enter' key. The keypad gave off a red light.

"No, that didn't work," Felix reported back.

"Oh. Hmph. That's concerning." Luther made a few humming sounds. "Oh, I was wrong. No, it's not that. That's the password for my safe."

Felix widened his eyes, as did I. "Uh, Father, did you forget that Seraphine's listening to this conversation?" he said slowly, meeting my gaze.

"Oh!" Luther exclaimed. "Seraphine, dear, erm, just pretend you didn't hear that."

"I'll have forgotten it by the time we get back," I admitted.

"Ah, like me. Memory of a goldfish?"

"More like overcrammed storage."

"Father." Felix clenched his teeth. "Pass. Code. Please."

248

"Yes, yes, all right, I'm thinking! I've got a lot of passcodes, you know!" Luther exclaimed. "Erm…try four-three-two-one."

Felix snorted. "Creative." He attempted the combination and received another red light. "That didn't work."

"Uh, how about one-two-three-four?"

"Father, I don't need your help taking shots in the dark."

"Just try it, you cantankerous boy!"

Mumbling, Felix tried the combo. Red light.

"Nope. Got any other innovative combos, old man? Perhaps one-one-one-one?"

I heard Luther groan in annoyance over the phone. "Okay, I think this must be it – two-zero-one-two."

Felix pressed the numbers on the keypad. It lit up with a green light, and there was a click.

"That worked!" I told Luther.

"Ah, excellent. Stay safe, you two. It's back to work for me." And he hung up.

Felix put his phone away and then opened the door into the home's massive living space. It had an open floor plan, with a spacious kitchen at one end, a dining area at the other, and several seating places in the middle. The high, vaulted ceilings and the floor-to-ceiling windows gave the space an airy feel, and much of the light wood was uncovered by furniture, leaving plenty of space to breathe. The colours of everything in the home were all light – whites, creams, beiges. At the right end of the room was a hall that led to four bedrooms and their attached bathrooms. On the left, there was a room that had been turned into a study and another that contained a pool table. While still luxurious, the space had a much different aura than that of Felix's villa, Luther's mansion, or Julius' calamity – it was more soothing and tranquil. It also appeared like much of the space opened up into the gardens, allowing for the easy merging between indoor and outdoor during the warm days. Though our flight had been a few hours, a wall clock above the kitchen showed we'd gone back in time, putting us at around one o'clock in the afternoon.

"We've got some time to kill until dark," Felix said, and I turned to see he'd followed my gaze to the clock. "Don't want to run into any hikers on the volcano." He looked at me. "You hungry?"

I nodded. "A little."

"Pizza sound good?"

"Pizza sounds great."

He went into another room to make the call while I decided to head out to the gardens. I found a patch of grass underneath a large palm tree that overlooked the ocean ahead, and sat myself down comfortably. The breeze that brushed across my skin and through my hair was heavenly.

A little while after I'd sat down, Felix approached and sat down beside me, a piping hot box of cheese pizza in hand. He placed it between us and opened it. "Dig in," he said.

We ate the pizza quietly, the view before us more than enough to absorb as I chewed slowly and methodically. As I watched the waves come again and again to the shore, I became aware of a peculiar, melancholic air washing over me, an emotion so real I thought it was tangible. It flickered and faded within me, that strange rope wrapping itself around my spine as the gloom dripped down its woven strands like tears. I slowed my chewing to a near halt, trying to process why I'd suddenly been overcome with such a sorrowful feeling.

Then, I realized it wasn't me.

I turned to look at Felix. "What's wrong?"

He met my gaze, first with confusion, but then with a simple blandness. "Nothing," he tried, but his voice was so forlorn that I think even he knew I wasn't convinced.

I studied him. Like violet drapes being drawn and reopened, his irises dimmed and brightened with an uncertainty and tentativeness I found melancholy. There was a desire in there to get out, to be free of those walls that had been so

250

harshly built and so mercilessly concealed in all its lavender glory. And after putting up a fight, I saw something break in him. The curtains were drawn. The music faded to silence. The lights dimmed. The act was over.

I could hear him inhale deeply and let the air travel throughout his entire body before he turned to look at the home. "This place holds a lot of memories," he said softly. "Being here…it makes me think of a lot." He paused. "It makes me think of my mother." He paused again. "I miss my mother."

He frowned to himself. "It bothers me that I even miss her, because she clearly doesn't miss me. But I'd be lying if I told you I never wanted to see her again. She left so long ago; she didn't see so much of me, or my accomplishments, or anything I did. There was so much I wanted to show her – there still is. Every milestone grew more and more agonising as time went on. Learning to ride a bike, elementary school recitals, getting my driver's license, graduating high school, and her not being there to see any of it…the pain of it is unbearable. The fact that it's her choice. The fact that she never even made an effort."

He shook his head. "I'm disgusted with her killing Ohên. I'm mortified that she never even tried to apologize. And that was partially my father intimidating her so much that she left. But she was still in the wrong. She almost killed my Phoenix. She almost took away something that mattered so much to me. And when she couldn't take him away, she tore herself away from me instead."

He sighed loudly. "For a while there, I couldn't even believe she'd left for good. I thought, 'Oh, she'll be home soon. She has to be home for Christmas.' But Christmas came, and she still wasn't home. And then New Year's came, and then my birthday…and you know, nothing really struck me about her disappearance until I realized the very person who brought me into the world wasn't there to celebrate the anniversary of the event. Whatever hope I had of her coming back vanished then. I knew that if I wanted to see her again, I would have to be the one to go and find her. But I didn't even know where to start. I still don't. So I never really tried. And all of these years later, I haven't gotten any closer to seeing her than I did on my sixth birthday."

He cleared his throat. "I'm sad about it," he went on. "And I'm confused about it. And I'm cross about it. But worst of all, I can't get past it."

His lavender eyes met mine; they were injured, war-torn. "I trusted her. And then she left. And she took all of that trust away with her. I thought it would get better with age. I thought I would get over it somehow. But as much as I'm emotional, I am also logical. And logically, I think, 'Well, if I can't trust my own mother, how can I trust anyone else?' And I've gotten so caught up in this that it's hard for me to escape it."

He turned away. "I've destroyed myself. I'm lonely, and reclusive, and hard to understand. I've got so many unusual things going on in my head that it scares me. And I've had to hide it all from everyone so that nobody will ever care enough to figure any of it out. You remember how I treated you when we first met. I act in ways that make people hate me. But I am hurting so badly deep down inside, and truly, I believe I am the world's most overrated person. I don't care for my wealth. I don't care for my name. I don't think I'm anything special. I am the world's weakest man, and that is the truth, for I have caved to my problems for the longest time. I've never taken the time to truly heal. All I do is band-aid my issues. And I have run away from anything that had the potential to hurt me more, because I'm terrified to know what will happen if I get hurt like this again."

His breath wavered. "I live a life of cowardly fear," he muttered. "And it isn't the life I wanted to live. But I have no choice. It keeps me up at night – very rarely do I get the blessing of a perfectly restful sleep. I have nightmares about it.

Some nights it makes me panic. Others, it makes me cry. And sometimes, I lay awake the whole night, blinking at the ceiling until morning. I have no doubts my fragility will lead to my own demise. Water doesn't crack, but ice sure does."

All I could do was watch. I watched the beautiful man before me reduce himself to nothing; the sorrows he carried burst from him like the eruption that destroyed the town of Pompeii. I watched the agony I felt encasing my own heart, burying my sense of self in a desperate need to make things better for the soul that touched mine. He'd entrusted a story to me, a story he didn't normally share, a story that broke him down and weathered him away, that he was afraid would give others power over him. But perhaps he was so desperate to feel any sort of trust again that he simply couldn't be the only one to hold the pain any longer. And here I was, having made it my own, having had it drown me in an anguish that felt like it had come from within me.

I swallowed. "I feel it," I whispered.

His eyes were misted and distant, like he'd lost himself in his mind somewhere. It seemed like he had something he needed to say, but couldn't find the right words. So instead, he said nothing.

I clutched at my own chest. "The pain. When you cut yourself this morning, I felt it on my own hand. And now, I feel how sad you are." Tears welled in my eyes as I patted my chest harshly. "In here – in my heart. It's so overwhelming. I don't really know how to explain it well, but it feels like there's this… chain, or rope, or *something* wrapping around my heart, constricting me." The tears fell as a surge of desolate emotion buried me six feet underneath myself. "Felix, I'm so sorry."

His eyes widened as he watched me crack underneath the weight of his agony, and I had to look away from him to try and get a grip on myself. It wasn't helpful to confide in someone and have them break down at the information you shared. But it was so overwhelming that I was rendered defenseless. Whatever powers I'd acquired from having two Phoenixes were stronger than I was.

I felt his hand on my shoulder. "I'm sorry, too, Seraphine," he said solemnly, his voice cracking when he said my name. But it was not enough to stop my heaving sobs as they escaped me.

I didn't see much of what happened next; my vision became blurred with relentless waves of tears as they billowed beneath my eyelids and rushed down my cheeks.

But I felt the next few moments.

I felt him lift me with ease, cradling me in his lap as if I were a small, helpless child. I felt him hold me close, wrapping his arms around me and pulling me in towards him as if he intended to pull me through his own skin. I felt the gentle caress of his fingers as they traced the paths all my tears left behind, then the soft stroking of his hands through my curls.

I felt him try to soak all the sorrow – *his* sorrow – back into him. And it worked, curiously; slowly, my wailing softened, and my torrent of tears became mere trickles. But I didn't dare try to leave his grasp. The comfort of his embrace was a prison I would commit the most heinous crimes for if it meant I could rot there for eternity.

An overwhelming wave of exhaustion crept into the crevices left by the wake of the dissipating sadness. Like a snake, it slithered menacingly up my spine, filling my bones with fatigue and forcing my eyes, still sopping wet, to close. The sea of weariness drowned me mercilessly as Felix held me in his arms.

- F -

A part of me couldn't bear to part with her, but I knew she needed the propriety that came with pillows and a mattress. I carried her as if she were the finest silk spun in all the years of the craft, draping her as delicately as lace on one of the beds in the vacation home.

She did not stir as I gently lifted the duvet over her angelic body. I admired her for a moment; the softness in her warm cheeks glistened with the remnants of her tears, like morning dew on the petals of a desert rose.

Guilt swirled within me as her cries replayed in my mind. The sight and sound of her sobbing destroyed me; I never wanted to see her like that again. It raised some fiend within me, a fiend gone so mad with a hunger for vengeance that it would claw through seven layers of hell to kill the devil who made her feel that way.

The remorse twisted and turned with the bile in my stomach.

It was *me.*

I was the devil who had ruined her.

I shut my eyes and looked away, the sight of her resting after the grief I'd caused now despairing me.

My burdens broke her. Just as they had broken me.

Clenching my fists, I hurried out of the room as silently as I could. By the time I had reached the gardens, my breaths were coming in heaves. My hands shook. My chest was tight.

This was *my* fault.

I let out a series of enraged, disgruntled sounds as I fell to my hands and knees in the grass, gripping the strands of greenery between my whitened knuckles as I cursed myself, over and over.

I was *breaking* her.

I slammed a fist into the ground, then again, then once more. The curses flowed smoothly from my lips in rage, unending and pitiless.

"Felix – enough."

It was Fuego's voice that slashed through my mind. Though I was still seeing red, I turned to see where he and the other Phoenixes were nestled in between the fauna. They all watched me curiously, but the look in Fuego's familiar, ruby eyes…it was intent.

"*Get a grip.*"

It took a moment for me to fully process the command. I lifted myself on to my knees and threw my head back, swallowing harshly as I shut my eyes. I forced myself to breathe with intention, to bring the furious gasps back into calm, rhythmic normalcy.

"*You need to be strong. For her.*"

The words dazzled my mind like fireflies. I opened my eyes, taking in the cerulean blue sky above me. The soft wisps of white clouds looked like haphazard brushstrokes against the endless sea of blue. My gaze lowered to the ocean in the distance, the endless serenity of the water lapping against the shore. Such tranquility before me…

I took a deep breath in as I tried to absorb it – for her. The thoughts of bringing her peace, calmness…

I swallowed again. "*Thank you.*"

But Fuego's words still held weight when they bounded into my head. "*You need to take better care of yourself. I'm worried about you. She's worried about you.*"

I cleared my throat. "*I know.*"

And though true, it only scratched the surface of how crucial it was that I got things under control. The truth extended far deeper than that, far deeper than even the ocean before me. It was imperative that I stopped running from my problems and faced them, especially given that the impact of my actions landed well beyond me.

I glanced at the Phoenixes, all their gazes still fixed on me.

I needed to do it for them.

My eyes fell to the ground directly beneath me, my head hanging between my shoulders.

I needed to do it for *her*.

CHAPTER 23

- S -

I AWOKE with an eerie sense of calm and composure.

I sat up groggily, rubbing my eyes as I looked around. The bedroom was blithe; the mint green colour of the room's fabrics was a pleasing, almost soothing colour. Outside the window, I could see the sun was beginning to set in what was undoubtedly going to be a stunning array of sunset colours across the Hawaiian sky.

I blinked at the sight out the window, recalling the last moments filled with sobs and sadness prior to me drifting away. I stood slowly, adjusting my clothing as I walked into the adjacent ensuite, bursting with pops of the same mint green colour. My eyes were red and puffy from the remnants of my crying. I sighed as I washed my face with cold water several times; the swelling under my eyes decreased, but the redness didn't disappear much.

When I emerged from the bedroom, I could see movement through the windows out of the main seating area. It was Felix on the other side of the pool with a camera pointed out towards the ocean.

I stepped out into the gardens. "Hey," I said as I approached.

He turned and gave me a small smile. "Hey," he said back. "Feeling better?"

"*Oui.* Sorry. I...don't know what overcame me."

"Don't apologize. There's no need."

I nodded at the camera. "Is that the new one you were telling me about?"

He nodded. "Thought it would be a good idea to get some photo therapy in," he noted with a hint of humour.

I smiled at this, extending a hand. "Can I see?"

He came to my side and showed me the camera's saved photos. He'd managed to capture some magnificent photos of the setting sun over the horizon, the movement of the waves both stilled yet somehow animated in the frozen stamps of time.

"They're gorgeous," I mentioned.

He seemed delighted that I liked them. "Thank you," he said, motioning out towards the water. "I mean, it's hard for a photo to turn out poorly when the subject is so lovely." Felix glanced at me, and I met his eyes as they glistened. Then, without warning, he raised the camera and took a picture of me. Proudly, he then turned the camera around and showed it to me. "See what I mean?" he said, his voice amorous.

I let out an amused breath as I beheld the red eyes and sleepy face. "I wouldn't consider that the most flattering photo of me, if I'm honest."

"I don't think any photo of you can be unflattering," he retorted.

I narrowed my eyes at him, the corners of my mouth pulling. "Is that why you stare at me so much?" I questioned. "Am I just that beautiful?"

As if they were being tugged with strings, his lips curled upwards. "It's an admirable thing for one to be so self-aware in such an age of uncertainty," he replied quietly.

My eyes locked on his. A wild thought crossed my mind, and I could see it echo in the way the embers in those lavender eyes flickered back at me. But nightfall was nearing, and so was our window of opportunity to fly to Mauna Loa.

"We should get going," I said next.

He cleared his throat. "Yes. I suppose we should." I could hear the faintest twinge of disappointment in his voice.

I gave him a smirk. "A little let down, are we?"

"Was it that obvious?"

I rolled my eyes. "There are certain explorations we can make in broad daylight. But ascending a popular hiking destination with four mythical birds is not one of them."

He raised an intrigued eyebrow as a grin flashed across his lips. "Oh, do humour me with some of those appropriate explorations when we're back, hm?"

"Appropriate isn't the word I'd use," I noted slyly, "but you have yourself a deal."

———

When we had gathered our things, we returned outside to where the Phoenixes were lounging in the gardens. The sun had conveniently gone to sleep, and night brushed the skies of Hawaii.

"All right, everyone," I called to our flock. "Off we go."

I mounted Aurora before turning to Felix. After he'd clambered onto Fuego's back, we wasted no time taking off into the newly darkened sky, trailed by Lumina and Suelo.

From where we were on the island, it only took us about fifteen minutes before we were flying over Mauna Loa. The huge, rocky crater was hard to miss, even as it blended in with the night. At the base of the mountain, the ocean waves rushed up against the rocks harshly.

Felix and I directed our Phoenixes to land at the edge of the summit. To my surprise, there was no hole in sight anywhere on the crater volcano. It was flattened, filled with ashy volcanic rock that we could walk over.

I frowned. "I don't get it," I said.

Felix studied the sight before us. "Me, neither," he said. "I thought volcanoes – "

"Were open at the top," I finished for him.

"Huh." He paused. "It must be only when they're erupting," he then concluded. "The lava that spews out must melt the rock that sits on top. Or force its way through. Whichever happens first."

"Hmph," I replied. I hopped over the edge of the crater and onto the black volcanic rock. It was evident that it had hardened stiffly since the last eruption. Felix followed me, and so did the Phoenixes. We walked towards the center and then stopped.

I glanced around for a moment, then turned to him. "All right. Got any ideas?" I asked.

He thought for a second, then walked a little ways away from me, creating a ball of fire in his hand. He knelt down and held it to the crater for several minutes before making it disappear. He then took his foot and pressed on where he'd heated the rock. His shoe sank down into what was now a much more malleable surface.

He looked up at me. "Get back a bit."

I obeyed. When I was far enough away, he created a much larger ball of fire, raised it in the sky, and then harshly smashed it against the volcanic rock. A large dent formed as a result, and so he created another one, and then another, smashing it repeatedly against the rock and deepening the impact time and time again.

At last, Felix released a ball of fire that broke through what remained of the layer of rock. Peering through the deep hole he'd made, it was evident that we now had a pitch-black pathway down the main vent of the volcano.

He looked up at me. I nodded, turning to Lumina and

Suelo. "Wait here," I told them. They sat down at the edge of the crater, Suelo giving me a single nod in return.

We hopped atop Fuego and Aurora, and I led the way down, lighting the vertical tunnel as we dove into Mauna Loa. As we flew further and further into the vent, the air around us became warmer and warmer. Eventually, a glowing mass of reddish-yellow appeared in the distance.

"That must be the magma chamber," Felix called from behind me. "We're getting to the base of the volcano."

As we neared the magma, I could feel the heat on my skin rise. Sweat dripped from my hairline down the rest of my face, and my blood pulsated beneath my skin. The tunnel widened into a bit of an expanse, forming the shape of the volcano's base and giving us more space to spread out. Beneath us, in the midst of the magma chamber, was a rock formation that jutted out from the lava. On it, I could see a pedestal topped with a sparkling, orange egg.

"There!" I exclaimed. I had Aurora dive towards the formation. Felix and Fuego followed suit.

The magma moved slowly around the rock formation, the heat radiating around us intensely. I looked at Felix and motioned to the egg.

"Well, go ahead," I told him.

He shook his head. "I already have a Fire Phoenix. You go ahead."

"But I hatched the last one," I told him. "It's your turn."

Felix sighed, then pulled out a coin. "Heads it's mine, tails it's yours."

I held back a humoured smile. "All right."

He tossed the coin up into the air, let it fall to the rock, and then stepped on it. Removing his foot revealed that it was tails.

He raised his eyebrows at me. "There. Now go."

I smiled, reaching out and placing my hand on the citrine egg's soft surface. Orange light erupted from its cracking shells, and out popped a baby Phoenix with the same-coloured feathers.

It handed me its pendant, which I pried open. "Ignacia," I said, picking up my new beloved baby girl and cradling her in my arms. Ignacia let out a happy little squeak as I looped the new pendant around my neck. Even though she was the third Phoenix I'd hatched, a fluttering excitement bounced around my chest. Nothing would ever make the incredible experience any less magnificent for me.

Felix rubbed her soft, little head. "She's beautiful."

She indeed was. It was as if the tips of her feathers were dipped in fire, the way the tangerine colour blended with the deeper, more robust orange reminiscent of pumpkins along her main body. Her eyes were indescribably bright sunstones, even in the dark of the magma chamber.

I nodded towards the broken eggshells. "Check for the next riddle."

He did as he was told, brushing the remnants aside and revealing an inscription on the pedestal:

> *"Burn warmly and searing through flight*
> *as my darkness now appears in sight.*
> *Speak with the moon goddess near Thalamae*
> *and she will guide you to where the night lays."*

Felix took a picture of it with his phone, and suddenly, there was a low rumbling sound that shook the loose stones on the formation we stood on.

We glanced around us before our eyes returned to each other. "What was that?" I said.

"I don't really want to find out," Felix replied. "Let's get out of here. Lead the way."

I grasped Ignacia tightly in my hands as I turned towards Aurora. But as I did, the rumble came again, louder this time, and suddenly, the rock formation was riven by spurting lava.

I gasped, stumbling backwards as the piece of rock we were standing on split into several pieces. I could hear Fuego and Aurora shrieking, and could feel Ignacia's panic in my arms. The lava rose and fell like fountains in the magma chamber, blocking my view of Felix and the Phoenixes.

"Felix!" I cried among the roars that echoed off the rocky walls.

"Seraphine, you need to jump!" I heard him bellow. "You need to jump to me!"

My heart leapt into my throat, down to my stomach, and back up again. "Jump?" I exclaimed. "Felix, there's lava everywhere!"

"You won't burn!" he yelled, and one of the fountains of lava paused just briefly enough that I could see him. He was standing on the other piece of rock, a distance away. I could make the jump – provided the magma burst stayed down long enough for me to land on the other side. But it was broiling unpredictably; a mere second passed before it surged in front of me again.

"Felix, she just hatched!" I screamed. "I won't have her ability to withstand fire – "

"Just listen to me!" Felix begged. "It's too narrow for Fuego to fly to you, and the overhang of rock above you will crumble and kill you if you don't!"

My gaze shot upwards. I hadn't even realized where the rock had drifted – Felix was right. The rumbling was splitting the curve of the magma chamber above me, the cracks forming large pieces of a certain written death if I didn't move. But to not burn in the lava – how? There was no way.

Tears welled in my eyes as my panic and anxiety swallowed me whole. There was bursting lava and tightening chambers, and seemingly no reasonable options.

"Seraphine, trust me!" I heard Felix yell.

And seeing as I had no other choice, I did.

As soon as the magma fountain in front of me lowered, I leapt towards Felix. But the moment my feet left the rock, the lava rose again, engulfing my legs in the oozing, molten liquid as I moved overhead.

And where I expected excruciating pain and an awful series of fatal burns, there was none.

I landed on the rock beside Felix, dumbfounded. My skin remained unphased, unscarred, though my pants and the bottom half of my shirt were singed into ash. I didn't have time to contemplate or ask questions. Felix nearly threw me onto Aurora's back, and with Ignacia still tightly held to my chest, we began hurtling upwards towards the exit of the crater.

As we burst out of the volcano, I felt a rush of considerably cooler air and tumbled harshly onto the ground with a loud, thumping sound. I turned to see we'd flown well out of the way of the lava that was spewing out of the hole behind us. Aurora had gotten us to the first safe bit of rock she could find.

I gasped several times, still clutching Ignacia, shakily trying to right myself but not making much progress.

I suddenly found a hand on my shoulder, and I turned and met Felix's gaze.

"Hey, we're okay. Take it easy," he assured me.

I clutched my chest, forcing myself to hold my breath before releasing. When I gained control of one breath, I then gained control of another. The escaping lava eventually weaned and subsided; relief flew through me at the recognition that we hadn't set off a full eruption. I didn't really understand why – maybe we hadn't released enough pressure, or maybe there was some magic at play. I wasn't about to start pushing my luck with too many questions, though, so I just accepted it for what it was.

A flurry of movements produced the shirt off Felix's back

in a crumpled ball, outstretched towards me. And when I was sure I wouldn't send myself into a tizzy, I grabbed hold of it and threw it over my head.

His hand remained offered to me – an invitation to help me up. I looked at it for a moment and then pushed it away with a force driven by irritation.

His confusion was palpable as I stood on my own, glaring at him. "What haven't you told me?" I growled at him through barely parted lips.

He frowned deeply. "What are you – "

His shirt blew in the breeze like a dress on me, the various shreds of my burnt clothes clinging to my suspiciously unburnt skin underneath. "You've been hiding something," I snarled, pointing a finger at him. "In Colombia, I told you my powers had grown overnight, and you told me it was because I was nearing my full bond with Aurora. But here we are, still not fully bonded, and yet my powers are bursting within me – especially, might I add, when I'm around *you.*"

I ground my teeth together, the very powers I spoke of surging within me with blistering ire. "I asked if you knew why it bothered us to be apart from each other, and you told me you didn't know – *supposedly.* I asked about how I could feel your pain when you sliced your hand, and you told me it was *possibly* because of the other Phoenixes I acquired – not a straight answer. And then, your sadness – your emotions…they became mine on the beach so overwhelmingly that I broke down before you under no weight of my own."

His eyes were frenzied.

"Now, here I stand, with clothes burnt to a crisp, yet my body unscathed. I don't have a fully grown Fire Phoenix. This should be impossible." I lowered my eyes at him, my anger bubbling like the magma chamber beneath us had. "And you *knew* I wouldn't burn. You've known something I don't, for a while now. And I want to know what that is."

He swallowed, glancing at Fuego, at the other Phoenixes,

and then back at me. He opened his mouth to respond, but all that came out was a series of stammers before he shut it again, looking down at the ground.

I took a step towards him. "I'm not fucking around, Felix," I scowled. "I need to be able to trust you, and that's hard to do if you're keeping secrets. I want to know what the hell is going on."

Felix didn't bring his gaze up to meet mine. Whether it was fear, or shame, or a combination of both, I couldn't tell. All I knew was that the crater beneath us was the only thing he could face.

"Felix," I said with annoyance again, taking one more step towards him. "I'm going to ask you one last time. Why haven't I burned?"

Slowly, he lifted his eyes to mine. In them, there swirled remorse, and bleakness, and distress, and apprehension. Those lavender eyes were storms of a violent kind.

"You haven't burned," he said slowly, "because we're bonded."

I lifted my chin, my eyes darting over his face with an offended disbelief I could feel deep in my soul. "Bonded?" I repeated with dissatisfied astonishment.

He cleared his throat. "Yes. We have bonded. And when two Phoenix Keepers bond, several things happen," he went on. "They can use each other's powers and special abilities. They become more closely connected to one another, beyond a realm of mortal understanding, making them able to tap into an awareness of their feelings and pain. And they strengthen these capabilities as they strengthen their bond over time. The Keepers become more tightly entangled in each other's souls, stronger in their mindfulness of each other, and more powerful than the unbound."

I stared at him, my mind racing. The tether I'd felt all this time, drawing me to him...

"And how, exactly, did we bond?"

His eyes were panicked, his stature threatened. He couldn't bring himself to say it. But from the look on his face, I was able to piece it together myself. And I was far from pleased.

"You didn't think," I rumbled, my hands shaking slightly, "to warn me that we would bond before we had sex?"

His face dropped with mortification. "Seraphine, I didn't know that – "

"That what? That I might have sex with you? Or that I would be pissed we would be bonded? Or both? Or something entirely fucking different?"

"What I'm trying to say is – "

"What, Felix? What exactly are you trying to fucking say?" I snapped, my eyes alight with fury. "Did you know I would react this way, and that's why you kept it a secret? Hm? Were you hoping you were going to just get away with me never finding out?"

"I was going to tell you – "

"Well, apparently not soon enough!" I screamed, motioning at myself angrily. "Not before I had to fucking figure it out myself!"

He shook his head slowly, his hands raised in a pleading motion. "Seraphine, please – "

"You're begging me? For what?" I spat. "Haven't you already gotten what you wanted? Your balls are empty, and your powers are strong. What more do you fucking want?" My entire body was shaking. "You got in my pants knowing what it would lead to, knowing full well that I had no awareness of it because you never taught me. Was that intentional? So you could bond to me without my knowledge or consent?"

He gave up trying to speak. Deflated and desolate, he lowered his hands and gaze to the ground, sinking so far within himself it was as if the ground beneath him had gobbled him whole.

My mind was searing, my teeth clenched. "How long are we bonded for?"

He didn't reply right away. "For life," he then said.

"For *life?*" I repeated, stepping back in incredulity.

He nodded once without looking at me, his next words rapt with a regretful dismay. "If one of the Keepers dies, the bond is severed. If one of the Keepers loses their Phoenix, the bond is also severed. And if one of the Keepers bonds to another Keeper, the first bond is severed to form the new bond. Barring those three scenarios, Keepers are bound for the duration of their lives. In our world, it is viewed as a sort of marriage."

Marriage. *Marriage.*

I stepped back from him, shaking my head as my brain churned and thrashed and reeled.

Bonded for life to Felix Clarkson, married to him through some charmed magic bond, and I hadn't even had a say in the matter. I hadn't even known. I hadn't gotten a choice.

Furious, I dug deep within myself. I didn't have to dig very far before I found it – the inferno resting within me. The warmth he'd given me. The fire I didn't ask for.

Livid was an understatement – I felt disrespected, betrayed, used, taken for a fool. Had he planned this all along to strengthen his own powers? What else was he hiding from me? How could I ever trust him again?

I erupted with such wrath that flames burst from my fingertips as I shrieked curses into the night sky. Then I turned and made for Aurora, stepping harshly onto her back and rushing her into the air without so much as a glance back.

PART THREE
THE DEMISE

CHAPTER 24

MY ANGER KEPT me tossing and turning for the rest of the night. When I finally drifted off, I suppose it festered, for it had barely subdued upon my awakening the next morning.

I sat up in bed, glancing out the window of the mint-green bedroom at the Clarksons' vacation home. Dawn was sparkling on the ocean water in the distance. I watched a bright yellow butterfly flutter around some of the hibiscus bushes, landing for a moment on one of the petals. Moments later, movement in the bushes scared it back into flight – perhaps a squirrel, or a cat. The butterfly didn't stay to find out.

I sighed, turning to look at the empty spot in the bed beside me. I didn't know where Felix had slept. I didn't even know if he'd made it back to the vacation home. I'd only stormed in and slammed the door shut behind me before crawling into bed and sulking my way into a bitter sleep.

I replayed the conversation we'd had on the summit of the volcano, shaking my head slowly with unchanged disbelief. How could he not have warned me? How could he have hidden something so significant from me? I'd trusted him with my body, and now it seems I had no choice in trusting him with my soul, too. The Three Fates must have been having a ball, twisting and winding our strings, bonding us eternally.

I threw away the covers and made for the door, stepping out into the rest of the home. He was in the sitting area, a tray of pastries and fruits in front of him on the coffee table, alongside mugs of coffee.

He looked at me immediately when I entered, his body tensing slightly. Those eyes were whorls of sadness and guilt and fear. I felt the billowing clouds of remorse and regret as they swallowed him, felt the downpour of shame and despondency as it filled him from within. They morphed and merged into darkened shadows, more concentrated, more inexorable, like a penitentiary of darkness he couldn't escape.

He stood, "Seraphine, I –"

His voice broke, and he hurriedly motioned to the food in front of him. "Please. Come eat. I – there's something I didn't get to tell you yesterday."

I studied him; I'd reached the point in my storm of rage where it had died down enough to behold the destruction it left in its wake. A dangerous tempest within itself, almost like a cobra, poised to strike up and rise again should the right conditions present themselves. I was so mad that I was no longer going to scream, or yell – if anything, I would whisper so quietly, the words would slither into his soul like a plague and sicken him from within.

But…

I thought about the pain he'd divulged, about what he'd told me about the way his mother had made him feel. I thought about the immense burden that caused, the same burden he'd carried since she left. And then, I thought about how it was now my burden to carry, too.

Despite none of this being my choice, I didn't have the heart to hurt him any more than he already was.

I inhaled slowly, containing the storm that billowed in me,

and sat across from him. My eyes scanned the pastries and fruit slowly, methodically. I reached for a strawberry and bit into it, chewing with intention as I avoided Felix's gaze.

He cleared his throat. "I, um…"

My eyes were delayed in meeting his. Those beautiful lavender irises were so petrified, it was as if they had seen death itself.

"The bonding process," he stammered, almost as if it were a struggle to speak. "It's…not just about sex. There's one other piece."

I didn't interject. I simply maintained his gaze.

"In order for the magic to work, for the bond to form," he went on, taking a deep breath as he did, "the Phoenix Keepers must…be in love."

I stopped chewing.

"I didn't…"

He huffed as his words failed him. "I thought…I *knew* that I loved you. But I didn't think you…"

He trailed off, and whatever words were supposed to come next never came.

I swallowed. I felt every part of my body go numb as the knowledge, the realization, started creeping its way through me.

He *loved* me?

Was it…could it be…true?

Was love what I had felt all along? Why I would risk myself to save his life? Why I was devastated that he would bargain with his?

I didn't know that love could feel like that…

I knew of the love I had for my family, and the love I shared with friends. I knew the love that stemmed from passion or the fulfillment of purpose. The love I had for myself, the devotion I had to my own life…

But I'd never been *in* love.

I'd been infatuated, charmed, lustful, heartbroken. I'd kissed and dated and felt the touch of men. But love…it wasn't a word I'd used before to describe any of it. It wasn't a feeling I was familiar with.

Perhaps this *was* love.

Or perhaps…this was another lie.

He'd lied about this – or at the very least, withheld the information – until I'd figured it out, after all. Was it truly absurd to think he wouldn't try again?

My brows furrowed as I studied Felix intently, his body language, his expression. I tried to wrangle any knowledge I had of deception cues – psychology facts I'd learned in my high school class, or random information I'd come across in various literature. I could recall mentions about fidgeting, shifty eyes, rolling the lips back…

But he was still. Utterly still. There was no fidgeting, no movement of the lips or the eyes. The only thing he did was stare back at me, unwavering and willful. He was intent on my seeing and hearing the truth in him. The lavender in his eyes begged, pleaded for trust.

I broke eye contact, rubbing my temples with my fingers. "I don't know what to say," was the honesty that spilled out of my lips. "I need…" I shook my head to myself slowly as silence rolled in. "I need to think."

Think about what exactly, I wasn't entirely sure. But I indeed needed some time to think.

When Felix spoke next, his words were careful and measured. "I understand," he said softly. "For now, let's go home. And then, take the time you need."

My only response was a single, dawdling nod.

———

Felix and I didn't say a word to each other on our flight back to San Diego. It was late Sunday afternoon when we all arrived back in the cellar, the forest I'd created still thriving as it had been when we'd left.

I emerged from the cellar first, the sound of his footsteps trailing a ways behind me. My jaw was tight the entire walk to the villa, and it didn't loosen much as I stared out the window of the Koenigsegg.

When he parked, he said, "I'm sorry. Again." They were the first words he'd spoken in hours.

I cleared my throat, nodding. Despite having a lot on my mind, it seemed I had very little to say.

He bit his bottom lip. "I'll see you soon," he added. The way he said it made it sound like a wistful, nervous question.

I could only meet his gaze for a brief second before I turned to exit the car. "*Oui*," I replied. "See you soon." I didn't look back at him as I made my way up to my dorm.

I shut the door to my room, leaning against it with a long, heavy sigh. The dorm seemed smaller, more compact than I remembered it – I could almost see my thoughts bouncing off the walls as they echoed in my head. I almost regretted leaving Felix's side, as the fact that he wasn't there certainly didn't bring me any relief. But I didn't know what I would say to him, either. I didn't want to risk saying or doing anything I would be rueful about.

I meandered to my bed, plopping on its center as I threw my bag haphazardly on the floor. Then I sat there, alone with my mind in the isolation of my dorm, blinking up at the ceiling. Just my feelings and me, the latter completely silent, the former louder than a thousand gulls calling over the ocean breeze.

I allegedly loved Felix Clarkson.

My nose crinkled with confusion at the entire fiasco. A bond formed by and with love. How was that even possible? How could our magic even recognize love? Was it triggered by our emotions? A phrase? An action?

How could we be sure it wasn't wrong?

My eyes darted across the popcorn ceiling, my mind swirling. After all I'd been through, all that I'd been given, all that I'd experienced...it seemed ridiculous to question the limits of magic.

But perhaps that was the power of fractured trust. Or denial.

Everything felt heavier than it needed to be. Between the irritation and the perplexity and the suspicion, I couldn't settle on one emotion to focus on; sitting with the discomfort of any revelation would have been near impossible, let alone that of such profound devotion to another person.

I heaved a frustrated huff of air and sat up. Being alone wasn't helping. It was becoming much too crowded and imperious in my head. And I was...wary of what I might come to terms with.

What if it were true? Then what?

My steps were deliberate as I made my way to the floor lounge, my homework in hand. Emmanuella, Keiffer, and Chenoa were working on assignments at a table while Roscoe and Sajan watched a football game on the sofas, snacking on chips.

"Hey, guys," I said, plopping down at the table next to Emmanuella.

She gave me a sly smile. "You look exhausted. Fun weekend?"

Try as I might, I couldn't bring myself to humour my features. "Tiring one," I countered with a sigh.

Her smile shook a bit. "You okay?"

"Yeah, yeah. I'll be fine."

Em eyed me as I opened my textbook. "This doesn't have anything to do with the whole Everly episode, does it?"

Everly. Right. I'd almost entirely forgotten.

I shook my head. "No, I'm over it."

"What Everly episode?" Chenoa piped up at the mention of her roommate.

I rubbed my eyes as I recalled the weird encounter. "She was cleaning her room last week, and I offered to help her, and then I…"

My eyes flickered to Keiffer as I pondered my next words. He was completely focused on his homework and didn't seem to notice. "…gave her some advice. With the best intentions, of course. But she seemed to take it as me judging her, because she started yelling at me about it all."

Chenoa's reaction was a mix of shock and concern. "That's odd."

"I was there. Odd doesn't do it justice," Emmanuella noted.

Chenoa frowned as she took this in. "What kind of advice did you give her?"

I exchanged a glance with Emmanuella. "Boy advice," I then replied simply. If Keiffer's interest was piqued, he surely wasn't making it known.

"But she wasn't mean about it," Em chimed in again. "It was solid advice."

Chenoa considered this. "Hm. Everly usually loves talking about boys, so that doesn't make sense to me." She paused. "Maybe she was having a bad day or something. I don't know. Would you be willing to talk to her, you think?"

"Well, of course. I'd love to sort things out." I shrugged. "I just haven't seen her since."

"Neither have I," Emmanuella added.

Chenoa chewed her lip. "She's been partying a lot recently. I think she's enjoying her freedom." Her voice seemed a bit distant. "To be honest, I don't see much of her anymore, either. I think the last time I saw her was a week ago."

I studied her – she seemed bothered. "Sometimes people have a hard time adjusting to new situations," I offered. "Or get lost in the moment."

She nodded slowly. "Yeah, I guess you're right."

But the mention of the absence admittedly had me glancing around the room, and it suddenly occurred to me that she wasn't the only one I hadn't seen in a while. "Where is everybody else, anyways?" I noted aloud. "Feels like forever since I've seen Myra and Hakeem." Elijah, too, but I didn't feel the need to mention him.

Roscoe looked over at me from the sofa. "Not sure. I texted Hakeem the day he stood us up at the gym, but I never heard back."

"Haven't heard from Myra in a bit, either," Sajan said. "Actually, I don't think I've seen her since our beach day."

My brows furrowed a bit. The beach day seemed so long ago.

"You don't think they could be upset with us or something, could they?" I questioned, looking over at Emmanuella.

Em shook her head. "Over what?"

A fair question. Apart from the entire debacle with Everly, nothing even remotely tense had happened in the friend group.

Keiffer finally looked up from his homework. "People are fast and loose, dude," he droned. "Especially in college. They meet other friends, or they find other things to do...I wouldn't worry too much about it. They're probably figuring themselves out or something."

Emmanuella blinked at him. "Whoa – you can be smart?"

Keiffer stuck his tongue out at her. "I'm always smart. Some people just don't understand true genius."

She snorted. "True genius doesn't usually obsess over cheese."

"That isn't true genius, then. Every true genius knows the importance of cheese."

"So, what, lactose-intolerant people can't be true geniuses?"

"Of course they can!" Keiffer objected. "You don't have to indulge in the great wonders of cheese to know it's a masterpiece of a creation. I mean, I might not understand what birth feels like, but I can still recognize it's a painful experience, right?"

Emmanuella seemed taken aback. "That's, like, the second time in minutes that you've made sense. Are you running a fever?"

He smirked. "Nah – you're just realizing you've never given me enough credit."

She stared at him. "The first time I met you, you ran my hair straightener through your hair. Unplugged. And then said something about hair being like pancakes."

Keiffer grinned at me. "If you set the bar low, you don't have to work very hard to exceed expectations."

To that, I only rolled my eyes and buried my nose in my work as the two continued bickering. I did not find it a nuisance – if anything, I felt indebted to them for the distraction, the background noise to tune out my own thoughts and feelings.

- F -

The whiskey was the only thing that felt smooth, uninterrupted, as it coursed down my throat.

I brought the bottle, now empty from the last swig, away from my lips, and plopped it on the floor beside me. It clinked on the spotless white tiles of my kitchen, disturbing the perfection with an obvious eyesore that didn't belong. The warmth oozed through my body as it travelled down my esophagus, spreading slowly in the pit of my stomach – the pit that seemed to grow deeper and deeper by the moment.

I groaned, leaning back against the wall, shutting my eyes. So much whiskey in so little time. I'd ruined myself like I'd ruined everything else.

That's all I ever was, all I'd ever be. A ruin.

My eyes creaked only slightly, watching as I thumbed the keychain I'd traded her for the Legend of Sedaurea the night I'd rescued her from Alchnost. Even in my stupor, there was no denying it was, indeed, what I thought it was. Would the jagged, faded metal of the charm be the only thing I'd have left of her?

Would this be the end of us?

The thought of the look on her face when I'd finally confessed made me grimace. My heart suddenly weighed a ton, sinking into an abyss carved so far within myself it could be considered forsaken. Many things about me seemed to feel empty and irrecoverable; I'd suddenly become an entity solely carved of caverns and chasms. More hollow than solid. More meaningless than man.

"Felix, you've got to stop."

It was not the first time Fuego's voice had bounded between my ears throughout the course of the evening. It was also not the first time I ignored him. He wasn't wrong. But facing that truth, in my state…

For a man so full of holes, my mind was certainly dense.

There was a reason I was in this mess, after all.

I reached into the inside pocket of my jacket, pulling out the three grams of cocaine I'd snagged on my way home. Any reason I'd had to fix myself had disintegrated with each scathing look she'd given me. My reason couldn't stand me. And in no way did I place blame on her for the fact that I chose to engage in an endless devil's dance. I was the one who had let my desire for her fuel a crashing car – one that I was driving, and that she wasn't in.

She was not responsible for my bad habits. She could not be held accountable in any way for my sobriety or lack thereof. And though she was compassionate, kind…Seraphine had her limits, as all humans do. It was unfair of me to ascribe my vulnerability to her.

Nobody could change me but *me*. Nobody could do this for me, but *me*.

And the reality, however tragic it may be, was that I didn't have it in me. Because change, no matter how necessary it may be, was frightening, challenging, and painful.

It was much easier to just give up on me.

It always had been.

CHAPTER 25

- S -

I DIDN'T SLEEP VERY WELL.

I felt unsettled and restless the entire night, sleeping for only an hour or so at a time, only to wake desperate for more rest that came sparingly. My thoughts felt like cobwebs I could get laced in, but try as I might, I couldn't seem to burn the spidery, sticky threads. Monday morning was unwelcome; my alarm was met with my own series of chiding curses, as if I were trying to rouse it back.

I sluggishly got ready for my classes, my makeup turning out a little ragged, my outfit a tad more wrinkled than I would have liked it to be. I couldn't find it in me to care. I slung my purse over my shoulder as if it weighed a thousand pounds, my textbook in one hand as I dragged myself out the door.

As I was locking my dorm, I noticed the door to Everly's was open.

I paused for a moment, debating whether I should wait or walk away. The dread of another bizarre confrontation stirred in my mind with a desire to clear the air. But then the length of my delay, combined with the lack of sounds coming from the room, made me suspicious. Perhaps she wasn't leaving and had just opened the door for…some purpose I couldn't quite place.

I inhaled and exhaled quickly, then made my way to the open doorway.

I stopped outside the room, confounded. I felt my face contort with my frown.

She wasn't in her dorm. More pertinently, her room was still a mess. In fact, it almost looked worse than the last time I'd seen it.

I stepped inside carefully, as if I were afraid the floor might crumble beneath me like it did in the blending temple. I tried to remember if certain items were still in the places I'd last seen them – was that book in its same spot? What about those candy wrappers? I couldn't recall; the room was in such disarray it was difficult to tell if she had simply given up on cleaning it, or if it had been cleaned only to be destroyed yet again.

I pursed my lips, thinking. Then I remembered there was one particularly problematic item that had been in the room before.

I glanced at where Keiffer's lighter had been. It was gone. And noticeably, the other items that had been next to it had shifted – that small piece of a bigger picture I could recall.

Perhaps she'd given it back, then. And perhaps this was a new mess after all. Perhaps the door was left open because she'd scurried out in a hurry.

I turned on my heel and was about to leave when something on her desk caught my eye. It was a piece of paper, seemingly torn from a notebook. And on it, written in bold, black letters, were the words 'FINDERS KEEPERS.'

I stared at it, my frown deepening. Then I slowly, hesitantly, reached for it. As I held it closer to me, I studied the two words intently. The way the writing shone in the morning light indicated it was rather fresh.

"What the hell?" I murmured to myself, setting the note

back down and glancing around the room again. Nothing else caught my attention in the same way. The fact that the note itself had stood out amongst the entire clusterfuck of chaos was quite incredulous.

I sucked in my lips and turned back to the note. It simply stared back at me, unchanged. And there was nothing more I garnered from pondering it further, so I shook my head a bit and departed the cluttered, untidy room, shutting the door behind me.

———

The day dragged on like a three-hour documentary on rocks and boulders.

Felix became a recurring intrusive thought, creeping through my head anytime I wasn't preoccupied with anything else. Between following chemistry lab instructions, I caught the memory of our first-ever flight atop our Phoenixes drifting through my inner vision. My mind failed to keep various things he'd said to me – about the stars, about his mother, about me – at bay as I struggled to pay attention to my Greek Mythology lecture. And despite my best efforts, the replay of all our most intimate moments was far more stimulating than whatever my physics professor was droning on about.

The pleasantness, of course, was still swirling around with all the uncertainty and irascibility that came with the unexpected bond and refused to let my soul know peace. Nothing in my day's routine was distracting enough to tempt my focus; there was no pause in my cyclic spiraling of reminiscences and feelings. Felix was as much a part of my autonomous functions as my breathing.

I didn't know how long it would take me to sort the disarray within myself out. But given I had a text message from Felix waiting for me after I'd finished my last class of the day, I assumed the uncertainty was already starting to nibble at him.

Felix Clarkson

I hope this doesn't bother you. Just checking in to make sure you're okay.

I chewed on my lip. I'd calmed enough that I could, at the very least, separate my emotions from the logistics of the situation. And, at the foundation of it all, I knew two things with certitude.

I knew I cared about Felix.

And I knew he cared about me.

Again, the thought of his woes flashed through my mind, the vulnerability he'd passed on to me. And once more, I found myself distraught at the thought of contributing to any sort of discomfort, especially if it could be avoided. Although I couldn't say exactly what I wanted to do next regarding the nature of our relationship, I knew for sure I didn't want it to take a turn for the worse. And, it went without saying that I didn't want him missing from my life, either.

If anything, the communication…

It made me realize I missed him already. Even more so than that annoying tether of our bond that thrashed within me, begging me to be near him again.

I took a deep breath and began typing as I walked to my dorm.

Me
I'm okay. Are you all right?

Felix Clarkson

I'll be okay. Don't worry about me.

Me

I don't think I'm ready to talk about everything just yet. I still don't really know how I feel about it all. But I'd still like to see you and the Phoenixes. Maybe we can get started on the next riddle or something. Focus our attention elsewhere.

Felix Clarkson

Of course. My last lecture ends in fifty minutes. Meet me in the parking lot then.

Me

Thank you, Felix.

I didn't even bother trying to salvage whatever pathetic excuse of a makeup look I'd slathered on my face, or the disheveled outfit. I scrolled through my phone and half-heartedly worked on an assignment while I waited for Felix's class to be done. When fifty minutes had passed, I grabbed my things and left my room.

When I arrived at the Porsche parked by the curb, I opened the passenger door and immediately froze.

If I had seen better days, then Felix had seen them thrice over. He looked as though he'd been yanked from a witch's cauldron after simmering in it overnight; his hair was unkempt, the lines on his face etched unforgivingly deep, and dark circles shadowed the skin under his eyes. Even the quality and expense of his dark clothing could not make up for the fact that they'd clearly been slept in – or worn for much too long. The black Prada bomber jacket he donned even had what looked like a little stain on the sleeve. He hesitated to meet my gaze, his head sitting low between his shoulders. Those lavender eyes were hazed and reddened – whether it be the bond or the contagion of his weary gaze, I could *feel* the weakness behind them.

I stared at him with shock and concern. "You look awful," I couldn't help but blurt.

His face moved as if it were laden with stone, his throat bobbing. "I had a lot of homework to catch up on," he feebly explained. "I've been up all night."

I didn't need to know him as well as I did to detect the hint of deception lingering in his voice. But he seemed like he might shatter into a thousand pieces before me, so I didn't pry. I simply swallowed as I sat down beside him, buckling myself in.

He turned the car on. In the most unusual manner, considering how smoothly he usually drove, he then proceeded to accidentally reverse, bumping into the parked car behind us.

I started at the sound of the clanking metal. "Shit," I heard Felix grumble, and he proceeded to step out of the car. I watched him walk around to the back and inspect the two vehicles. Then he returned and fumbled around in his wallet, pulling out a receipt. He wrote what I could only assume was a brief explanation and his phone number on the small paper before setting it in the windshield and sitting back down in the car.

"Is it bad?" I asked as he closed the car door.

To this, he let out a long breath and simply rubbed his eyes. "Could be worse," he muttered.

I studied him as he hid his face, his demeanour so unlike what I was used to from him. Eventually, he put both hands on the wheel and began driving.

The strangeness of his handling didn't cease; I was used to Felix's evenness and capability when he drove, but it seemed that skill set had dissipated. He came to jerky stops at red lights and stop signs. His reactions, either to start again at a green light or to slow down as we approached another vehicle, seemed delayed. When we made it to the winding road that led to the estate, the scenery around us seemed to whizz by faster – a little too fast.

"Felix?" I queried as I instinctively gripped the handlebar above me.

"What?" was his bleak reply.

The tone was so foreign that I could only look at him with concern once more. The tiredness, the dullness, the darkness not only under his eyes, but within them. The lavender seemed to be struggling, a candle in the wind just vying to stay alight as best as it could.

And then, before I could tell him to slow down, there were flashes of red and blue in my peripheral vision. I glanced out the rear window just as the sirens started blaring.

"Fuck," I heard Felix groan. He slowed the car roughly and pulled over to the side of the road, putting the car in park starkly and thrashing himself over the steering wheel in frustration. He rubbed his face as he muttered more curses under his breath, his movements teeming with anxious energy.

I sighed a bit, glancing at the police car that had pulled up behind us in the rear-view mirror. The male officer looked to be in his late thirties or early forties, and he was skimming through some electronic device on the dash. When he began making his way out of the car, I turned to look at Felix, who was still hunched over the steering wheel.

"He's coming," I said to him. There was a pause before he straightened and rolled down the window.

The officer presented himself a second later – his badge read *Officer Larson*. "Licence and registration, please." Felix handed it to him. "Do you realize you were going sixty miles per hour in a thirty, sir?" he then asked Felix gruffly.

Felix took in a deep breath as he stared out the front windshield. "Yes, officer," he muttered.

Officer Larson leaned one pale forearm on the window frame. "It's much too dangerous having you on this road at that speed. Or anyone else, for that matter."

Felix swallowed. "I agree, officer," he responded, still avoiding eye contact.

The officer glanced at me briefly before turning back to Felix. "You normally have trouble looking at people?" he asked provokingly.

Felix cleared his throat, his eyes falling to the steering wheel beneath him for a few moments. Then, he hesitantly brought his eyes up to the officer's.

I felt the tension in the air as Officer Larson scanned Felix's face. "Have you been drinking today, sir?" he asked him sternly.

I'd never seen Felix falter like he did under the officer's leer. "No," he replied unevenly.

Officer Larson's eyes narrowed ever so slightly as he surveyed Felix, then the inside of the car. His steel-coloured eyes didn't seem to latch on to anything of importance, but he still met Felix's stare again with hefty, unconvinced suspicion.

"Any firearms in the car?" the officer asked.

Felix shook his head. "No, officer."

"Mhm. Do you mind stepping out of the vehicle for me, sir?" he then asked in a way that made it clear it was less of a question and more of a demand.

That didn't stop Felix from saying, "Is that really necessary?"

The officer's lips twitched with the most unamused smile I'd ever seen. "Hmph. Let me rephrase – step out of the vehicle *now*, sir."

I heard Felix huff slightly, but he proceeded to unbuckle his seatbelt. I felt his weight leave the car as he opened the door and stepped out, the officer giving him just enough room to exit the vehicle and nothing more.

"Face the car and place your hands on the roof," Officer Larson instructed.

Sluggishly, Felix complied, his exhausted gaze falling to the floor as the officer began patting him down aggressively. He had made it about halfway down his torso when he paused and began feeling around the side of Felix's ribs.

"Does this jacket have an inside pocket?" the officer questioned.

The delay in Felix's response, combined with the officer's inquisition into something he'd clearly found, ran my nerves ragged. "Yes."

"Open it for me."

My heart began thumping as Felix slowly stood straight and unzipped his jacket, presenting the inside pocket to the officer. I noticed he purposefully avoided the cop's gaze as Officer Larson reached into that inside pocket and pulled out –

No. *No.*

"Hmph." The officer held the little plastic baggy up closer to his face, the remaining white powder inside clouding its clarity. "Care to tell me what this is before they tell me back at the station?"

Felix's eyes were glued to the ground. "It was three grams of cocaine. Now it's about two."

I thought I might vomit. I fought back tears in my eyes as I turned to look out the passenger side window.

"And when did you last use?"

A pause. "About two hours ago."

I bit my lip as tears fell.

I should have followed up. I should have been more involved. I should have said something, done something, *anything* more.

I couldn't tell which guilt I was feeling – his or my own. It was so substantial that it felt like a living thing that had festered in my gut, morphing into some kind of horrid monster that began eating me from the inside out.

But it was too late now. My culpability was inconsequential. No amount of remorse would change the consequences he'd now found.

I lurched as I heard the handcuffs being clicked around his wrists, the sound a vicious mockery resounding through my ears.

CHAPTER 26

BENJAMIN'S FACE was warm when he greeted me at the doorway to Luther's mansion. "So good to see you, Seraphine!" he exclaimed heartily, before he glanced around and his expression morphed into one of confusion. "Where's Felix?"

I threw a quick glance behind me at the Porsche I had parked carefully in the driveway. After I'd assured Officer Larson that I myself had not been snorting cocaine and agreed to a breathalyzer and pat down that proved so, he had said it was all right for me to drive the car with Felix's permission. Felix didn't say much in terms of argument, and merely nodded his head when the officer suggested the idea. It was a smooth ride – smoother than anything I'd ever driven in my life – but I was so worried about damaging the car and so frustrated and saddened by what led to me driving it that I hadn't driven nearly as fast nor as enjoyably as I could have.

I cleared my throat as I turned back to face Benjamin. "Felix sort of got arrested."

Benjamin stared at me, blinking several long, increasingly dumbfounded blinks. "What do you mean he *sort of* got arrested, miss?"

I sighed. "He got arrested. The word choice was to soften the blow."

"Arrested?" came George's voice from around the corner as he himself did, too. "Who's been arrested now?"

"Why, Felix has been," Benjamin answered him as he offered to remove my jacket. I let him. "What for, I don't know."

George looked at me. "Do you know?"

I ran my teeth over my lips, considering whether or not Luther would want them to know. "For being an idiot."

Both of the butlers exchanged glances with one another, and they seemed to understand my hesitancy to provide a direct answer. "Luther is in the lounge. Let me escort you there," George offered. I followed in his footsteps, and Benjamin followed behind me.

We arrived in the lounge quickly, where Luther had his nose in a report he was reading as he sat on one of the armchairs. "Miss Seraphine has arrived, and she's brought news that your son was sort of arrested for, and I quote, 'being an idiot,'" Benjamin announced to him blandly.

Luther shook his head away from the report as he scrunched his eyes, his face twisting into a deep, bewildered frown before his gaze reopened on me. "I beg your ever-loving pardon?"

Benjamin nodded once at me with a trying smile. "We'll leave you two some privacy," he said, before he and George hustled out of the lounge and shut the door behind them. I wouldn't have been surprised if they had their ears pinned to the other side of it.

I sighed as I made my way to the other armchair, sitting down tiredly. "He was – "

"*He* is Felix, correct?"

I blinked. "*Oui.*"

"I see. Just clarifying." He threw the report grumpily on the desk. "I have two sons, both of whom tend to be idiots at different times, you know," he griped matter-of-factly. "They plan it quite nicely between themselves."

I pursed my lips. "No comment."

He motioned to me. "Right, now go on. You were saying?"

I folded my arms across my chest and glanced down at the floor. "Felix was driving under the influence," I said in a bit of defeat. "I didn't realize until we'd been pulled over for speeding."

"God help me." Luther let out a huff of dissatisfaction as he rubbed his face with his hands. "Of all the things, driving while drunk."

"Oh, no – not while drunk. While high."

Luther's normally bright eyes were the very definition of devastation as they peeked at me through parted fingers. "Come again?"

There was no use in sugar-coating – the words came with a blunt sort of disillusionment. "He was driving while high on cocaine. So he was arrested on a count of possession and a count of driving under the influence."

Luther's eyes snapped shut again, his head falling between his hands as he clasped them behind his neck. The room fell so silent that the only sound for many minutes was the ticking of the lavish grandfather clock in the corner of the study.

"So he's in jail?" Luther finally asked after heaving a long, disappointed sigh.

"There wasn't an accident, and he doesn't have any prior criminal history, so they're only giving him two misdemeanour charges. He's spending at least four days in jail and got a thousand-dollar fine, but moreover, his license will be suspended for six months and won't be returned until he completes a DUI program." I paused. "He can request a hearing with the DMV before ten days is up to get it all reconsidered, though."

Luther groaned. "Fabulous," he muttered. "Just fabulous."

I watched as he lifted his face and tapped on the armchair with his pointer finger several times, seemingly deep in thought. "Well, I suppose I ought to call my lawyer for him," he finally said in exasperation, turning to look at me with eyes that bore irritation. "Do you know if they've posted bail?"

"I don't know. I haven't really done this whole 'getting arrested' thing before."

He ran a hand through his greyed hair. "Right. You and me both, darling." He stood. "Let's you and I have supper, and then we'll head down to the station later. I'll have my lawyer meet us there."

I blinked. "We're going to see him?"

He shrugged. "Yes. And if we can, we're going to bail him out."

It was hard for me to maintain eye contact with him. It was as simple as that in his eyes – pay the fee, bail his son out of jail. And I could understand why he'd want his son out, too. But if Felix didn't face the penalties for his actions, who would? There would be no accountability. I'd been taught that we pay the price for our mistakes. If you don't pay a price, you just keep making the same mistakes, over and over…

I could still feel some sort of weird guilt toiling through my insides amongst all the disappointment and anger. I wondered if he knew Felix's bad habits were as much of an issue as they were, if this had been a point of contention before. And if he did know, had he done anything about it?

As I looked away, Luther asked, "Is there something else that's troubling you, dear?"

I thought I should tell him, should confess what I'd seen Felix do, what I'd heard Felix say about his struggles and strife. But try as I might, I couldn't bring myself to tell him. Maybe it was from fear of hurting him, or because I'd promised Felix I wouldn't – however much of a broken promise that now had become, given I'd had to divulge his drug use. Perhaps a part of me felt I could still salvage the promise if I didn't share the reason why Felix used. I didn't know.

I simply shook my head. "No, just a long day."

"I can imagine. Come, you must be hungry," he said, standing.

I nodded as I stood to follow.

- F -

There was nothing in jail – just a bed and a toilet, which I had told myself I would not use unless absolutely necessary. The officer had seemed pleased to lock me in here. It almost made me want to burn him alive. I could have done it when he'd stopped me. But it certainly would have followed with a trail of inescapable problems – I definitely didn't need more of those.

I swallowed, circling my thumbs over themselves, one by one, over and over. There was nothing else for me to do, so I thought I would simmer in my own self-hatred. As if I needed another reason to hate myself, my actions, and my being.

My record was blemished. My wrists were reddened and sore from the handcuffs. Whatever was left of my pride had seeped out of me like a leaking wound. My father would be livid. My brother would be laughing. And Seraphine…

Tears welled in my eyes. Perhaps the bleakness of jail finally made it all sink in. We would never be the same. That dream had died in the corner of this miserable space and buried itself within the decaying floor. There was no way she would ever look at me the same way again. I'd butchered that hope with this latest stint.

I buried my head in my knees, trying my hardest not to cry. I felt pathetic, worthless, like a blunder that kept spiraling in some kind of never-ending snowball. When did it end? The only person to blame was myself. But I was so far gone…

I heard the door to the hall open, and I hesitantly lifted my head.

He looked like the face of anguish. The air around him felt like the shadows and weight of a miserable gloom that physically knocked the breath from my lungs. There, in the corner of the cell, did I finally see how weakened and fragile he truly was. He was so pale, the lights gone from his eyes. Those swirls of lavender were beaten and numbed. The weary circles, the permanent frown, all prominent and highlighted in the faint light of the jail. He was deflated, the handsome features overcast by this hanging, darkened cloud. Somehow, before my very eyes, Felix Vaughn Clarkson had been eaten alive.

Officer Larson strode to the cell door and inserted a key. "Your bail's been covered, Mr. Clarkson," he said with the least bit of enthusiasm as he opened the door. "You're prohibited from driving until your court date. In the meantime, you're free to return home with your dad."

Felix couldn't make eye contact with me. He was avoiding me like a cat avoids water. And he couldn't look at his father, either, who stood by my side. He simply nodded, swallowing as he stood, and slumped out of the cell.

Nobody said anything as we left the police station. The drive back to the Clarkson estate was so silent that a pin could be heard dropping on the vehicle's floor. When we finally arrived at Luther's mansion, I exhaled as I left Luther's car, not realizing how tightly I'd been breathing the entire ride until then.

Luther fumbled with his keys before managing to open the door. As we strode inside the dimly lit entryway, soundless as fatality, I noticed a figure lurking in the grandiose archway to our right.

The sight of Julius strained every muscle I had even further than I thought possible. I hadn't seen him since the edgy conversation we'd had in his kitchen, since I'd revealed his mother's infidelity to him. This certainly wasn't the circumstance I'd wanted to be our next encounter. Whether he was harboring any ill feelings towards me, I couldn't tell from his face or his stature. He seemed surprisingly impartial as he leaned almost casually against the wall, his eyes fixed on his brother and only his brother as we made our appearance.

Felix's shoulders and back were still as tense as I'd seen them when he got arrested – the step inside his father's home didn't seem to relax him any further, and neither did his brother's presence. He stopped in the foyer, glaring at Julius without turning towards him.

To this, Julius only asked with careful evenness, "Are you okay?"

Felix didn't reply right away. "What do you think?" he asked with stark shortness.

Julius flexed his jaw, but didn't say anything.

"Why are you even here?" Felix pestered on.

Julius straightened. The humour and playfulness I'd come to expect from him were nowhere to be seen. Behind what became a rather stoic, impatient expression at Felix's words, I could see hints of concern hiding in the depths of his features.

"I helped bring some of your clothes over," he replied bluntly. "So your staff didn't have to go through your stuff."

To prevent them from finding anything they might not expect, and to avoid unnecessary conversation. For Felix's privacy and protection. A courtesy.

Felix didn't soften; if anything, he grew even more steeled as his glare shifted to his father. "I think it's best if you stay here for a bit, son," Luther explained. His tone left no room for argument.

"I put everything in your old bedroom upstairs," Julius went on, his own stance stiffening at the hostility that cascaded from Felix in droves.

Felix's gaze returned to him, his eyes sizing his brother up with a look akin to something of disgust. I knew the two didn't get along on a good day, but I couldn't help but be bothered by his reaction.

The lack of a response seemed to drain whatever patience Julius had left. "The words you're looking for are 'thank you,' *hermano*," he nearly spat. He turned on his heel and disappeared through the archway before Felix could react.

The three of us were left again in our icy, barren silence, motionless as a tundra. When Felix made to take a step, Luther's voice suddenly sliced through the air again, halting him. It wasn't normally powerful, but given how quiet the room was, it felt jarring.

"A moment in my study, Felix," he instructed frigidly. "Please."

Felix's eyes flickered to him. There was nothing said – only a quick, shallow nod.

Luther moved next, towards the archway opposite the one Julius had vanished through. Felix followed, leaving a large gap between him and his father. He didn't muster even the briefest glance back at me before they were swallowed by the mansion.

Then, he was gone. And suddenly, I was left alone.

I bristled at the wave of unease that overcame me, desperate for anything other than deathly quiet. Decidedly, I turned and began hurrying down the archway to the right – the one Julius had left through.

I hadn't even the remotest idea where I was going. Luther's mansion was difficult to navigate during the day, but at night, it was unmanageable. Mercifully, light drew me to a room off one of the hallways I somehow found myself wandering through.

I'd never been in the room before – I would have remembered the striking, dome skylight in the center, underneath which grew a purple weeping willow tree. Not a small one, either. A fair-sized tree, a size I didn't know was possible to grow indoors, occupied the bulk of the space. The stunning, almost implausible leaves – a sprightly, lilac colour – seemed to glisten in the moonlight that wafted through the dome. But it was not the soft, white glow that had drawn me to the room, but rather the warm twinkle of the string lights that were splattered amongst the leaves of the tree. It illuminated the room comfortingly – perhaps that was the reason Julius had found himself here, too. He stood across from the tree, a glass of red wine in his hand, watching it intently. It was almost as if he were waiting for it to do something – morph into a woodland creature, perhaps, given the fantasy of its essence.

I stopped in the archway of the room, throat bobbing a bit. I hadn't rehearsed anything on my quest to find him, but I suddenly found myself wishing I did. The pressure of how to word any of the emotions I felt became insurmountable as my arrival drew his attention. He turned his head towards me, nothing definitive written on his face.

I chewed my bottom lip.

Then, I blurted, "I'm sorry."

It took Julius a few moments to react. To my surprise, I saw a half-smile twitch his lips.

"There's no need to burden yourself with quirks that aren't yours," he replied lightly. "Save yourself the trouble." He paused, adding with a half-hearted chuckle, "Unless you particularly enjoy apologizing every waking moment on Felix's behalf."

I blinked at him, unable to comprehend how he didn't realize it was not Felix's entire fiasco I was sorry for. "I meant to apologize for the other day," I clarified. "What I did – said. It was spiteful, and it wasn't right." It was hard to look at him, so I glanced at the floor. "I'm really sorry."

I could feel his movement across the room, a shifting of his posture as I assumed he processed the information. "Water under the bridge, as far as I'm concerned," he then responded calmly.

Relief flooded through me, and the edges of my mouth

lifted as I brought my gaze back to his. "I'm not sure I would be so gracious, but I appreciate it."

There was an airiness to his dark features. "Felix explained you'd had a bit of an…unwelcome encounter with one of the other guests. I chalked most of your wording up to that bitter aftertaste."

I tried not to show my aversion for Valentina on my face, difficult as it was.

"And all things considered," Julius went on, "you told me some important truths. The truth about my parents, the truth about my actions. That's some very valuable information I don't take for granted."

My smile wavered slightly. "I don't think you're a bad person."

"I know." He cocked his head slightly. "Which is why your anger with me was important for me to see." He took a casual sip of his wine. "We often lose sight of reality, given our public image. You get so used to tuning out people's grievances about you because there are so many other people singing your praises. But that's not a good way to be – not if you intend to make a positive impact in this world, and not just appeal to people who already like you."

Julius nodded towards me. "If someone close to me, someone whose opinion I hold in high regard, is thinking so ill of my actions, then it means something. It means I've lost my way. I won't say I wasn't initially a bit…upset with you. But I came to realize your frustration with me was more about expecting better – a reflection of how you truly feel for me. You care if I'm making an ass of myself because you know that's not who I really am. That is something I feel inspired to rectify."

He shrugged. "And I have. I told Nina everything. She wasn't pleased – I'll likely never see her again. But I was honest. It worked out for the best. I want to have fun, have a good time. I'm not looking to settle down. But she wanted more, and I pretended to be it. Eventually, the truth would have come out. It was better that it happened this way. I felt better after coming clean. And now, I can be better, too."

I let his words wash over me, my eyes widening a bit at the astonishment I felt. "That's...a really mature and profound observation."

He flashed a smile, the cheeky Julius smile I'd come to know and love. "Not just a pretty face, you know."

I was grateful for the opportunity to smile back, given the heaviness of the evening.

He held his wine glass out to me. "Come – you probably need this more than I do."

My feet moved before my brain gave them the order. Within seconds, I was drinking from the glass as if it were water. I received a breath of amusement in response.

I brought the glass away from my lips, swirling what remained and watching the red liquid dance. "Will he be okay?"

He didn't answer right away. "He better be," he then replied solemnly. "Because I don't know what I'd do without him."

The words hit me like a ton of bricks. The two could barely exchange a kind sentiment. But the way Julius spoke of him, despite every nasty interaction I'd seen between them – it was how family spoke of each other. No matter how difficult Felix made it, Julius still cared for him. Loved him. It showed in his face even more than his words as his eyes fluttered about the floor of the room.

I swallowed the lump that formed in my throat. "Today was...not good," I said weakly.

He inhaled sharply as he wrapped an arm around my shoulders, pulling me in close. "No. It was not."

Neither of us said anything for a long time as we stood before the twinkling tree, exchanging sips from the wine glass until there was none left. I passed the empty glass back to

Julius, who took it before studying me. Whatever he saw made him loose a long breath.

"Let me show you to a guest room. It's late. Sleep would do that worry on your face some good," he offered.

There was no reason nor desire for me to argue, so I simply nodded once as he began walking.

As I went to follow Julius out of the room, I noticed the lights flicker behind me in the reflection of the windows sprawled across the outside walls. I turned to see the string lights faltering within the lilac leaves, breaking the air of loveliness around it and instead speckling the tree with uncertainty. My brows shook as they struggled to fully brighten again, the remaining dots of light eventually fizzling into a dimness that slowly, diffidently, faded to black. All that was left to illuminate the space was the light of the moon that came from the skylight above; the tree was swallowed within the shadows that seemed to creep towards it from every corner of the room, drowning it slowly in a woeful obscurity.

The light had fought to prevail, and it could not. Despite the struggle, the darkness fell abruptly – much too quickly to simply be night; no, this was a fate more finite than the end of day. It felt more like the end of life.

A chill ran down my spine, the hairs on my arms rising as my body shivered.

I had to turn away immediately at the discomfort, hurrying after Julius with a newfound sense of urgency.

CHAPTER 27

I COULD HEAR his footsteps fade further and further down the hall as Julius left the guest room he'd shown me to. A small part of me wished he hadn't left.

I had almost no bearings about me anymore; I couldn't tell which side of the mansion I was on, or where I was in proximity to Luther, to Felix, or to the many, many other rooms. Half of that was due to the darkness, and the other half due to the sheer size of the structure. It made me wonder how much of a home it could truly become to its inhabitants. Perhaps they had gotten used to it – but did they ever feel the comforts of the coziness a family felt in a snug living room?

The guest room was massive, the plush king bed taking up only a small portion of the baroquely decorated space. A cloud-white chaise sat in one corner with a dark wood book-shelf; I questioned if all the other guest rooms had bookshelves, and tried to think about how many books this entire place had. Considering the size of the shelves in the study, in Luther's office…this mansion most likely held more reading material than a public library.

I eyed the luxurious bed. As inviting as it appeared, and as drained as I was, I couldn't quite bring myself to crawl in just yet. Sleep seemed like a foreign concept.

I glanced around the room again, this time pausing at the doorway to my right. It led to an adjacent ensuite, and through it, I spied a fabulous soaker tub.

The resounding craving for a bath clanged across my body. I found my feet dragging themselves to the ensuite, and I gratefully turned the tap on, deciding on the hotter side.

I managed to collect a soak and some bath salts from one of the drawers, mixing them in with the water as the tub filled slowly. I could see steam drifting from the surface of the water as I turned the tap off. I slowly removed my clothes and stepped into the tub.

It was hot – much hotter than I anticipated. I took a sharp breath in as I continued lowering my body down anyways. It was only several degrees away from being scalding; I could see my flesh redden as I submerged myself further and further. I let the fiery water envelope me as I shut my eyes.

For some reason, I found solace in it.

My skin's protests faded to soft whimpers as it became accustomed to the heat, and as I let myself become one with the water, I felt my body growing lighter. It was as if the bath were burning the remnants of the day, washing it away from wherever it had burrowed and festered – my pores, my hairs, my stretch marks, the bends and hollows of my figure.

My breathing slowed as I leaned back, resting my head against the edge of the porcelain. The bath solved nothing in a pragmatic sense, but at least it allowed for a temporary peace. The loudness of my mind, the frantic thoughts – for just a moment, they were muted. Still there, but unheard…

A violent cough abruptly escaped me, yanking my body upright.

My eyes popped open as I hacked, instinctively clutching at my chest. I gasped at the tightness, at the constriction that hadn't been there seconds before. A sensation of heaviness exploded across my upper body – in seconds, my breaths were laboured.

I became frenzied, trying to stand but stumbling in the midst and collapsing over the edge of the tub in a fit of coughs and heaving. Tremors overcame me, my entire being shaking like the leaves of a tree in a hurricane. I desperately tried to grasp any extra air, my breaths shallow and uneven. My lungs cried out for more, more I could not give them, more I could not find. Panic spread throughout me as I reached forward with my free fingers, trying to steady, trying to make it all go away –

It stopped as suddenly as it started, a snap reverberating through me that brought me back to myself.

My inhales were long and loud as I quickly refilled my lungs, thankful for the stillness in my body that returned. Startled and hesitant, I brought myself to standing, the hot water trickling down my body and into the tub as I tried to collect my thoughts.

Confusion swarmed me like a plague of locusts as I stared at my hands, no longer trembling. It had all come out of nowhere, like they were symptoms of a sickness that didn't belong to me –

I brought my gaze to my own reflection in the mirror, my eyes doubling in size.

Felix.

I leapt out of the tub, yanking a robe off a hook in the corner of the ensuite. I flung it on, the front of my naked body still exposed as I bolted out of the guest room and fumbled to tie it closed at the same time. I didn't care that I was dripping wet. I didn't care that I probably didn't do the most effective job tying the robe closed. All that mattered was Felix.

I tuned my senses into his presence as I ran down the hall teeming with classical art of figures who looked nearly as distressed as me; none of the doors seemed to respond to my magic. He felt distant, and I gritted my teeth as I spun around from the last door in the hall – wasn't he supposed to be here?

Frenzied, I ran to a set of stairs and clambered down, following my magic as it weaved me through rooms and archways in the dark. Suddenly, I was in the front foyer, and the presence…

I let out a distressed sound.

He was at his villa.

I threw the door open as if it were made of straw and bounded down the steps, racing in the direction of his villa as my heart pounded in my chest. My bare feet hit the ground so fast, I barely had time to consider how they ached as I ran.

"Felix!" I cried, the breathless scream a culmination of fear and despair as I sprinted. It wasn't like he could hear me, but his name escaped me as though he could.

I bolted the entire way to the villa, nearly tripping over myself as I ran up the front steps and began yanking on the front door. It was locked. I cursed out loud and began banging with both fists against it.

A frazzled, freshly awoken Francis whipped the door open minutes later. "Miss Pierre, what in the – "

"Where is he?" I screamed as I blew past him.

Francis blinked, befuddled. "Felix is at Luther's mansion, I believe."

I was trembling with desperation. I squeezed my eyes shut as I tuned my senses into Felix again – he was close. Closer than before. But his presence came from further beyond the villa…

The cellar.

"Miss Pierre, are you all right?" Francis inquired, but I didn't have time to respond as I turned on my heel and began dashing further into the home, towards the room that led to the gardens.

I flung open the garden door and ran as though I were carried on a wind, the robe fluttering behind me as I struggled to see straight in all my movement. The only things that truly kept me guided were my senses and the muscle memory from making the trek to the cellar countless times over.

The door to the cellar was open, and I bounded down the steps. "Felix!" I shrieked. "Felix!"

I made it to the bottom, my feet landing on the indoor forest floor I'd created, and I halted.

My breathing came in heaves as I took in the sight before me.

Our Phoenixes stood in a tight half-circle, all their wondrous, beautiful colours seeming to blend as they peered down at the forest floor. For before them, sprawled like a fallen angel, lay Felix – unmoving amidst the foliage. His hand, outstretched beyond his head, seemed to be reaching for something – perhaps the little bag, clouded with the remnants of that damned white powder, that sat just out of reach of his fingertips. Not the one the police had confiscated. Not the one from Colombia. One I'd never seen before. A secret stash? A new purchase?

My heart sank beneath my feet.

"Felix?" I exhaled.

Aurora was the first to look at me, her usually bright, yellow eyes tragically dim. Lumina and Suelo followed suit, their gazes no less morose. Ignacia, so little next to her flock, looked at me with an expression that indicated she lacked understanding. But it was Fuego, who only stared regretfully at Felix and didn't let his eyes leave him – not even to acknowledge my arrival – whose actions told me the most.

I involuntarily started quivering again, my legs weak as I stumbled over to Felix. My knees buckled just before him; I had to crawl to reach his side. With unsteady fingers, I turned him towards me, frightened about what I would see.

Those handsome features, every angled line of his jaw, every defined bone in his face, were frozen. The way his mouth remained parted, soundless and without breath, unresponsive to my touch – it was as if he'd been stilled in time. And his eyes, the lavender eyes I'd seen within inches of mine, that I'd kissed with my own gaze…they were shut with permanence.

An inhuman sound of despair escaped me as I dragged my fingers, plagued with tremors, down the side of his pale face. His skin held warmth still, but it was only a matter of time before it froze like his entire being. No pulse lived beneath that broad chest.

Felix Vaughn Clarkson was dead.

I went to scream and found no sound in me. Tears fell past my widened, disbelieving eyes, dripping onto the body of the dead man below. My shuddering became uncontrollable – afraid I would drop him, I clutched him closer to me, into my chest, holding him to me as if my heartbeat, my life, might seep into him, might wake him, if only for a moment.

Ringing ricocheted in my ears, drowning out all my other sensations as my head filled with the painful sound. I stared beyond the Phoenixes, beyond whatever lay past them, without truly seeing anything as my vision blurred with more tears. My throat caved in on itself, suddenly as dry as desert sand.

I reached within myself, desperately grabbing for that bond, frantic in my search. But where the tugging usually came, there was only a desolate stillness. I was devoid of the sensation I'd come to expect, that once annoyed me, and that I now would have given anything to feel again.

I was convulsing without reprieve, my breaths jagged and uncertain. My vision had left me, my body no longer my own. Then the ringing in my ears, in my mind, became a recollection.

"*Because I don't know what I'd do without him,*" Julius had said.

And neither did I.

I did not know what to do without Felix.

I did not *want* to do anything without Felix.

I felt as though a piece of me had died with him, and now, I was not fully myself.

Not without him.

TO BE CONTINUED

IN

THE PHOENIX KEEPER
AND
THE UNDYING FLAME

ABOUT

Margarita Artista was born and raised in British Columbia, Canada. She has been writing since she could hold a pen, and as a child, she often found herself scribbling silly little stories in her notebooks. Margarita's lifelong dream has been to write a story that inspires her readers the way her education and favourite books have inspired her. She holds a BA in Sociology and a Master's in Public Administration.

Margarita resides with her husband, Chris, their miniature daschund, Simba, and their three birds – Iago, Zazu, and Jewel – in British Columbia.

Margarita Artista

www.ingramcontent.com/pod-product-compliance
Lightning Source LLC
Jackson TN
JSHW021943020625
85253JS00001B/1